"You are going to ruin this investigation," she hissed. **"Could you have looked any more appalled at playing the role of my fiancé?"**

"Are you mad?" Edward countered, keeping his voice equally low. "Of course I'm going to be shocked and downright annoyed when you announce such a ridiculous fiction."

Maggy crossed her arms and glared at him. "There wasn't time to ask how you felt about it. Besides, I told you that I was coming up with a role."

"Yes. But I didn't think that would be pretending to be my fiancée. This is madness." He threw his hands in the air, then spun to face the fireplace. "There is surely some other role for you to play."

He sensed her stepping toward him. "T̶̶̶̶̶̶̶̶̶ best way. You said it yourself. E̶̶̶̶̶̶̶̶̶̶̶̶ ̶̶̶̶̶̶̶̶̶ay I can gain access into th̶̶̶̶̶̶̶̶̶̶̶̶̶̶̶̶ your wife or fianc̶̶̶̶̶̶

He had only a mo̶̶̶̶̶̶̶̶̶̶̶̶̶̶̶̶̶̶̶̶̶̶̶̶ ̶̶̶̶̶̶̶̶ g her say his name be̶̶̶̶̶̶̶̶̶̶̶̶̶̶̶̶̶̶̶̶̶̶̶̶̶̶̶ve me, I wouldn't choos̶̶̶̶̶̶̶̶̶̶̶̶̶̶̶̶̶̶̶dn't think it absolutely necessary t̶̶̶̶̶̶̶̶̶̶ssion."

Edward wasn't sure whether to be offended by that remark or not.

Stacy Henrie has always had a love for history, fiction and chocolate. She earned her BA in public relations before turning her attention to raising a family and writing inspirational historical romances. The wife of an entrepreneur husband and a mother of three, Stacy loves to live out history through her fictional characters. In addition to being an author, she is also a reader, a road-trip enthusiast and a novice interior decorator.

Books by Stacy Henrie

Love Inspired Historical

Visit the Author Profile page at Harlequin.com.

STACY HENRIE

The Rancher's Temporary Engagement

HARLEQUIN® LOVE INSPIRED® HISTORICAL

Recycling programs
for this product may
not exist in your area.

LOVE INSPIRED BOOKS

ISBN-13: 978-1-335-36955-0

The Rancher's Temporary Engagement

www.Harlequin.com

Printed in U.S.A.

But if we hope for that we see not,
then do we with patience wait for it.
—*Romans* 8:25

To my editor, Elizabeth.

Thank you for believing in that first story
and the ones that came after. I'll be forever grateful
for your outstanding help with this part
of my writing adventure.

Chapter One

Near Big Horn, Wyoming, April 1898

Edward Kent studied the gaping hole in the barbed wire fence and the trampled posts. This wasn't the work of an animal—at least not the four-legged kind. Anger heated his neck more than the weak spring sunshine did as he slapped his cowboy hat against his leg.

"How many horses wandered off?" he asked his ranch foreman, West McCall.

"Ten, maybe fifteen. Some of the boys are rounding them up now."

Edward dipped his chin in a curt nod. "Good. See that one or two of the others repair the fence."

"Yes, boss."

"We'll put as many of the horses in the main barn and the corral as we can at night, for the time being, so we can post guards."

"Will do." McCall mounted his horse and rode off in the direction of the large barn and the wranglers' quarters.

After jamming his hat back on his light brown hair,

Edward wrestled one of the toppled fence posts until it stood moderately upright. New wire and fresh post-holes would fix the fence. But it wasn't likely to fix the rash of mysterious occurrences hobbling operations around the Running W ranch or end the threatening notes he'd been receiving over the past four weeks.

Go back to where you came from, Brit, the last one had said. *Or else there will be trouble.*

Edward cringed at the memory. His gaze swept the rolling hills and scattered trees where they touched the feet of the Big Horn Mountains. If he squinted, he could almost imagine himself back home in England. Though that wasn't where he wished to be—not since leaving five years ago. The longstanding stigma of being a castoff, a throwaway, as the third son of an earl, stole over him and gripped his throat in a choke hold.

Coughing, he climbed onto his horse, Napoleon, and steered the animal toward the ranch house. Even at a distance the white, two-story home with its three-sided porch stood out like a pearl against a velvet-green backdrop. A swell of pride loosened the bitter taste of old memories. He'd come here, armed with only a dream and his inheritance. And now he ran the largest horse ranch in the Sheridan area.

But all his hard work would be for naught if he couldn't figure out who was sabotaging him. He urged Napoleon faster, his stomach grumbling with hunger. McCall had come to the house at the start of breakfast with the news of the damaged fence and runaway horses. Edward had left without eating a bite.

Outside the small stable near the house, he dismounted and led his horse inside. "Time for your version of tea and crumpets, isn't it?" he murmured affectionately to the black horse. The gelding whinnied and tossed its head, eliciting a chuckle from Edward. The horse wasn't as tall as its predecessors, hence Edward's choice of name. What the animal lacked in overall stature, though, Napoleon made up for in strength and agility.

Once he'd given the horse its grain and a rub on the nose, Edward headed into the ranch house through the front door.

"I've returned, Mrs. Harvey," he called to his housekeeper and cook as he removed his hat and hung it on the hall tree. A pile of mail from yesterday's post still sat undisturbed on the table. He'd been so busy overseeing the breaking-in of a horse yesterday that when he'd finally returned to the house, he hadn't bothered to do much more than grab a late supper and head to bed.

He carried the mail to the dining room. On the top of the stack, he found a letter from his mother, no doubt asking when he planned to visit. Edward wished he could convince her to come here instead. He wanted to show that, although he wasn't an earl and the estate heir as his oldest brother had been these last five years, that he'd worked hard at creating a good, successful life here.

Though a bit of a lonely one, his conscience prodded.

Edward ignored the thought. He'd discovered early on that the daughters of Sheridan's wealthy ranchers weren't so different from their English counterparts. In both countries, he was the sum of his bank account and supposed good looks, with little thought to his character or integrity—and no consideration at all to their own. He'd never loved the idea of money or appearances being the basis of a marriage. Living alone, in his opinion, was far more tolerable than entering into a marriage that wasn't founded on mutual affection and respect. It was something his younger sister had helped instill in him.

"Just remember to be true to who you are, Eddie," Liza had often reminded. "You are of worth, most especially to me and to God."

Though one year his junior, his sister had exemplified wisdom and vision beyond her years. Perhaps that was the reason she'd left this world too soon, at the tender age of fourteen. Edward missed her still and hoped she knew that he'd tried to live true to himself in the fifteen years since her death.

Taking a seat at the polished mahogany table, he started sifting through the rest of the mail. There was a newspaper and some sort of penny dreadful—or dime novel as he'd heard them called here in America—for Mrs. Harvey.

As though she knew what "treasure" awaited her, Mrs. Harvey bustled into the dining room, a tray in hand. "Here you are, sir. Nice and warm once more."

"Thank you for accommodating my erratic schedule of late, Mrs. Harvey." Edward scooted aside the mail to make room for his breakfast. The poached egg, crumpets and hot tea made his mouth water. "Looks splendid as usual."

The older woman's round cheeks pinked with pleasure. "Best eat up before it goes cold—again."

After laying his napkin across his knees, he extended the dime novel toward her. "I do believe this is yours, madam."

Her face went from pink to red as she snatched the thin book from him. "Thank you, sir."

"What is this one about?" he asked as he lifted his fork.

Mrs. Harvey's brown eyes lit with excitement. "It's about a detective in disguise—a real Pinkerton agent, no less. I'm hoping it's as good as one I read by E. Vanderfair about five years ago."

"Ah. Sounds intriguing."

"I'll see that you're hooked on them before too long, sir." She wagged a finger at him. "Just you wait and see."

Edward shook his head with amusement as his housekeeper left him to his meal. The fifty-year-old woman had been the family's cook for years at their London residence. Edward had always liked her and her food, so when he'd concocted the idea of coming to America, he'd asked if she might be interested in joining him as a housekeeper and cook. Mrs. Harvey, a widow with no children of her own, had readily agreed. She could be doting at times or downright cheeky, but they got on as well here as they always had. She was still the creator of the finest food he'd ever sampled, and she hadn't lost her propensity for sensationalized stories, either.

As for himself, he didn't see the appeal of those overblown bits of nonsense. His reading tastes had changed since leaving England, consisting of mostly equestrian books and the newspaper. Facts, reality, knowledge, those were his forte—not melodrama.

After offering a blessing over his food, as well as his ranch and staff, Edward began to eat. He decided to read his mother's letter later, since hers had the potential to spoil his appetite. The address and English postmark on the other letter he found in the stack of mail set his heart beating double time as he opened the envelope. This must be an answer to his inquiry, at last.

He read the words through carefully. By the time he reached the end, he was grinning. His father's contact in the British Cavalry had come through after all. They were, indeed, interested in securing a large quantity of horses from his region.

A rush of satisfaction rose within him as Edward dug heartily into his breakfast once more. All of his hard work would be worth it if he could secure a contract with the British Cavalry. Then his mother and brothers would surely have to acknowledge that, in spite of not being the heir or the spare to his family's wealth and title, he'd done quite well. Soon the name and ranch of Edward Kent would mean something, far beyond his small corner of the world.

He couldn't wait to tell McCall the good news. Thoughts of his foreman brought the memory of the trampled fence and escaped horses to mind and doused his excitement like water against hot coals. He couldn't afford any more mishaps, not if he wanted to supply the Cavalry with needed horses.

No longer hungry, he set aside his fork. He needed to stop whoever wanted him gone. But that meant finding out who was behind the disruptions. Pushing his dishes out of the way, Edward rested his elbows against the tabletop. Who in the area might hold a vendetta against him? He could think of no one. His staff treated him with the same respect he showed them, and the other ranchers he associated with at the Sheridan Inn were uniformly friendly to him.

He climbed to his feet, fresh frustration chewing at him as hunger had earlier. He stacked his dishes on the tray and carried it into the kitchen. "Here you are, Mrs. Harvey," he said, setting the tray on the center table. "Thank you again."

She glanced up from the dough she was kneading. "Didn't know you were done, sir, or I would've collected the dishes myself."

"Not to worry."

His gaze fell on the dime novel that lay open before her, giving him a sudden idea. Perhaps this might be an answer to his anxious prayers over the last four weeks. "How efficient are these Pinkerton detectives?" He motioned to the novel. "In real life, I mean."

"Quite, sir." Her expression conveyed her confusion at his question. "They always get their man."

Edward clapped his hands. "Excellent. If you need me, Mrs. Harvey, I'll be in my study." He had a letter to write.

"Yes, sir."

He exited the kitchen, feeling a return of his good mood. He would employ the Pinkerton's finest, most reliable man for his case, and soon life would resume to normal at the Running W once more.

Denver, Colorado, one month later

Maggy Worthing yanked the maid's cap off her head, causing her straight auburn hair to tumble around her shoulders. "The counterfeiter is sitting behind bars as we speak," she announced with triumph as she propped her boots on the edge of her supervisor's desk.

"Well done, Maggy." James McParland, superintendent of the Pinkerton Agency's Denver office, leaned back in his chair and peered at her through his round spectacles, his chestnut-colored mustache twitching. "You do make a rather convincing maid in that getup, minus the arrogant look."

"Ha." She loosened the top collar button of her borrowed uniform. Once she'd finished talking with James, she could return to her boardinghouse room and change back into her regular, more comfortable clothes—a well-worn button shirt and men's trousers. "I make a rather convincing detective, maid getup or no."

James inclined his head. "Touché. And that is why I have some news for one of my best detectives."

A frisson of excitement, similar to what she felt each time she knew she'd nabbed her man, unfurled inside her. "What news is that?" she asked, dropping her boots to the floor.

"The Pinkerton brothers in Chicago are looking for a woman to head up the training of all their female operatives." He shot her a knowing smile. "I've a mind to recommend you."

Maggy blinked, hardly daring to believe his words. This was her dream, one born into existence the moment James had hired her as a Pinkerton operative six years earlier. Now it was so close she could nearly grasp it within her fingers. The twenty-one-year-old widow she'd been then had been as scared as she was determined to make a career out of being a detective. And now, she not only had a solid career for herself but the chance to mold and assist with the careers of other female detectives, too.

"Have a mind?" she echoed, erring on the side of

caution rather than unbounded hope. "Something I can do to make things more definitive?"

James separated a short stack of papers from the others on his desk. "Complete this mission in Wyoming. The other operative I sent last month wasn't able to make any headway on it, which hasn't made the best impression on the rancher who requested a detective. So far all we've managed to do is sour his opinion of the agency. I would've put you on the case from the beginning, but you were deep in the counterfeiting mission."

"Why does he need an operative?"

"Someone's sabotaging his ranch." He slid the papers toward her. "The man's initial request is on top, along with the other operative's report."

Picking up the letter first, Maggy carefully read through its contents. Edward Kent, a horse rancher in Wyoming, had experienced a rash of threatening notes and acts of vandalism to his ranch, the Running W.

It was apparent from his choice of words that the man was well educated and had likely attended school well beyond the completion of the second grade as Maggy had done. The rest of her education she'd garnered on her own—mostly from secretly reading the newspaper and any books she could get her hands on.

She leafed through the other operative's notes next. The man, working undercover as a wrangler for Kent, had noted no nefarious behavior or ill feelings among the rancher's staff—they seemed to be loyal to their employer. He had uncovered no leads as to the identity of the saboteur.

"Appears to be a straightforward job." She set the papers back on the desk. "Though I'm not sure which sort of role I ought to play. It sounds like pretending to be a wrangler didn't exactly help."

"See what Kent suggests, but only after you smooth his ruffled feathers. He's expressed reluctance at hiring someone new from us. But I trust you to convince him that the Pinkertons can still help him and that you'll crack this case."

His confidence in her skills and ability to solve a case where the other operative had failed had Maggy feeling on top of the world. "I can leave for Sheridan tomorrow."

"Excellent." James stood, signaling an end to their conversation. "Find this ranch interloper and I'll send my recommendation to Robert and William Pinkerton to hire you as the head of all female operatives."

She rose to her feet as well as she excitedly crushed her cap inside her fist. "Thank you, James. I won't let you down."

"You never do. That's why I'm sending Get-Her-Man Maggy to complete the job."

Chuckling, she maneuvered around her chair. She had garnered the nickname after her first undercover mission, in which she'd pretended to be a hapless female traveling alone and had successfully tracked down a ring of train employees swindling hundreds of dollars from the company every month. Several more triumphant undercover missions over the next couple months had secured her a position as one of James's top operatives.

"Would you miss Colorado?" he asked, trailing her to the door. His head barely reached her shoulder, though she wasn't considered overly tall. "If you get the position in Chicago?"

She didn't hesitate to shake her head. "I'd miss working for the office here. But there's nothing keeping me from leaving."

No husband, no children, no family. A prick of loneliness, of the old abandoned feeling, threatened to uproot her enthusiasm of finally being in reach of her dream. Maggy steeled herself against it. She was strong and safe and could take care of herself. There was no need for any deep relationships—those brought only weakness, fear and pain.

"We'd miss you, too," James said with sincerity in his tone.

Warmth filled her at his words—no one had ever told her they'd miss her before. Not even her pa the day she got married.

"I also know how much you want this." He opened the door and stepped back. "Wire me after you've spoken with Kent and let me know how long the mission is likely to take."

"I will." She would solve this case and be one step closer to fulfilling her dream. Twirling the cap around her finger, she shot James a saucy smile. "You can count on me."

Frowning, Maggy tapped the toe of her shoe against the wooden platform of the Sheridan train depot. Mr. Kent was late. That or he'd already changed his mind about employing another detective to solve his case. Maggy's gloved hand strayed to her collar, and she forced it back down to her side instead of plucking at the scratchy lace for the umpteenth time. The ridiculously small, plumed hat she'd chosen to wear to complete her outfit did little to shade her face from the afternoon sun.

Without knowing what sort of role Edward Kent might want her to play for this mission, she'd chosen the part of a female relation—middle-class and independent—for her journey to Wyoming to visit *her distant cousin*. But now that she was here, she longed to be free of the smothering, stiff fabric of her traveling suit.

"Where is he?" she muttered to herself as she glanced around the emptying train station. She'd been hoping to convince him that he still needed help, get to his ranch right away, then take stock of the situation, not stand around waiting.

When another ten minutes had crawled by, according to the watch pinned to her lapel, Maggy dragged her trunk into the train's waiting room. She cajoled the ticket clerk with a pretty smile and a nickel to watch her luggage until she returned. Then she asked for directions to the nearest livery stable. Once there, she requested a horse and buggy.

"How far is it to Big Horn?" she asked the livery owner as he hitched the bay he'd selected to the vehicle. The animal looked a little docile for Maggy's tastes, making her wish she could saddle up the sleek mare she'd seen inside the building. But she couldn't risk the talk that would surely follow if she rode astride a horse in her dress.

The owner peered over his shoulder at her. "Big Horn would be 'bout nine miles from here. You visitin' someone that a ways?"

"Edward Kent." She smiled demurely. "I'm a distant relation of his."

"Kent's place is just seven miles away." He eyed her thoughtfully. "You're from England then, are you?"

"Come again?"

"Mr. Kent's a Brit. Figured you must be, too."

Maggy inwardly cringed at not knowing such an important detail sooner. Her repertoire of accents didn't include the most convincing British one. "Actually I hail from the part of the family that immigrated to America a few generations ago. Dear Edward followed in our path. But I've only just been able to leave my obligations at home in order to come see him."

The man took her explanation in stride without even blinking. "Your buggy's all ready, ma'am. This here horse don't move as quick as he once did, but he's real easy to handle."

"Thank you for your help."

Maggy accepted the reins from him as she took a seat in the buggy. Once he'd given her directions on how to find the Running W, she clucked to the horse and drove away from the livery. It didn't take long to collect her trunk from the station—a train porter insisted on carrying it out to the vehicle for her and tying it down with some rope.

She maintained a cordial smile to passersby as she drove through Sheridan. Once she left the stores and homes behind, though, she dropped the friendly, slightly vacant expression as her sharply honed observation skills kicked in.

The green hills and distant mountains reminded Maggy of the Colorado town she'd called home before escaping to Denver. She immediately locked her mind against any thoughts of *home*, if she could even call it that. Instead she concentrated on paying attention to the landscape she passed and the other ranches in the area.

Before long she reached the lane the livery owner had indicated led to Kent's ranch. She turned the horse to the left and drove the buggy down the side road. The Big Horn Mountains were closer now, their peaks stretching towards the overcast sky. After crossing a stone bridge that spanned a river, Maggy glimpsed a large house and outbuildings among the trees. Ahead stood an iron archway with the ranch's brand prominently displayed at the top. She drove beneath the arch, and a feeling of anticipation had her urging the horse faster. This is where she'd spend the next while, where she'd "get her man" and hopefully where she'd secure her promotion as lead female detective for the entire Pinkerton Agency.

Maggy glanced to her right, her gaze snagging on a small cabin beside the river. It had likely been Mr. Kent's residence prior to the building of the larger house. But that thought barely registered in her mind before her lungs squeezed tight, forcing her to gasp for breath. At the same time, her heart began to pound. Sweat collected beneath her hat brim and along her strangling collar. Her hands trembled so badly she could hardly hold the reins.

Not another attack. Not here. She hadn't experienced one in months, and yet, the tiny cabin eerily matched the one she'd grown up in and the one she'd shared with Jeb as his wife.

It required all of her strength to stop the horse. Unpinning her hat, Maggy used it to fan her flushed face. She shut her eyes and willed herself to breathe through the pressure in her chest. She was safe—no one was going to harm her ever again. Especially not a man. Detective skills weren't the only things she'd learned in the last six years; she'd also learned how to take care of herself.

If she'd only learned those skills sooner…

Feeling faint, she lay down on the seat and pressed her cheek to the tufted leather, desperate for something real and solid beneath her. Her pa was dead and so was her husband. Neither of them would ever lift a hand to her again. But the old fear and panic refused to release her from their iron grip. Hot tears burned her face as they slid onto the buggy seat.

"May I help you?" a male voice asked from nearby.

Maggy scrambled up, her heart thrashing for an entirely new reason. Mortification scalded her cheeks at being caught in the middle of one of her episodes. Brushing away her tears, she discovered a man watching her from the seat of his wagon, his expression a mixture of curiosity and concern. He had light brown hair, cut short, beneath his cowboy hat. And his eyes were an interesting shade of gray.

"I'm here to see to Mr. Kent," she said, hastily poking pins back into her hair where it had fallen from its coif as she'd removed her hat.

His eyebrows shot upward. "I'm Edward Kent. And you are?"

She'd been too flustered to immediately identify the British accent she now plainly heard behind his words. This was her employer. Maggy cleared her throat.

"Pleased to meet you, Mr. Kent." She straightened her shoulders and pasted on what she hoped resembled a smile. "I'm your new Pinkerton detective."

Chapter Two

"I beg your pardon?" Edward shook his head, certain he hadn't heard her correctly. There was no way this woman with her messy auburn hair and tear-filled blue eyes could be a Pinkerton detective. Besides, he'd been informed the new operative would be waiting for him at the train station, and probably had been for some time. He'd spent longer than he'd intended watching a group of strangers who'd ridden close to the edge of his property that morning.

The woman's smile increased, appearing less tremulous and more confident by the second. "I said I'm your new detective. My name's Maggy."

"You can't be the new detective. I was supposed to meet him…" He cleared his throat when she lifted a haughty eyebrow at his use of a male pronoun. "What I mean is, I was supposed to meet *the detective* at the train station." Before Edward promptly sent the chap back to Colorado.

Despite the agency's insistence about sending another agent to the ranch—likely in an attempt to restore their good name with him—Edward had decided just that morning that he would find some other way to solve his case.

The woman consulted the watch pinned to her jacket. "Yes, you were to meet me more than an hour ago. But I got tired of waiting. It was easy enough to get directions and this horse and buggy. I may be able to count the livery as expenditures. Then again, the rental was necessary because you were late, so you might need to reimburse the expense."

Frustration rippled through him, its waves growing more pronounced the longer he sat here glaring at her. The last detective had incurred an *expense* from him as well, and Edward had not been satisfied with the results.

"I regret I was not at the station on time," he conceded. He shifted on the wagon seat, his fingers tightening their grip on the horses' reins. What was the most polite way to share with her that he no longer required a new detective, male or female? "I was attending to business related to the case that the last detective found too difficult to—"

To his astonishment, she clucked to the old nag pulling the buggy and headed up the drive as if Edward hadn't spoken. "You'll find that I don't back down from a challenge as easily," she called over her shoulder.

Giving a low growl, he hurried to turn the team and wagon around to catch up with her, but she made it to the house before him.

"If you'll pardon me, Miss…" He waited for her to supply him with a last name.

"It's better for both of us if you simply call me Maggy."

Edward could think of several other things to call

her at the moment—none of which his proper English mother would approve of. "Maggy," he bit out. He prided himself on sounding marginally calm. "I can't afford any more interruptions to my ranch." Not when the British Cavalry was interested in his horses. "However, I no longer wish to shoulder the expense of another agent, only to be disappointed with the results once again."

She climbed from her vehicle, her head held high. Apparently she was as stubborn as she was striking. "I promise you won't be disappointed with my results." She proceeded to untie the rope that secured a trunk to the back of the buggy. "If you need credentials, I can supply those. But you should know..." She paused to throw him a penetrating look. "I'm known in the Denver office as Get-Her-Man Maggy. And that is why Mr. James McParland himself sent me."

He recognized the name McParland. After Edward had sent his letter to the agency, Mrs. Harvey had illuminated the more renowned cases of the Pinkertons, including McParland's own role in infiltrating a gang of assassins in Pennsylvania in the '70s. The man might know what he was about in sending Maggy.

Still, Edward wasn't sold on the plan. It seemed a waste of time and money to employ yet another detective from the same agency. Their methods of investigation would likely prove similarly unfruitful.

"That last gentleman pretended to be a new hire," he said, climbing down from the wagon, "but that won't be as easy to explain if you were to assume such a role, would it?"

He'd hoped to deter her, but he was disappointed. Instead, she manhandled her trunk onto the porch and threw him a satisfied grin. "I'm sure we can think of a different, more effective role. This trunk of disguises will help." She slapped the top of the luggage as if it were an old friend.

"Disguises?" he repeated with a shake of his head. "This isn't a circus, *Miss Maggy*. This is a prosperous ranch. And I need someone to find out who's sabotaging it. Not entertain the populace with some masquerade."

His neck heated with greater anger as memories intruded, memories he typically kept locked away. It had been at a masquerade ball, several months after his father's death, when he'd discovered the woman he'd loved in intimate conversation with his oldest brother. He'd confronted them, only to learn Beatrice had thrown him over.

A mutual friend confided to Edward later on that Beatrice had cared for him, but a sudden and tragic misfortune with her family's finances had made her anxious to marry someone with the money to rescue her relations from ruin. Edward still felt the sting of rejection, though. Especially when his brother and Beatrice were married six months later. Two weeks following the wedding, he'd climbed aboard a ship bound for America.

"Are you always this obstinate, Mr. Kent?" Maggy asked, jerking his thoughts back to the unpleasant scene unfolding on his porch.

She was accusing *him* of obstinacy? He climbed the steps in an effort to keep her from barging her way inside. An action he wouldn't put past her. "Are you always this persistent?"

Her eyes brightened with amusement. "I wouldn't be one of McParland's best detectives if I weren't."

Running a hand over his face, Edward blew out an exasperated sigh. Clearly he wasn't going to convince this woman that he was done employing Pinkerton detectives. But if she were to prove her own inabilities…

"I will make a deal with you. You find some clue your predecessor did not, and I will hire you as my new detective."

Instead of looking defeated, a thrum of energy seemed to radiate from her. "How long do I have?"

"Until this evening." Then he'd kindly provide her with supper and a room for the night before sending her back to Colorado.

Undeterred, she stuck out her hand. "Agreed."

Edward eyed her hand, feeling a bit foolish at the idea of shaking it as if she were a gentleman. Then again, she'd been insisting since he stumbled onto her in the drive that he take her seriously. He wondered what had caused her to appear so upset earlier. Her expression no longer held any of the vulnerability it had upon first glance. In contrast, she raised her eyebrows again, challenging him.

"Very well. Welcome to the Running W," he said, shaking her hand. He even managed a polite smile. After all, he felt quite confident she wouldn't be unpacking. This would be her first and final day on the ranch.

"Should I bring my trunk inside?" Maggy gestured to her luggage. The sooner she started on her investigation, the better. She could tell by the determined gleam in Edward's gray eyes that he thought he'd given her a test she couldn't pass. And she couldn't wait to prove him wrong.

He frowned but moved to heft her luggage anyway. "I suppose we shouldn't leave it out here unattended."

Maggy opened the door for him, then followed him inside. The marble-inlaid hall tree where he hung his cowboy hat didn't surprise her in its tasteful opulence, nor did the polished wood paneling of the entryway where he set her trunk. The ranch wouldn't be the target of sabotage if it weren't doing well.

"May I ask you some questions about the ranch?" Or would he see that as a violation of the conditions of his test? Was she supposed to figure everything out unaided? She wouldn't interview the staff or hired hands yet, since she wasn't sure which role she'd be playing for the duration of her stay here.

And she would be staying.

Stepping to the open doorway on the right, which appeared to be a parlor, Edward motioned her inside. "You may ask questions but only of me. If you'll take a seat, I'll see that my housekeeper prepares some tea for us."

Maggy suppressed a grimace at the promised tea as she entered the parlor. Tea was a drink for timid, rich women. Not a female detective in the throes of an investigation.

The parlor was as tastefully and richly furnished as the hallway. A sofa and low table sat in front of the window, while a pair of armchairs stood before the fireplace. A large painting ruled over the mantel. Maggy went to stand before it. The green countryside might have resembled the one beyond the house, except there were no mountains and a man with a cart in the foreground didn't look like a rancher. Perhaps it was an image of Edward's native England.

Turning to view the other side of the room, her eyes widened when she saw the crowded bookshelves that stood on either side of the doorway. Maggy hurried over to inspect them up close. She'd never seen so many books in a private home before. She ran her fingers along the smooth surfaces of the spines, wishing for a moment that she could select a pile and curl up with them in one of the chairs.

"Do you like to read?"

She startled, as much at being caught staring as at not having heard Edward reenter the room. Spinning to face him, she knocked a notebook off one of the side tables. "Sorry about that." She picked it up from where the book had fallen open on the carpet. A list of names covered half the page, which Maggy couldn't help perusing. She'd learned long ago that anything might provide clues. "What's this?"

"It's a list of those who've borrowed a book from me this year." Edward took the notebook from her, shut it decisively, and returned it to its place on the table. "Please, have a seat."

Maggy sat in one of the armchairs, while Edward took the other. "Tell me what's been happening at the ranch the last few months," she said in a no-nonsense tone.

He rested his boot on his knee as he settled back in his seat. "Didn't the other detective give you a report?"

"Yes, but I would like to hear it directly from you. Maybe there's something he missed."

His earlier frown made another appearance. "Of

course there's something he missed—he didn't find who's trying to destroy my ranch."

She waited, knowing the importance of silence and patience. After another moment, Edward pushed out a sign of resignation.

"Very well. It began with a note…"

For the next while, Maggy listened carefully as Edward described the anonymous notes he'd received and the various acts of damage to the ranch. Fences had been broken, tack had mysteriously gone missing, and several feed orders never arrived. Four horses had gotten out several days earlier after another breach in a pasture fence, and the wranglers hadn't been able to find them this time. Edward's men rotated serving as guards at night and one patrolled the property during the day, but the new responsibilities meant less help around the ranch during daylight hours.

"Do you trust your employees?" she asked when he'd finished.

He nodded, but it didn't radiate as much confidence as his demeanor earlier. "I do… I *did*. At this point, other than my housekeeper, who came here from England with me, I'm not certain who to trust."

A tug of compassion pulled at her. "You can trust me, Mr. Kent."

"I can, can I?" The briefest of smiles touched his lips. "I suppose we shall see."

"Your tea, sir." The housekeeper appeared to be in her late forties or early fifties. She had gray hair and carried a tray in hand, but she stopped inside the doorway when her gaze fell on Maggy. "Oh, dear," she admitted, her British accent as strong as Edward's. "Had

I known you had a *female* visitor, I would've used the good china."

Edward lowered his foot to the floor. "This is not a female visitor, Mrs. Harvey."

"Then what would she be, sir?" The older woman bustled forward and set the tray on the low table. "She's female and a visitor, is she not?"

Maggy swallowed a laugh at the woman's clever retort.

"This is Mrs. Harvey, my housekeeper." He waved at the older woman, then at Maggy. "Mrs. Harvey, this is Maggy. She's here to…to possibly help with the trouble around the ranch."

"What will you do?" Mrs. Harvey asked.

"I'm a detective, so hopefully I'll find out who's behind all the trouble." Maggy kept back a sigh, though she knew what would come next. The look of disapproval, the sad shake of the head. She didn't feel the need to justify her reasoning for being a detective, but she did wish for more acceptance from those of her own gender.

Instead of horrified shock or blatant condemnation, Mrs. Harvey's face registered plain awe. "A female detective? Oh, how exciting. Sounds just like something from one of my penny dreadfuls."

Maggy released a surprised chuckle. Edward's housekeeper might be the first female she'd met whom she might actually get along with.

"If you'll excuse us, Mrs. Harvey," Edward intoned with a note of impatience. "We are discussing sensitive matters."

"Of course. If there's anything else you need, sir. Or you, Miss Maggy." Mrs. Harvey offered her a kind smile. "Let me know what I can do to make your stay most pleasant."

Edward mumbled something that sounded like "she won't be staying."

"Thank you, Mrs. Harvey," Maggy said, ignoring Edward.

The woman inclined her head, then exited the parlor.

"I believe I have at least one champion in this household." She arched her eyebrow at Edward in a self-satisfied expression.

"Time will tell if she is the only one." His gaze darted to the clock on the mantel. "And time is slowly running out." He stood and moved to the tea tray.

His reminder robbed her of some of her smugness. She had the details of what had occurred at the ranch, but she wasn't any closer to identifying a suspect, or even uncovering an important clue.

"Tea?" He lifted a cup toward her, but Maggy shook her head.

"No, thank you."

Edward returned to his seat to drink his tea. He was all stiff politeness, giving rise to a strange and irrational thought within her to see him laugh or grin with abandon. Or perhaps he wasn't given to humor at all. Did his austerity hide a darker side? Maggy mentally shook her head at the idea. There was nothing about him that smacked of dishonesty or aggression. Why she hadn't been able to read those things as clearly in Jeb, she'd never know.

Pushing thoughts of her late husband from her mind, Maggy drummed her fingers on the chair arm, thinking over the information Edward had shared. "Do you still have those threatening notes?"

Nodding, Edward set aside his teacup and rose to his feet. He opened a box on one of the bookshelves. "I kept all of them," he said, removing a sheaf of papers.

He handed them to Maggy as he sat back down. After reading the menacing message on each, she went back through them, this time studying the handwriting. "Whoever wrote these is likely educated. Or, at least, comfortably literate."

"How can you tell?"

Maggy lifted one for him to see. "There are no misspellings, contractions or slang. The letters weren't written with a heavy hand, either. Which means the person didn't have to think too hard before writing the words or struggle to keep up as someone dictated them."

A flash of admiration filled his gray eyes, but only for a moment. "That is rather impressive. However, it doesn't tell us who the culprit is."

"Or does it?" Maggy muttered to herself as she peered harder at one of the last notes in the pile. The curves on the capital *B* in Brit seemed vaguely familiar. "May I see your library notebook?"

She glanced up to find Edward watching her in confusion. "Whatever for?"

"Testing a theory."

Rising to his feet once more, he collected the book and brought it over to her. "I don't see how this is going to help."

"Which is precisely why I am the detective and you are the rancher." Maggy opened the notebook to the page she'd surveyed earlier. Carefully she reread each name, then compared it to the handwriting on the note. Sure enough, her theory proved correct when she reached the most recently penned name.

"Ah-ha," she exclaimed with a surge of victory as she glanced at Edward. "I found one of our potential suspects." Which was one more than the last operative had discovered. She'd won Edward's little challenge, which meant he would have to hire her as his new detective.

Snatching the book from her, Edward shook his head. "That's not possible."

"Look, here." She bent forward to show him the handwriting on the note and how it corresponded to the name in the book. "This one has a curve in the *B* like the one in Bertram there."

Another of the names was written in handwriting she was sure she'd seen on one of the other notes. She sifted through them again until she found it. "Here's another. This note has the same flourish on the *W* as it does on the name…" She leaned forward and read the notebook upside down. "Right there—the name Winchester." Now they had two suspects! "Who are these men?"

The furrow in Edward's brow increased as he handed back the book. "They are both wealthy ranchers who live in the area."

She nearly blurted out that she'd been right—the culprits *were* educated—but she clamped her teeth over the remark as she saw the color drain from Edward's face. She'd had plenty of practice keeping her thoughts to herself—she wouldn't do well at undercover work if she told the criminals how absurdly dim they were to brag about their exploits in front of her persona as a harmless-looking scullery maid or a mousy store clerk. But holding her tongue for the purpose of sparing someone's feelings was new, and she wondered why she didn't wish to add to his discomfort. Especially given that he hadn't believed she could sniff out any clues at all.

Edward stood and began to pace the rug in front of the sofa, his expression one of consternation and confusion. "I can't understand it. I dine with these men nearly every week at the Sheridan Inn. They've visited me here and I've been to their homes. Why would they sabotage me?"

That was still another matter to solve—motive. Though she didn't share his surprise that the attacks came from those he considered friends. She'd seen too much of mankind's duplicity to be shocked by it anymore. "It makes more sense that a fellow rancher would be behind all of this havoc rather than a lone wrangler or cowboy. What more can you tell me about these men?"

Pocketing his hands, Edward frowned further. "They've done well for themselves, though their spreads aren't nearly as large as the Running W. Winchester is married and his wife belongs to that little club in town."

"Little club?" Maggy sat up straighter. The niggling of an idea had started to form inside her mind, though it wasn't fleshed out and ready to present itself yet. "What sort of club?"

Edward waved his hand dismissively. "All of the ranchers' wives belong. They get together for their teas and tête-à-têtes and head up a number of society functions in Sheridan, as well."

"Do you have to be married to a rancher to join their club?"

He didn't slow his pacing. "I believe so, yes. That or engaged."

"And their husbands?" she asked. "Do they gather socially, as well?"

Edward nodded. "Nearly all of the ranchers attend weekly dinners at the inn. Sometimes it's with their wives. Other times it's only the men."

"Perfect." She slapped the chair arms for emphasis. Things were definitely looking up for this investigation—and for restoring the Pinkerton name with Edward. "Now we know where to concentrate our efforts."

"What do you mean?"

Maggy stood, ready for some tea after all. It would be tepid by now but could still serve as an honorary toast to her first successful hour on the ranch.

"You already know two of these men and you attend the same social events they do. Since there's a strong likelihood others in their social group are involved in this plot against your ranch, you need to become better acquainted with all of the well-to-do ranchers in the area." She bent and lifted her teacup from off the low table. "You need to know their closest friends, enemies, ambitions, fears."

He threw her a perturbed look. "And what will you be doing while I am ingratiating myself?" His tone still rang sharp and full of frustration.

"I'm working on that," she reassured him as she took a sip.

"Boss?" a voice called from the hallway.

Edward turned toward the sound. "In here, McCall."

A man with a handsome face and curly black hair poking out from underneath his hat strode into the parlor. "Some of the boys just learned about that detective pretending to be a wrangler. They're worried that since he didn't find the culprit…" He broke off when he saw Maggy. "Sorry, boss. Didn't 'spect you to have company. Especially not feminine company." Removing his hat, he nodded politely at Maggy. She inclined her head in return.

She was beginning to get a picture of Edward Kent, and it didn't include the man having numerous female visitors. He was handsome, she conceded, and fairly affable. But clearly his ranch, his horses and perhaps his staff were all his heart had room for. She couldn't help wondering why.

"This is West McCall, my ranch foreman." Edward collected his cup and poured himself some more tea. He was stalling, which meant he was either grappling with how to introduce her or reluctant to reveal to the man that she was a detective. Perhaps both. "McCall, I'd like you to meet…" He took a swallow of tea, his gaze darting to Maggy's in a silent plea for assistance.

His unexpected show of confidence in her abilities to come up with a solid cover story brought her earlier idea forward at last, in full form. "I'm Maggy. Edward's fiancée," she finished with a triumphant smile. "Isn't that right, darling?"

Turning toward him, Maggy only had a moment to register the shock in Edward's gray eyes before his mouthful of tea came spewing out—all over her.

Chapter Three

Edward mumbled an apology, avoiding eye contact with both his foreman and Maggy. *Of all the foolish, rash, ridiculous plans*, he thought as he set down his cup, scooped up a napkin, and thrust it at Maggy so she could dab her tea-soaked dress.

Feigning affection for someone, as Beatrice had done five and a half years ago, was the last thing he wanted to do, least of all toward a practical stranger. He fought to keep his expression impassive, but his jaw began to twitch with the attempt.

"Didn't know you were engaged, boss."

"It is rather sudden," Edward managed to get out between his clenched teeth.

Maggy glanced up from wiping her dress and frowned at him. Was his scowl leaking through, or had she heard the sharpness in his tone?

"So how did you two…" McCall shifted his weight, looking every bit as confused and uncertain as Edward felt. "Are you from England, as well…Maggy?"

She set down her napkin as she offered the foreman a brilliant smile. "No, I'm not from England, Mr.

McCall. But I have come a very long way to see Edward here, so if you'd be good enough to allow us another few minutes in private." With impressive skill, she linked her arm through the foreman's and guided him toward the parlor door as if the idea to leave had been his all along.

"If you didn't meet in England, then where—"

"Oh, we have a shared acquaintance," Maggy said with a nonchalant wave of her hand and a tinkling laugh as she led McCall into the hallway. "Our friend introduced us, and after that Edward and I struck up a lively correspondence."

Edward nearly forgot his fury as he watched her win over McCall. The poor man looked a bit in awe of Maggy. Edward had to admit himself that she'd accomplished much in the last hour and with great aplomb. She acted quickly on her feet and had successfully discovered two possible suspects.

If only she hadn't gone and ruined everything with this harebrained scheme of them pretending to be engaged.

"We'll be just a few minutes, Mr. McCall."

Her back was to Edward, but he could tell from her tone that Maggy had graced the foreman with another smile before she shut the parlor door. An outlandish, irrational thought had him wondering what it would be like to have the full power of that charming smile directed at him.

It certainly wasn't her smile that she aimed at him when she whirled around. "You are going to ruin this investigation," she hissed. "Could you have looked any more appalled at playing the role of my fiancé?"

"Are you mad?" Edward countered, keeping his

voice equally low. "Of course I'm going to be shocked and downright annoyed when you announce such a ridiculous fiction."

Maggy crossed her arms and glared at him. Her eyes had turned a dark cobalt. "There wasn't time to ask how you felt about it. Besides I told you that I was coming up with a role."

"Yes. But I didn't think that would be pretending to be my fiancée. Who will believe it?"

Her eyebrows rose in a haughty look as she motioned to the closed door. "I have no doubt that your foreman believes it."

"This is madness." He threw his hands in the air, then spun to face the fireplace. "There is surely some other role for you to play."

He sensed her stepping toward him. "This is the best way for me to ingratiate myself into that club for the ranchers' sweethearts and wives. If I can get them to trust me, they'll share their secrets, which will likely include hints or knowledge of their husbands' nefarious activities."

"What about playing a servant at the inn? Or my… my visiting relation?" Edward jammed his hands into his pockets, his chin dipping low. He didn't need to hear Maggy's rejection of those ideas—in his heart, he knew they wouldn't work in the way they needed.

Her voice came out surprisingly kind and placating. "It's not enough to overhear their conversations, the way a servant would—I need to be someone they can confide in. You said it yourself, Edward. The only way I can gain access into that club is to pretend to be your wife or fiancée."

He had only a moment to realize he liked hearing

her say his name before she went on. "Believe me, I wouldn't choose this role if I didn't think it absolutely necessary to this mission."

Edward wasn't sure whether to be offended by that remark or not. Turning to face her, he glimpsed a touch of vulnerability on her face, as he had earlier, but it disappeared as quickly as it had come. Had she also been hurt in the past?

"Care to elaborate?" he inquired.

It was the wrong thing to ask. Maggy jutted out her chin and peered down her nose at him. "I have my reasons, which I do not need to discuss."

"And if I refuse to go along with this charade?" He felt compelled to ask the question, though he could feel himself relenting—against his better judgment. Maggy had effectively bested his challenge, and if he let her go, he wasn't sure where he'd look for another detective.

"Then I suppose I'll drive myself back to the station. There's nothing more I can do to help you."

The words themselves were spoken with clipped finality, but the flicker of desperation that entered her blue eyes belied their strength. Did she stand to gain or lose something from this case? Something beyond a paycheck for her time and efforts?

Edward pushed out a frustrated breath as he eyed the ceiling. The intricate plasterwork was a unique fixture of his home, a nod to his English heritage. He'd been hard-pressed to find someone who could do the work and had been relieved and proud when the old chap he'd hired had finished. This place represented Edward's hard work and ambition, not to mention his confidence in himself and his place in the world. He couldn't imagine watching everything he'd accomplished be picked off and destroyed bit by bit.

And that meant making a rather large concession now.

"If I go along with this…" He emphasized the word *if*, though Maggy still lit up with interest. "I don't want it to be an outright lie."

Her brow furrowed in confusion. "I don't understand."

How to explain? He didn't know if she was religious or not, but even if she wasn't, he hoped she would honor his desire to be scrupulous. It was a way of life he'd attempted to live fully, in light of his sister's example—a determination reinforced by Beatrice's dishonest behavior.

"What will we do to end this charade?" he asked, trying a different approach.

Maggy shook her head and shrugged. "Decide we don't suit and I go back to Colorado."

"Then I would like to make the engagement official."

Her eyes widened as a look of near panic and suspicion crossed her face. "Official how?"

"Will you…" Edward cleared his throat—he could well relate to the alarm she felt. It was as if he stood at the top of some great mountain peak and had been commanded to jump. "Will you agree to be my fiancée, for the duration of your time here? I only ask it that way," he hastened to add, "so that we won't be living or telling a lie when we tell people I asked for your hand."

She took his measure, making him wonder what she saw. "All right then. I'll agree to be your fiancée for as long as I'm needed here."

Then her lips curved upward in a dazzling smile, similar to the one she'd bestowed on McCall, leaving Edward as charmed as his foreman and thinking this temporary engagement might prove to be a decent idea after all.

Maggy resisted the urge to shout with triumph. Things were going splendidly and she'd only been at the Running W less than two hours. "Since we've already established our plan, I'd like to change." She motioned to the tea splotches on her dress. "And then I'd like to see the rest of the ranch."

"One moment," Edward said, scrutinizing her with those gray eyes. "Have you played the role of someone's fiancée before?"

"Well, no, but—"

"Have you ever been engaged before?"

The question pushed memories best forgotten into her mind and she frowned. She and Jeb were betrothed just two days before they married. That hardly counted. "I don't see how that's relevant, but no, I have not."

"Then how do I know this plan of yours will actually work?"

Now he was simply being obtuse. She'd already proven herself twice over, and she'd agreed to be his fiancée so they wouldn't be lying. Crossing her arms, Maggy challenged his probing look with one of her own. "Of course it will work."

"We also have your reputation to consider."

He was worried about that now? "I'm a female detective, Edward. I have little to no reputation as it is."

"Be that as it may," he clasped his hands behind his back as he paced the room again, "as my fiancée and a hopeful member of the ranchers' wives' club, you must be seen as the consummate image of propriety."

Concern nagged her, causing Maggy to tighten her arms against her bodice. "Fine. I will be."

"That would entail things like staying in the guest cottage rather than here inside my home."

She nodded with impatience. "I can do that. Now I'd like to—"

"What about your wardrobe?"

Full annoyance sparked inside her. So she hadn't factored in every detail; at least she'd come up with a plan. "What about it, *darling*?" she ground out.

The merest hint of amusement lit his gaze before he shuttered it. "You only came up with this scheme a moment ago—I doubt you packed with this role in mind. How up to snuff are your clothes?"

"They're a bit out of style. But, again, I'm a detective, not a socialite."

He stopped and stood in front of her. "A socialite is exactly what you must be, Maggy, if we are to pull this off."

Fear began chewing at her frustration, riddling her thoughts with doubt. "I can show you what I have to wear to social functions." While most of her dresses were simple in style and adornment, they would surely do. "I'll get my trunk…"

She let her voice fade out when Edward slid his fingers around her wrist to stay her exit. Icy terror froze her for a moment, except for the painful, rapid beating of her heart.

"Unhand me," she said in a firm whisper.

Edward blinked in obvious confusion, then glanced down at her hand. "My apologies." He released her at once, restoring Maggy's ability to breathe normally. His contrite expression was further proof he'd meant nothing by his gesture. "I only wished to detain you another minute."

Gripping her hands together, to hide their trembling, she lifted her chin. "What more did you want to say?"

"I want to address this."

Maggy eyed him, feeling puzzled. "Address what?"

"What just happened." He motioned between them.

Fresh dread washed through her and she clasped her hands more tightly together. She would not divulge her past to him. "I don't see how that's important to your case."

"I disagree." His mouth and brow were both drawn downward. "As an engaged couple, we have to appear as if we share genuine affection for one another. But if you can't abide my hand on yours…"

He wasn't asking about her past. Maggy allowed a small breath of relief. "I can certainly feign affection." Her tone came out far more self-confident than she actually felt. Surely she could play any role she needed to. She always had before. "Can you do the same?" she countered.

To her surprise, Edward didn't rattle off a quick retort. Instead he lowered his head and shut his eyes in what appeared to be a silent prayer. A prick of guilt stung Maggy as she tried to remember the last time she'd prayed. Probably not since she'd been a girl. She shifted her stance, feeling uncomfortable and at a disadvantage. It wasn't an emotion she enjoyed.

Edward opened his eyes and took a decisive step forward, which meant they were standing toe-to-toe. Maggy had a strange urge to ask him what he'd concluded. However, when he scooped up one of her hands in his, she had a guess what his answer had been.

"I believe I can act the part of a devoted fiancé." He gave her a lopsided smile. "At least I shall try."

The gentleness of his voice and the warmth of his fingers on hers inspired a renewal of her trepidation but also an unfamiliar and entirely unexpected sensation of safety. Could she play this role as thoroughly as Edward was implying they must?

"I... I need to change." She pulled her hand free and fell back a step.

His brow creased again, but he didn't attempt to stop her this time. "I'll show you to the guest cottage then."

Nodding, Maggy waited for him to lead the way. The hallway was empty, which meant his foreman had decided not to wait. Edward easily shouldered her trunk a second time and she trailed him out the front door. A stone's throw away stood a stable and another small building. The guest house sported the same white clapboard as the main one and its own tiny porch.

Edward set her trunk down to open the door. "Here you are."

"Thank you." Maggy stepped inside. The single room was spacious and clean, and the window revealed a lovely view of the mountains.

He placed her luggage on the bed. "Is there anything else you need?"

"No." She shook her head.

Slipping out the door, Edward paused. "How shall I introduce you to the rest of my staff?"

"While I'm here, I'll be Maggy Worthwright." She liked to keep her maiden name, which was the surname she went by since becoming a widow, to herself to preserve her anonymity and ability to be anyone she needed.

He nodded. "I'll be at the main barn, when you're ready to see the ranch."

"I'll be there soon."

Once he shut the door, Maggy sank down on the bed beside her trunk. What if she couldn't effectively play the part of Edward's fiancée? She hadn't exactly thought through what that would mean. And she'd all but panicked when he grabbed her hand. Could she endure days, possibly weeks, of pretending to adore him in the company of others? As if she were young and in love…all over again?

Maggy shivered, despite the room's pleasant temperature, and folded her arms tightly against her tea-soiled jacket. The thought of being under another man's thumb made her stomach roil.

What did she know about love or being betrothed to someone? In the past, love had been a weapon used to hurt or a dangerous path leading to foolish choices and weakness. She'd vowed at Jeb's funeral that she would never, ever allow herself to be tied to another man. Instead she would live alone—and free. Free of belittlement, hurt and pain.

You're nothin', Maggy. Just you remember that.

The deep-rooted, ugly words repeated in her mind and made it hard to breathe. She rubbed a hand along the fabric at her collarbone and sucked in several breaths.

"I am not nothing," she fiercely told herself. "I am one of the best Pinkerton detectives out there."

And that meant seeing this mission—this role—through completely. Maggy jumped to her feet and opened her trunk, fresh determination battling her fears. She could do this. The next few weeks would be worth the sacrifice, especially if her success here meant she secured the position as head female detective.

She removed her trousers and shirt from the trunk, eager to exchange her traveling dress for more comfortable clothing. After all, she was about to tour a working ranch. The feel of the loose material eased some of her trepidation. She tucked in her shirt, laced her shoes back up, and pulled her worn straw hat from its equally tattered box. Positioning the hat on her head, she eyed herself in the bureau mirror.

Did she look the part of Edward's fiancée? Maggy frowned at her reflection, pulling her naturally pink lips downward. Whether she did or not, this was the part she would play. She'd navigated far more complicated roles in her six years as a detective. But as she exited the cottage, she couldn't help a faint tremor of misgiving that this charade might prove to be her most challenging yet.

Chapter Four

"Uh, boss." McCall tipped his head toward something outside the main barn doors. "Is that your...um... fiancée comin' this way?"

Edward turned. He was actually looking forward to showing Maggy around the ranch and hoped her drooping spirits had been restored, now that she had a clean dress on. As he watched, the wranglers in the yard parted like the Red Sea, mouths agape in shock, as another...young man...strolled through their midst. Only this *chap* had auburn hair peeking out from beneath a straw hat and a womanly figure that was still obvious in spite of the loose-fitting clothes.

His eagerness faded. "Yes," he managed to say with only slight weariness in his tone. "That would be Maggy."

She'd berated *him* earlier for not keeping up the charade well enough and here she was dressed like a man. He frowned, his forehead pinching with the effort. Perhaps their plan was destined to fail from the start.

Belatedly he remembered his foreman. "Probably didn't want to ruin one of her dresses as I show her around," he explained with false cheer. He walked out of the barn to greet her, doing his best not to clench his hands into fists at his sides.

"Hello, darling," she called as she approached. "I'm ready for my tour."

He managed a tight smile as he gently gripped her elbow and steered her away from the wide-eyed looks of his staff. "A moment in private first, *dearest.*"

"All right." She glanced up at him, her expression one of cautious confusion.

Edward led her toward the nearest pasture so they wouldn't be overheard. When they reached the fence, he released her, keeping his back to his wranglers and foreman. "What exactly are you wearing?"

Maggy looked down at her clothes as if she'd forgotten what she'd put on. His staff certainly wouldn't forget any time soon. "A shirt and pants?"

"Precisely." He shot her an impatient look. Was she truly unaware of the stir she'd caused or her breach of propriety in dressing in such a fashion?

She folded her arms and her countenance hardened. He may have only known her for a few hours, but Edward could easily identify when her dander was up. "And what is so abhorrent about my clothes?"

"Nothing," he said with a module of patience, "if you intend to lasso one of my horses or muck a stall. However, if you plan to parade around town as my fiancée, then I'd ask you to please not do so looking like a man."

Her pink lips parted as if she were about to throw out a rejoinder. Then she obviously thought better of it and shut her mouth. She glanced back the way they'd come, a never-before-seen look of consternation settling onto her pretty face. "You're right. It's just that these clothes…" Her blue eyes flashed with momentary vulnerability before she lifted her chin. "It won't happen again. I will endeavor to act and look as a proper society fiancée should."

"Thank you." But he felt less victorious than he'd expected. While clothes and appearances were critical to playing their respective roles, he had a hunch that Maggy felt most comfortable, most like herself, in the clothes she wore at this moment. He felt a pang of remorse at the thought of taking that comfort away from her.

Pushing out a sigh, she faced away from him. "I'll go change."

"No need just yet," he said. "I already told McCall that you'd chosen your outfit for the express purpose of not soiling one of your gowns during your tour of the ranch."

A small smile appeared at her mouth. "That was rather quick scheming on your part."

"A first, I'll admit." Edward chuckled. "But I've had a rather effective albeit persistent teacher today."

Was it his imagination or did she blush? Before Edward could decide, Maggy took a step forward. "Let's see this ranch of yours."

"Maggy." He waited for her to turn around, then he offered her his arm. "I'm supposed to be showing my betrothed around the ranch."

She hesitated, her gaze riveted on his sleeve. "Right, of course." Determination etched her features as she strode back to his side and linked her arm through his. He could feel the tension radiating through her fingers, though.

He placed his hand over hers, hoping it would be reassuring this time. "Ahead of us is the main barn. Shall we start in there?"

"Yes."

He was relieved to see a flicker of gratitude in her eyes, which meant that right now she found his touch more comforting than jarring. And for some reason that felt as much a victory to him as anything else today.

By the time he'd finished showing Maggy around the ranch and introduced her as his fiancée to every member of his staff, Edward was wound tighter than a lasso inside. She hadn't said much, though she didn't look bored, either. There had been a succession of nods, a few questions and plenty of bright smiles for the wranglers. But what did she think of the Running W?

It surprised him that he cared about her opinion of the ranch, unlike the last time he'd shown a Pinkerton detective around the place. That had been all business. This time, however, Edward had a peculiar desire to impress Maggy. Which made little sense. It wasn't as if they were really engaged.

After watching her rub the nose of his horse, he worked up the courage to finally ask her estimation. "Well? What do you think of the place?" He feigned disinterest in her answer as they exited the stable.

"It's beautiful, Edward." She stopped walking and removed her straw hat, giving him a full view of her face. "Very impressive what you've managed to do in five years."

Was she being truthful? He hoped so. "I am proud of it."

"As you should be." She offered him a brief smile. "And we need to ensure that it remains as it is."

"Yes, of course." The reminder of why she was really here sobered him and returned his thoughts to the necessary success of their temporary engagement. "I believe my staff is quite taken by you."

Her eyebrows arched in a look of haughty amusement. "Even in my unladylike attire?"

"Even then," he replied with a deadpan expression.

Rolling her eyes, Maggy started for the house. "I'm glad to hear it. And now I'm ready for that supper you promised."

"One moment." He caught up to her near the porch. "Around here we dress for supper."

She shook her head. "What do you mean? I don't understand."

"We... *I*...change for supper." He motioned to his dust-speckled trousers and shirt. It wasn't necessary to be more formal for the dinner table—particularly when he usually dined alone—but it was a throwback to his growing-up years in England. Truth be told, he rather liked putting on a fresh pair of clothes after a hard day's work, then sitting down to a delicious meal.

"Change into what?" Her arms were tightly folded again.

Edward cleared his throat. "I'll put on a suit as I would if we were going to the Sheridan Inn for dinner. And you...well...you can dress in one of those gowns you said you owned."

"This is a nightly ritual?"

He nodded.

For a moment, her eyes fell shut as if she were summoning patience from deep inside herself. "All right," she said, opening her eyes. "I shall dress for dinner, *darling.*"

"Excellent, *my dear.*"

Spinning on her heel, Maggy marched toward the guest house, her straw hat smacking her pant leg. "But I am not rearranging my hair," she called back loudly.

Edward chuckled as he headed inside. His good humor continued as he changed into a fresh shirt, trousers, tie, vest and jacket. Normally he looked forward to the quiet that came with taking his meals by himself. Mrs. Harvey ate when she wanted, and McCall felt it important to eat the meals she prepared for the outside staff with the wranglers. Which meant Edward ate alone more often than not. Tonight, though, he found himself looking forward to dining with Maggy. She might be stubborn and far from demure, but he supposed he could see why those qualities were important in a detective, especially a female one.

Had he really almost sent her away hours earlier? He was grateful now that he hadn't. Did the Lord have a hand in that? Edward wondered as he headed back downstairs. He entered the dining room to find it empty. Should he wait for Maggy by the front door then, or take a seat?

As he was debating what to do, he heard the door swing open and shut, then the clack of heels across the entryway floor. He moved to the doorway of the dining room to meet her. She gripped her trailing skirt with one hand as she approached.

"Suitable for supper?" She did a spin, giving him a full view of her dress.

While it appeared well made, the pale yellow gown looked a few years outdated as Maggy had said, and the dull color of it washed the pink from her cheeks. Surely this wasn't what a vivacious, engaged young woman ought to wear. Worse still, the carefree, open demeanor she'd displayed during their tour of the ranch had disappeared. She resembled a dressed goose awaiting execution.

"It does suit for supper."

"But?" She pinned him with a penetrating glance.

Edward shifted his weight as uneasiness coursed through him. "Are all of your dresses similar to this?"

"Yes, I suppose they're all the same style. Neither noticeably fashionable nor unfashionable. Light colors that don't catch the eye. No ribbons or trim to come loose and betray that I've been poking around where I'm not supposed to be. Simple. Practical."

Needing a moment to think, he led her by the elbow into the dining room where he pulled out a chair for her.

"What's wrong with my dress, Edward?" She gave him an arched look as she took a seat.

He helped push her chair in, then sat beside her at the head of the table. "There's nothing inherently wrong with it," he hedged. He placed his napkin across his lap and felt relief when Maggy artfully did the same. Apparently, dinner etiquette would not be something they had to master, as well.

Mrs. Harvey's fortuitous entrance into the dining room kept him from having to think up a polite reply to Maggy's question. "Evening, sir," his housekeeper announced as she placed full plates in front of them. "You, too, miss." She beamed at Maggy.

"There's been a new wrinkle to the detective plans, Mrs. Harvey." He hadn't taken the opportunity to let her know yet. "Maggy will be..." He glanced at the door, then lowered his voice. "I've asked her to be my fiancée for the duration of her time here."

The older woman's eyes widened. "Your fiancée, sir? Was that your idea to become engaged like that?"

"No," Maggy interjected as she picked up her fork. "It was mine, Mrs. Harvey. I'm hoping it will allow me to become part of the ranchers' wives' club and gather critical information."

Edward was grateful she didn't disclose that they already had two suspects among the ranchers. As much as he trusted Mrs. Harvey, he sensed the less he discussed his case with anyone other than Maggy, the better.

Mrs. Harvey trained a shocked gaze at him. "You agreed to this plan, sir? Even after…" She let her words trail out, to Edward's relief. The woman knew of Beatrice's deceit, but it wasn't something he wished to share with Maggy, now or possibly ever.

"Of course. It's a brilliant one." He felt Maggy watching him shrewdly.

His housekeeper eyed them in turn once more. "I'll leave you to your meal then."

"Thank you, Mrs. Harvey." When the older woman left the room, Edward turned to Maggy. "I'll offer the blessing."

Her brows shot upward as she set her fork back down. She looked slightly startled—even a bit chagrined—at his suggestion, but she didn't appear annoyed. Wordlessly, she lowered her chin. Edward shut his eyes and began to pray. He thanked the Lord for the meal and asked His blessings upon his staff and the investigation, as well.

Maggy's disconcerted look remained as they began

eating. Edward wondered what she thought of faith and religion. If she were truly his fiancée, he would hope to share a similar belief and love of God with her. Beatrice hadn't. She'd attended church, of course, like the other wealthy families in their social circle, but her faith hadn't been the anchor that it became for Edward and his sister.

He sampled a bite of food, pushing aside thoughts of Beatrice and the past. "I think you'll find Mrs. Harvey's fare quite above any boardinghouse or restaurant." He shot Maggy a smile. "That's partly the reason I asked her to accompany me to America."

"The food is delicious," Maggy agreed. "So you've known Mrs. Harvey a long time."

It was more a statement than a question, but he nodded anyway.

"What did she mean about you agreeing to our plan 'even after?'"

Edward stifled a groan, though he wasn't surprised Maggy had not only caught his housekeeper's slip but remembered it, too. "Nothing of consequence." He took another bite, though he tasted little this time.

"Have you been engaged before?" Maggy inquired, her expression one of innocence. But Edward knew better. Her blue eyes were glowing with that same determination and tenacity he'd seen several times already.

He shook his head. "No, I haven't. Not officially anyway. Though I did believe there was an understanding between myself and a young lady."

There, he'd told her all he wished to reveal. Even his vague description of his and Beatrice's time together had resurrected the long-buried sting of her rejection. He didn't wish to dwell on it anymore.

"What you need is a new wardrobe," he declared, only too happy to return to the earlier topic. Maggy's irritation over what he thought of her dresses was far safer and less painful than reopening the past.

She studied him a moment and Edward had a sudden urge to ask what she observed. Did she see the often neglected, thrown-over third son of Lord and Lady Healey? Or did she see the successful rancher?

"A new wardrobe?" she repeated at last. "Is that really necessary?" She made a face as if he'd asked her to roll around in a stable stall.

Edward couldn't help the upward tilt of his mouth— both at her entertaining grimace and in relief that she hadn't hounded him for information about Beatrice. "Some women are actually thrilled by the thought of new clothes. Especially when they are at the expense of someone else's pocketbook."

"You're going to pay for new clothes...for me?" Her astonishment both amused and confused him. Had no one ever bought her anything before?

He picked up his water goblet. "I don't think it entirely fair to ask Pinkerton to foot the bill. Not when you need to be outfitted with an *entire* new wardrobe."

"Entire?" Her eyes narrowed. "What exactly does that mean, Edward?"

Taking a sip, he set down his glass. "You know— day dresses, evening dresses, hats, gloves, possibly even a ball gown. The wives' club will host their annual summer ball in another month."

"Why would I need a new hat and gloves?" Maggy

retorted, her expression darkening. "It all sounds rather excessive. Not to mention a great waste of money."

He had the impression she lumped herself in with the clothes as something—someone—unworthy to spend money on. Why would that be? She'd shown such confidence in herself as a detective. Did she not see herself as valuable outside of her profession?

"I agree it may be excessive." She looked as if she could breathe again, until he continued. "But a waste or not, that is what you'll need in order to convince these women you are one of them."

"Fine. If asked, I'll say my luggage was misplaced and I needed to replace what I lost." She jutted out her chin as she forked another bite, the tongs tapping the plate with force. "And when am I to be subjected to the joys of obtaining a new wardrobe?"

He chuckled—he was coming to like her cheeky humor. "Tomorrow. That way we can square things up with the livery stable to have transportation at your disposal during your stay."

"We're keeping the nag and the buggy then?"

Edward scoffed, shooting her a teasing look. "The buggy, yes. But not that nag. Something tells me you'd appreciate a more spirited horse to convey you to and from club meetings."

A mischievous smile chased the annoyance from her expression. "I believe that's the first sensible thing I've heard you say all evening."

Chapter Five

Maggy gritted her teeth, trying to appear patient and serene as the dressmaker tugged, poked and pinned. She felt like a peacock in the ready-made royal blue gown, with as many pins stuck in it as there were in the woman's pincushion. What she wouldn't give to see Edward submit to such ministrations. The thought pulled a smile from her. He might not think a new wardrobe so necessary after that.

She'd driven the buggy into Sheridan that morning, while Edward rode beside her on the horse they would switch for the nag. He made arrangements with the livery owner about keeping the vehicle for a few more weeks, then he drove her to the dressmaker's shop.

It felt strange, and unsettling, to have a man watching out for her like that. And she still couldn't understand why Edward would throw his money away on clothes she wouldn't likely wear again once this mission was solved. She needed to be convincing as his fiancée, yes. But to have a great deal of money spent on her? The uneasy feeling returned to her stomach, though a traitorous seedling of pleasure attempted to

sprout, as well. When had her father or Jeb ever purchased a gift for her? Never.

Her apprehension began to morph into choking
dread as thoughts of the past took hold inside her mind.
Maggy tightened her hands into fists and received a
scolding look from the dressmaker for not keeping still.

"Sorry," Maggy mumbled.

She had a job to do. And whether it felt nice or not
to have a man's help, no one else would be doing her
work for her. It was past time to do a little sleuthing.

"Ms. Glasen, was it?" she asked the dressmaker,
doing her best not to move.

The woman looked to be about Maggy's own age,
maybe even a few years younger. "Mmm-hmm." Ms.
Glasen had said little—beyond asking what sort of
gowns were required to replace the ones Maggy had
lost, if she had any preferences for colors, and if she
was new in town.

"How long have you had this dress shop?"

The dressmaker's amber eyes lit with pride. "Three
years."

Perfect. That meant the woman might be able to provide Maggy with some useful information. There was
no reason the odious task of being fitted for uncomfortable clothes shouldn't be profitable in other ways too.

"Do you know Mr. Edward Kent?"

Ms. Glasen's forehead crinkled in thought. "He lives
near Big Horn way, right? Owns a large ranch there,
I think."

"Yes, he does." Maggy affected a tender sigh. "He's
also my fiancé."

The dressmaker glanced up from her work. "Is that

so? I hadn't heard the gossip that he was courting any-one."

"It all happened rather fast."

Ms. Glasen rose to her feet. "I'm finished pinning this one. I have one other gown that may fit you with little to no alterations. Mrs. Druitt decided she didn't think the purple color would suit her daughter after all."

"Does that happen often?" Maggy stepped off the wooden box she'd been standing on.

"Now and then," the other woman admitted. "But I think the dark purple hue will look lovely with your auburn hair."

She disappeared through a door in the back of the shop and returned a few moments later with another trailing gown. Maggy suppressed a groan. What she wouldn't give to be back in her favorite trousers and shirt!

After accepting the dress, Maggy slipped behind the dressing screen and carefully traded the royal blue dress for the purple. Unlike the first one, this second gown felt more fluid. She did the buttons up the front, then stepped out to show the dressmaker.

"Ah, yes." Smiling, Ms. Glasen nodded. "That's the perfect color for you and the fit is exactly right, as well." She stepped away from the floor-length mirror, giving Maggy a full view of herself.

And the view startled her.

She couldn't say for sure that the color enhanced her hair, but the woman staring back at her looked more than confident and determined. She looked almost… beautiful. It was a notion Maggy had never allowed herself to consider before.

Tears burned her eyes as she glanced away, blinking rapidly. "It's a lovely dress. I'll take it, along with the royal blue one and the others we discussed." Ms. Glasen would be making an additional eight dresses for her.

"Wonderful." The woman beamed again. "I'll have the royal blue one ready for you to pick up tomorrow and the others next week. Are you staying in town?"

Maggy shook her head as she ducked back behind the screen. "No," she called over the fabric partition. "I'm staying at Edward's ranch. My chaperone fell through at the last moment, but we decided with his housekeeper and staff around and me staying in the small guest house, that all would be right and proper."

"Then I'm afraid you'll have to make the drive into town tomorrow, too."

She traded the purple dress for one of her old ones, hanging the other over the screen for Ms. Glasen to wrap. "Not a problem. I enjoy driving a buggy and the countryside is quite beautiful."

She finished dressing and stepped back into the room. The lovely gown had sidetracked her a bit from probing for more information, and now it was nearly time to leave.

"I wonder what gossip will be shared about me." She feigned a light laugh. "Being without a real chaperone and now engaged to Edward."

The dressmaker paused in wrapping up the purple gown. "I imagine the local ranchers' wives will be a bit surprised." A hint of pain flickered through her gaze. "They do enjoy new people and topics to discuss."

Maggy could easily guess what the woman hadn't admitted—Ms. Glasen had at one time been the source of gossip herself. "Is that who shares all the gossip? The local ranchers' wives?"

"Mostly, yes." She tied a string around the paper-wrapped parcel. "They have a rather exclusive club that holds weekly tea meetings."

"Oh?" Edward had been right! "Do you belong to their club?"

Ms. Glasen shook her head, another trace of sorrow flitting across her young face. "No. You must be married or engaged to one of the local ranchers to join."

"Who is in charge of this club?"

"Mrs. Dolphina Druitt," the dressmaker replied in a slightly flat tone.

This was a new and potentially important piece of information. Mrs. Druitt was the same woman who hadn't liked the purple dress for her daughter. Maggy would need to see what Edward knew about Mr. Druitt. Did he hold the same authority among the men that his wife seemed to hold among the women?

Keeping her countenance impassive, she asked, "Do you think Mrs. Druitt and the club would accept me into their ranks?"

The dressmaker extended the package toward Maggy. "I don't see why not. You meet their engaged or married requirement. Of course," she continued in a tone that hinted at more hidden pain, "if for whatever reason you chose not to marry Mr. Kent, you would be asked to leave."

It wasn't difficult for Maggy to piece together Ms. Glasen's untold story. The woman had likely been engaged to someone and therefore part of the local women's club, but when she or her fiancé ended the betrothal, the dressmaker had been banished from the group.

She felt a strange desire to offer the woman a measure of comfort. Not as part of a mission or a disguise but as herself. What could she say though?

"Tea meetings sound a bit boring for my tastes," she admitted with full honesty into the tense silence of the shop.

Ms. Glasen's tight expression relaxed and her lips curved upward. "I think they're dull too. Although, the club does host an annual ball every summer that everyone is invited to and that is rather nice."

The summer ball. Maggy had forgotten. "That does sound lovely. Perhaps I ought to have a ball gown made, as well."

"I haven't made a ball gown in ages for someone new." The dressmaker went to the counter and grabbed up a stack of magazines. Turning back, she eyed Maggy carefully. "I think I know just the thing to make you shine."

Maggy didn't want to shine; she wanted to solve this case. Used to staying deliberately hidden in the background, it went against the grain to draw attention to herself. But, this could very well be a means to the end of finding the saboteurs.

She followed Ms. Glasen toward a pair of armchairs. Perhaps it was also a way to help out an unmarried female entrepreneur like herself. As she took a seat beside the dressmaker and watched the woman's face brighten with enthusiasm, Maggy felt a glimmer of satisfaction that surprisingly had nothing to do with detective work this time.

* * *

With his left foot resting on his right knee, Edward hoped he looked the picture of casualness, though inside, he felt only agitation. He didn't like being idle, at least not during the workday, even if it was important to outfit Maggy for her role as his fiancée. The other reason behind his uneasiness was the two ranchers seated near him on the long porch of the Sheridan Inn—the younger of which, Gunther Bertram, happened to be one of the ranchers Maggy suspected of sabotaging the Running W.

"Did you enjoy that equestrian book?" Edward asked as he swiveled to look at Bertram. "The one I loaned you a while back?"

While Maggy was busy with her new wardrobe, Edward had opted to walk over to the inn to see if he could get a head start on their investigation. It was more than fortunate that Bertram happened to be one of the men seated out front when he'd walked up.

Bertram cleared his throat. "It was good, real good."

"You're welcome to borrow another."

Did he only imagine the slight paling of the man's face? "Real nice of you, Kent. I'll…uh…" Another clearing of his throat filled in his pause. "I'll have to do that."

"How are your horses this year, Kent?" Nevil Druitt, the other rancher, asked.

Edward threw him a confident smile, one that wasn't forced. Between the Cavalry's interest and Maggy's help, he was feeling more assured. "The ranch is doing well. And yours?"

"Never better." Druitt swiped a bandanna across his brow and balding head, his vest pushed to its limits by his rounded middle. "Heard from Harry at the livery that some woman came to visit you. A relation of yours?"

Bertram smirked. "Who else would it be? It isn't like Kent is interested in settling down. Not that I blame you one bit," he added. "Women are just plain trouble."

"Now, hold on there, son," Druitt said in a placating tone. "When you find the right woman, you'll think differently."

Edward lowered his foot to the porch floorboards. "Actually the young woman who came to visit is my fiancée. Her name is Maggy Worthwright."

He wasn't sure who looked more shocked at his news—Bertram or Druitt. The latter recovered more quickly, though. "Well, look at that. What'd I just say about finding the right woman? Kent here apparently has. Where's your little lady from?"

"Colorado." That was where the Pinkerton office was located, and he thought he remembered Maggy saying something at dinner last night about living there.

Druitt's eyebrows shot upward. "How'd you meet then? Is she one of those mail-order brides?"

"No." Edward shook his head. "We were introduced by a mutual acquaintance, which was followed by a rather whirlwind courtship." *Of one and a half hours*, he thought wryly as he recalled Maggy's shocking proposal and then his own to prevent them from living a lie.

Bertram regarded him as if he thought Edward completely mad. Time would only tell if that proved true. "What'd you go and get engaged for, Kent? I didn't think you'd be sticking…" He shot a look at Druitt and let the rest of his question fade out.

"You didn't think I'd be sticking to what?" Edward asked.

Shaking his head, his face now inflamed instead of colorless, Bertram jumped to his feet. "I just remembered I promised the saddle maker I'd take a look at some of his new saddles. See you boys on Saturday."

"See you Saturday," Druitt echoed. "Suppose I'd best be getting on myself if I want to avoid Dolphina's scolding." He stood, as well.

Edward nodded; he could easily imagine his late father saying something similar about his mother. At least nagging wasn't something Maggy seemed inclined toward. She might be satirical and stubborn, but she wasn't badgering.

"Will you be bringing your fiancée to dinner on Saturday?" the older rancher asked.

Edward rose to his feet. "Yes. I believe she might also like to join that ladies' club." He pretended to try to recall more information. "I think it's the one that the other ranchers' wives and sweethearts are members of."

"I'm sure they'd welcome her warmly." Druitt pocketed his bandanna. "A prosperous ranch and a wife-to-be? Congratulations, Kent. You're doing well for yourself."

The words sounded admiring, but Edward wondered at their sincerity. "Thank you," he acknowledged with a nod. "I'm looking forward to what the future holds and seeing the ranch prosper even more."

Druitt smiled. "Wonderful to hear. We'll see you and Miss Worthwright on Saturday."

Watching him slowly walk to his horse, Edward frowned. Bertram had definitely acted strangely, but Edward couldn't say for certain about Druitt. He didn't know the older rancher well. How many men were involved in the plot against his ranch? Who were the real culprits and who weren't? His jaw clenched with frustration at not knowing the answers, but he fought to relax it. One way or the other, he'd figure things out. Or rather, he and Maggy would figure them out. Because the alternative, where the wrongdoers won, was unthinkable.

Maggy tightened the twine she'd used to secure her pile of hatboxes and packages in the shallow compartment behind the buggy seat. She eyed her handiwork with satisfaction as she brushed her hands free of flecks of string and dust.

"We might have procured some rope for you at the livery stable or the saddle shop."

She turned to face Edward, her hands settling on her hips. "Now why would we do that when I figured out my own ingenious solution?" She moved toward the driver's side of the buggy. "Besides, if I have to enter one more shop this morning, I'm liable to scream."

"That miserable, huh?" He moved to stand next to her, his hand rising to lightly grip her elbow. Instead of helping her up as she'd expected, though, he tugged her back to the ground and steered her around the buggy.

Maggy frowned. "What are you doing?"

"Helping you into your side of the buggy," he murmured before offering a polite smile to some passerby.

"What do you mean my side—"

He leaned close to whisper in her ear. "It wouldn't look proper for you to be driving me around town, Maggy."

"No?" It came out far more yielding than she'd wanted, but Edward's nearness had a sudden and peculiar effect on her ability to think or reason. Standing this close, she could see his eyes weren't entirely gray in color. There was a slight blue hue to them as well. She could also smell the pleasant scent of soap and grass that clung to him.

Summoning her fortitude to stay focused and unaffected, she pulled her arm free and scaled the buggy herself. "Fine, you can drive," she muttered, though loud enough that he would hear.

Edward chuckled as he circled the vehicle and climbed onto the seat beside her. Did his laughter mean he thought her amusing, or was he entertained by the affect his close proximity had on her?

"I'll let you drive once we're out of town…" He held up his hand when she started to thank him. "But only if you can act with decorum until then."

Maggy smiled fully at him and linked her arm through his. "Why, I'm the picture of decorum!"

His laughter came again as he guided the horse and buggy into the street. "Of course."

"I am," she countered, nodding cordially to a woman and her young daughter walking along the street. "I got everything I needed for my wardrobe and some new information to boot, too."

He flicked his gaze to hers. "What did you find out?"

"Well…" Maggy let the word hang there to draw out the suspense. "I learned from the dressmaker Ms. Glasen that the wives' club is run by a woman named Dolphina Druitt. Ms. Glasen also confirmed that as your fiancée, I can join."

Edward gave a thoughtful nod. "I was doing a bit of investigating myself."

"You were?" She stared at him in surprise. Even in cases where people desperately wanted something to go their way, they typically still left everything up to Maggy—the questioning, the disguises, the clue gathering. This was the first time in her career that she'd worked with a partner, so to speak. "What did you learn?"

"Well…" he said, letting the word hang between them as she'd done.

She elbowed him in the side. "Very funny. What did you find out?"

"All right." Frustration replaced the amusement on his face. "It wasn't so much what I learned as what I observed."

Maggy couldn't help throwing him an admiring glance. "That's something even new detectives don't catch on to soon enough."

"Are you admitting I'm proficient at sleuthing, too?" A rather attractive smile lifted one corner of his mouth.

She glanced away, her answering laugh a bit forced. "I don't know about that. I think it all depends on what you observed."

"I went by the inn and one of your—*our*—suspects was there. Gunther Bertram."

"Ah-ha." She sat up straighter. "What did he say?"

Edward shifted the reins in his grip. "It was more his mannerisms that struck me as odd. I asked him about the book I had loaned him. When I suggested he could borrow another, he appeared uncomfortable."

"What do you mean?" More details might help them

understand if Bertram's behavior was truly suspicious or not.

"His face went a bit white and his whole demeanor was quite uneasy." He threw her a quick look. "Did I only see what I wished to see?"

She understood what prompted his question; it was one she'd asked herself often her first year as a detective. "Were there any other signs that he was uneasy?"

Edward appeared thoughtful. "At the end of our conversation, I mentioned that I was engaged and he was clearly surprised to hear it. He started to say something. He said he didn't think I'd be sticking."

"Sticking?" she repeated. "Sticking to what?"

He shook his head. "I'm not sure—he cut himself off. Though I wondered if he meant sticking around—as in staying on the ranch."

"That would make sense, given he wrote one of the notes meant to scare you into leaving." She reviewed in her mind all that they now knew about the man. "I don't think he's the one behind everything. Someone else is pulling the strings."

His brow creased. "Why do you think that?"

"Because the person behind all of this is likely too crafty to let something slip out like Bertram did."

"Then we are right back where we began."

Maggy could relate to his discouragement, but unlike with her other clients, she wanted to reassure Edward. She gave his arm a friendly squeeze, telling herself it was as much to encourage him as it was to play her part as his fiancée. "Not necessarily."

"Why not?" he countered, shooting her a questioning look.

"I think we can confidently rule out that Bertram is

our man. He's being manipulated by someone else—probably someone too clever to use their own handwriting on the notes. Which also means it's likely that Winchester isn't our man, either."

He nodded slowly. "I also spoke with Nevil Druitt."

"Is he married to Dolphina Druitt?"

"Yes."

Maggy brightened. "Perfect. How well do you know him?"

"Not well. He's never been to the ranch, though I've seen him every time I've dined at the inn on Saturday evenings." Edward cast a glance at her. "He asked if you would be accompanying me this Saturday."

The reminder that they had more to do as an engaged couple than Edward simply driving her about town and being seen arm in arm made her stomach twist with fresh nerves. She had no worries about pulling off her part while meeting with the women's club. But playing the part of a loving bride-to-be in a mixed group, with Edward right beside her?

"Is something wrong?"

His question sliced through Maggy's apprehension and jerked her back to the present. She glanced around to find they'd left the last of the buildings behind them. "Only thinking," she said as she pulled her arm from his. "And now it's time for me to drive."

Edward wordlessly studied her, but she refused to let him see her concern. After all, being his fiancée had been her idea. Instead she simply smiled and held her hand out for the reins.

After a moment, he passed the reins to her. "As promised."

"Thank you." She slid over on the seat as he climbed

down and moved around the buggy. An urge to tease him nearly had her driving away. But she suppressed the desire with a mental shake of her head. She had to be careful. Edward wasn't arrogant or rude, but he was still a client—and a man.

He took the spot she'd vacated, and Maggy guided the buggy forward. "I think you should try to get to know Mr. Druitt better," she suggested, "and any of the other ranchers whose wives are in Mrs. Druitt's club."

"Very well."

When she glanced at him, she found him frowning. "We'll weed out our man, Edward. I know it."

"On that score, I'm feeling more confident." He gripped the side of the seat with one hand. "Returning to the ranch hale and whole is something I feel less assured about."

Maggy laughed. "Too fast?"

"Not if we're in a chariot race." He grimaced, but she saw his gray eyes flash with teasing. "Be advised there is a rather large rut in the road a quarter of a mile ahead of us."

She slowed the conveyance a little. "This isn't nearly as fun as galloping on a horse."

"You ride?" He appeared to relax slightly.

"I love riding."

He shifted to face her on the seat. "Then what do you say to lowering our speed to something more conducive to a leisure ride through the country, and I'll take you riding this afternoon."

Could she afford to take a break in the investigation to go riding? But then they had spent all morning gathering information and securing their role as a couple.

It had been ages since she'd last ridden a horse, especially over acres of unbroken land.

It was too appealing a suggestion to ignore, even if it meant a meandering ride back to the ranch for now.

Glancing at Edward, Maggy tugged back on the reins to slow the horse. "You have a deal, *darling*."

Chapter Six

Leaning forward in the saddle, Edward urged Napoleon faster. They were in the lead, but a glance over his shoulder confirmed that Maggy and her horse weren't far behind. The tree they'd selected as the finish line for their race drew closer and closer. A rare grin pulled at Edward's mouth. It had been far too many years since he'd last raced someone on his horse—and even then, it had likely been one of his brothers or school chums, not a woman.

He wasn't surprised Maggy had suggested the challenge, though. Her insistence in swapping her dress for her men's clothes for the ride hadn't shocked him as much as before, either. She was the most unconventional woman he'd ever met, and at the same time, he rather liked that quality about her. Especially if it helped them solve his case all the sooner.

The tree loomed up ahead. He was going to win! Edward kept his horse at a gallop. He couldn't recall the last time he'd felt this free, this satisfied. Grinning all the more, he let his concerns about the ranch slip to the back of his mind.

He and Napoleon were nearly abreast the tree, when Maggy came thundering up alongside them. Edward's jaw went slack with astonishment that she'd caught up to him—then tightened with determination. Something about her compelled him to meet her challenges head-on as if she were a friend or a business partner.

Napoleon still had the lead by a nose, but the lead was narrowing. The two mounts vied back and forth for first until finally they raced past the tree, side by side.

Edward let his horse have its head as he sat up straighter. Turning, he saw Maggy doing the same with her horse. After another minute or so, he circled Napoleon back the way they'd come.

"Well done," he said with sincerity as he rode toward Maggy.

She threw him a smile that outshone the afternoon sunshine. "You too. I wasn't sure we'd beat you, at least not until right at the end."

He stopped his horse. "You're saying *you* won?"

"I do think Persimmon's nose was an inch or two ahead of Napoleon's." She patted the neck of her horse.

Edward shook his head in disbelief. "Preposterous. That was a draw if I ever saw one."

"I don't know..." Maggy's forehead creased in thought, then she laughed. "All right. Fine. We tied."

His sudden thought slipped out his mouth. "You don't want to admit that you might not have won."

The lightheartedness between them shattered like glass. Maggy's open expression disappeared, too, replaced by a frown.

"There's nothing wrong with liking to win," she said as she climbed to the ground. "Why do men think they're the only ones who do? The only ones who should win?" She seemed hurt, though she was trying to hide it behind her prickly demeanor.

As she stalked forward, leading Persimmon by the reins, Edward dismounted, as well. He led Napoleon after them. "My sister was quite competitive."

Maggy shot him a surprised look. "Your sister?"

"Yes," Edward said with a nod. "Perhaps that was inevitable, given she was the only girl in a family of three boys."

"Was she older or younger than you?"

"Younger by a year. But she still loved to best me in chess." He smiled at the memory of Liza's grin—not so unlike Maggy's of moments ago—when she was victorious at a game. "She was most competitive when it came to our education, though. She wanted to learn and know all of the subjects her brothers did."

They reached a stream and both allowed their horses to drink. "And did she learn those things?" Maggy asked, with a note of what sounded like more than curiosity.

"Not as well as she would have liked." Edward kicked at a clump of grass, remembering the times he'd found Liza crying in frustration that she couldn't go to school like he and their brothers had. "Our parents were adamant she learn the things other well-bred ladies learned, which didn't include commerce or politics or science. I did give her my school texts whenever I could."

He turned to look at Maggy. Her auburn hair glowed in the sunlight, but her blue-eyed gaze still appeared troubled. "It was not my intent to insult your desire to win, Maggy. I simply recognized in you the same spirit of competition I saw in my sister."

"Is she still in England? Your sister?"

Sadness rose inside him at the question. "No. She passed away when she was fifteen."

"Oh." She glanced his way, her expression one of surprise and compassion. "I'm sorry to hear that, Edward. Were you…were you two close?"

He dipped his chin in a nod. "Quite close. She might have been younger in age, but she possessed the wisdom of someone much older. At times, she was more a mother to me than our own."

Maggy faced the stream and nearby mountains, an almost wistful expression on her face.

"Do you have siblings?"

Shaking her head, she folded her arms. He recognized the telltale sign of her nervousness, of a need to protect herself. It reminded Edward of a horse they'd broken last year—one he'd been more than happy to buy, especially after learning the animal had been mistreated by its previous owner. At first, the horse had acted much like Maggy, stubborn and strong-willed and unwilling to let Edward or McCall get too close.

"It was just me and my pa," she said, her voice barely more than a whisper. "My mother died when I was a girl."

He sensed she didn't want his sympathy, so he changed the subject. "You ride quite well."

"For a woman?" she countered, though her posture had relaxed and her blue eyes now sparked with amusement.

Edward chuckled. "For anyone. And I mean that."

"I know you do." She spoke so softly again she almost missed her response.

This simple statement of trust—in him and his

word—struck him hard in the chest. He might have known her less than twenty-four hours, and yet, Edward had quickly realized Maggy did not trust lightly. But, in some ways, she seemed to trust him already. That revelation felt like a rare gift, something he didn't want to take for granted.

"Would you like to see the precise spot I stood when I chose where I wanted my ranch?"

Maggy lifted her head and blinked as if she'd been deep in thought. "Is it close by?"

"Just to the right of that rise," Edward said, pointing in the direction of the mountains.

Her lips tilted slightly upward. "Lead the way."

He gathered Napoleon's reins and mounted. Maggy did the same with Persimmon. After crossing the stream, he rode past the rise to a waist-high stack of rocks. He hadn't visited this spot in more than a year, and feelings of nostalgia swept through him as he turned Napoleon beside the rock mound to face north.

"I'd heard there was good grazing near the Big Horn Mountains, so after Mrs. Harvey and I arrived in Sheridan, I rented a horse and rode this way." He rested his arm on the saddle horn. "When I reached this spot, I stopped to gauge how far I'd ridden and that's when I saw that." He gestured at the fertile hills and distant stand of trees along the river where he'd built his ranch.

Maggy gazed in the direction of the Running W. "It's beautiful, Edward."

"I placed this marker here to commemorate the moment."

She stared down at the rocks. "You stacked these rocks?"

"I did," he responded firmly, though he was beginning to feel a bit foolish. He'd never shown another person this spot or the rock mound he'd created. "My ancestors were known to have erected stone monuments throughout Britain." He shrugged. "I suppose I thought it might be fitting to do the same in my new homeland."

She tipped her head, her gaze intent on his face. Could she read his past as well as he thought he was beginning to read hers?

"I think it's fitting," she said before turning away. "What about that fence? Did you put that up as a monument, too?"

It took a moment for her question to register in his mind. "Fence? What fence?"

"There between those trees." Maggy pointed a short ways off. "I spotted some fence posts as we rode past."

His confusion gave way to instant suspicion and concern. "I don't recall seeing a fence around here, at least not when I last visited this spot. There are no other ranches this far south."

"I'd like to check it out."

He didn't argue. The apprehension roiling in his gut was prodding him to investigate, too. Guiding his horse after Maggy's, he followed her toward the stand of trees. There, to his astonishment, stood a fenced circle.

Frowning, Edward dismounted and walked toward the nearest post. Maggy did the same. "It's a corral, isn't it?" she asked.

"Yes, though it's been hastily constructed." He motioned to the crude branches and logs that made up the fence. "What's it doing here?"

He traversed the fence line, searching for a clue as to the structure's purpose or ownership. Maggy circled the corral in the opposite direction. On the far side, Edward stopped to think. Why would someone build a corral way out here? And why would they need to gather horses so far from any ranch? He rested his forearms on the top rung of the fence.

The closest ranch was his, and yet, he didn't use this spot—hadn't even paid attention to its existence before today.

"Edward, come look at this."

He turned to find Maggy peering at something on the ground a few feet away. When he walked over, he saw it was the blackened remains of a fire. A large rock sat beside the cold ashes, its surface burnt, as well. Almost as if…

"They're changing the horse brands," he and Maggy exclaimed at the same time.

A clear picture of what had likely transpired formed inside his head, and with it came a wave of anger. "Whoever built this must have been planning to release some of my horses the other day. Somehow they hid them while my men were on the hunt, then the culprits rounded up the horses and brought them here to change the brands." He removed his hat and slapped it against his thigh.

"If that's true," Maggy said, her voice calm but confident, her blue gaze steely, "and we can prove it, we can have them arrested for horse rustling."

Edward stalked back to his horse, his hat choked between his fingers. He was barely aware of Maggy behind him. "That's the trouble," he half growled as he smacked his hat back on his head and climbed into the saddle. "We can't prove anything right now."

Glancing at Maggy, who surprisingly kept silent

as she mounted her horse, he realized he'd allowed himself to be caught up in her vivacity and company. They were business partners of sorts and temporarily engaged to one another, but he had to keep his focus on the weightier matters at hand. His ranch was on the line, and it was time to redouble his efforts to save it.

Maggy saw little of Edward the next three days, except for at meals. Even then, their conversation didn't flow with the same easy banter as it had during their buggy ride or when they'd gone riding the other day. Any talk revolved around the ranch and if either of them had observed anything new. Edward seemed intent on throwing himself into his ranch duties, so Maggy had turned her focus outside the Running W. She'd driven into town to collect the royal blue dress and one other gown Ms. Glasen had also completed and made a point to drive around the streets of Sheridan—as if she really were Edward's fiancée, driven by nothing more than simple curiosity to explore the town she would eventually call home.

She also rode back to the hidden corral to search for more clues, but she didn't find any. Mostly she felt bored and useless, feelings she despised. She wanted to make more headway on Edward's case, and for that reason, she was more than ready for her debut dinner at the Sheridan Inn.

By Saturday evening, though, her stomach felt so twisted in knots that she didn't think she would be able to eat a thing. She asked Mrs. Harvey to help with her hair, and the housekeeper kindly agreed. Maggy wore the royal blue gown. From her trunk, she even unearthed a strand of faux pearls.

"You look lovely, Maggy," Mrs. Harvey declared as she stepped back from finishing Maggy's hair.

Maggy couldn't see much of herself in the handheld mirror the housekeeper had brought to the guest house, but she was still grateful for the compliment. "Thank you, Mrs. Harvey."

"I mean it, love. See for yourself, in the bureau mirror there." With a smile, the older woman nudged her arm.

Pushing out a sigh, Maggy stood, fisted her train in one hand and moved to the mirror. The woman looking back at her tonight couldn't possibly be the same one who'd arrived here five days ago. This woman's hair and eyes glowed against the backdrop of the bright blue dress. Her cheekbones appeared prominent, elegant even, with the way her hair had been swept up off her face and neck.

Mrs. Harvey came to stand behind her. "Everyone'll be in awe of Mr. Kent's fiancée."

The reminder of what part she must play well tonight tightened her middle with fresh tension. *You can do this, Maggy. This is only temporary. You are engaged to Edward, and now you look like someone he would choose.*

A knock at the door set her heart racing. It was likely just Edward. Why was she blushing then, like a girl about to see her beau?

Lifting her chin in defiance of her nerves, she strode to the door and threw it open. "I just need to collect my gloves, then I'll be ready."

"Very good." His gray eyes widened as he gazed at her. Was it her brusque manner or something displeasing about her attire?

She snatched her gloves off the bed and put them on, thanked Mrs. Harvey once more, then marched out the door. "I know it's a bright color for an evening gown," she said as she passed Edward, "but you didn't like my pale ones. And for this situation, I do want to make an impression."

"Maggy." He took her by the elbow and tugged her gently backward. "You will definitely make an impression."

Was he teasing her? She couldn't tell, especially with her arm cupped warmly in his grip. "I can change into something more subdued—"

"And by impression..." He leaned close, his mouth quirked up at the corners. "I meant a rather stunning one."

She blinked, suddenly realizing how handsome he looked in his white bow tie and shirt and dark suit. "So the dress is fine?"

"The dress is fine." He chuckled as he released her. "Shall we?" He motioned to where the buggy and horse stood waiting.

Forcing a pert smile, she nodded. "Time for the show."

Edward helped her into the buggy, and she was grateful for the assistance. She wouldn't be able to maneuver on her own in the long evening dress. Thankfully this "disguise" wasn't what she normally had to wear for all of her missions. Though, she did have to admit, the fabric and cut of the gown were more comfortable than her older ones.

The drive to Sheridan seemed to take twice as long as normal, especially with neither of them saying much. All of sudden, though, the inn loomed before them.

Maggy swallowed hard, grateful the lace at her throat wasn't constricting. In spite of her long sleeves, she still shivered as she eyed the three-story white building with its dormer windows and long porch.

Her heartbeat pulsed faster as Edward helped her from the buggy. There were a number of carriages parked out front and a few guests seated in the porch chairs, but Maggy saw no other nicely dressed couples.

"Are we late?" she whispered when Edward offered her his arm.

He glanced around. "A few minutes perhaps."

"Oh." Her legs felt stiff as if she'd been riding in the buggy for a hundred miles instead of seven. "All right then."

Edward didn't move. Instead Maggy watched him shut his eyes and realized he was praying. It wasn't the first time she'd observed him doing so. He'd prayed before each meal she'd shared with him. And yet, unlike the other times, she didn't feel uncomfortable now—she felt marginally better.

A few seconds later, he squared his shoulders and guided her through the front door of the inn. Maggy found the inside of the building as tasteful and clean as the outside. Edward steered her past the desk, nodding a greeting to the clerk stationed there. Since he was busy speaking with some hotel guests, he simply nodded back, but his eyes went wide with shock when he saw Maggy. An unfamiliar desire to giggle rose inside her at the man's bug-eyed look.

Outside the dining room door, Edward paused again. "Ready?" he asked.

She pulled in a calming breath and lifted her chin. "Ready."

"Then here we go, Miss Worthwright," he murmured with a smile.

Releasing her arm, he placed his hand on the small of her back and directed her into the room. The murmur of conversation at the different tables ceased. Even one of the waiters across the room stopped mid-stride, a tray in hand. Every pair of eyes turned toward her and Edward.

Maggy's hands felt clammy inside her gloves and her heart pounded so loudly in her ears it sounded like cannon shot in the near-silent room. She might have stood there staring back at all those people forever if Edward hadn't nudged her forward with a whispered, "We can do this."

The confident words and his firm but comforting touch on her back propelled Maggy into action. She smiled brightly and swept toward the first table. "Good evening," she said with regal poise as she nodded to those seated there. "I'm so sorry we're late."

The silence in the room snapped as conversation and the clatter of cutlery filled the space once more. The waiter rushed forward with his food.

"Kent." A man with a long mustache rose from his chair at the first table. "Who's your enchanting guest?"

Edward reached out to shake the man's hand, then turned to her. "Miss Worthwright, may I introduce Sid Winchester?"

Maggy wanted to applaud him. Her name rolled effortlessly, almost tenderly, off his tongue. Perhaps it had been wise for Edward to officially ask her to be his fiancée after all.

Though she was sizing Winchester up, she feigned a pleasant demeanor as she held out her hand, fingers down. The rancher looked unsure of what to do, so he simply shook her fingers.

"It's a pleasure to meet you, Mr. Winchester."

"You, too." He released her to sit back down and motioned to the woman on his left. "This is my wife, Lola."

The introductions continued, then Edward led her to the next table and the next. At each, she smiled, shook hands, and committed to memory which wives went with which ranchers. Her mouth was beginning to feel sore from all the smiling by the time they reached the head table where two empty chairs stood.

"We'll be eating with the Druitts," Edward murmured in her ear as they moved forward.

"Excellent. I'm starving."

His lips twitched with a concealed smile. "Miss Worthwright," he said, when they reached the table. "This is Nevil Druitt."

"I'm pleased to make your acquaintance, Mr. Druitt."

"Miss Worthwright," the older rancher boomed, rising. "So good to meet you at last." Maggy shook his hand. "May I introduce my wife, Dolphina?"

Eagerly Maggy studied the older woman. She wasn't a great beauty with her sagging chin and graying hair, but unlike the other women Maggy had met tonight, Dophina Druitt had a commanding air about her. Her dress was in the latest style and her green-eyed gaze appeared sharp and observant.

"How do you do?" Maggy said. "So pleased to meet more friends of my dear Edward's." She linked her arm with his and leaned into him.

Mrs. Druitt gave an imperial nod. "A pleasure to meet you as well, Miss Worthwright. Do have a seat."

Edward helped her into her chair, then took the one beside her. "Quite a press this evening, isn't there?" Almost right away, the waiter brought their food and Maggy began to eat.

"Yes, quite a crowd," Mrs. Druitt said as she glanced at Maggy. "I think everyone was eager to meet your intended, Mr. Kent. I must say, I almost didn't believe Nevil here when he told me the news. None of us had the faintest idea you were courting."

Lifting his fork, Edward shot the woman a tight smile. "I wished to keep it private until things were official."

"And you certainly did." Mrs. Druitt turned to Maggy next. "However did you come to know Mr. Kent? Why, I daresay he's never left the area since he arrived here, save to buy those horses of his."

Maggy pressed her napkin to her lips, her heart drumming anew. Mrs. Druitt wouldn't be easily put off by the simple explanation they'd given others. "Another gentleman I highly respect became acquainted with Edward and recommended the two of us meet." She glanced at Edward and smiled fully. "I'll certainly be forever grateful that he did. I came to see right away that Edward is kind, hardworking and ever so patient."

Having taken a drink, Edward began to cough. Maggy suspected he was trying not to laugh.

"Are you all right, darling?" she asked, leaning toward him.

His gray eyes watered, but he nodded. "I'll be fine," he answered in a slightly hoarse voice.

Mrs. Druitt studied them. "Where are you from, Miss Worthwright?"

"Colorado."

"Denver, perhaps?"

Maggy nodded and continued eating. It wasn't as tasty as Mrs. Harvey's, but it was still flavorful and satisfied her appetite.

"You must be one of the Denver Worthwrights," the woman exclaimed with animation. "A rather prominent family you have."

The food tasted suddenly bland as Maggy swallowed. Mrs. Druitt kept chatting away, but her words didn't register. What would the woman say if she knew Maggy didn't come from Denver's upper class? She was the daughter of a drunken miner and their entire cabin would likely fit inside the Druitt's drawing room.

You're nothing, Maggy.

Her brow beaded with sweat, her pulse pounding hard and fast. Panic dried her throat. Then she felt Edward's hand clasp hers beneath the table and give it a squeeze. Reassurance swept through her, chasing away the old anxieties.

"Actually," she said calmly, "Denver has only been my home for six years. My family is originally from a different part of Colorado. Have you been to Denver, Mrs. Druitt?"

The woman's expression grew wistful. "Once." Reversing the questions did the trick of taking the focus off of her. Mrs. Druitt prattled about the tall buildings, shops and sights, most of which Maggy could comment on.

When Edward released her hand, she threw him an

appreciative smile, and he returned the gesture. The rest of the meal passed without incident.

"Your dress is lovely," Mrs. Druitt commented, once the meal had concluded and both couples were moving toward the door. "Who is your dressmaker?"

Maggy glanced down. She'd nearly forgotten she was wearing a new gown. "Oh, Ms. Glasen."

"Ah." A sour look pinched the older woman's face. Maggy recalled how Mrs. Druitt hadn't approved of the dressmaker's purple gown. "I thought perhaps you'd had your gowns designed in Denver."

"No, this dress was expertly made by Ms. Glasen to replace those I lost when my luggage went missing." Maggy smiled at the woman as she added, "I was most grateful to find someone so knowledgeable of fashion here in Sheridan."

Mrs. Druitt blinked in obvious surprise at Maggy's glowing praise of the dressmaker, but she recovered quickly. "Did you belong to any women's clubs in Denver, Miss Worthwright?"

"Sadly, no. But with Edward so busy with the ranch, I am looking for ways to stay entertained myself while I'm here." She linked her arm through Edward's. "Are there any women's organizations in Sheridan?" she asked glibly.

The older woman eyed her. "There are a few sewing groups."

"My needlework is limited, I'm afraid." Beyond buttons and darning socks, she couldn't sew a thing. "Is that all?"

"We do have a group for the ranchers' wives," Mrs. Druitt said with self-importance. "I'm the president."

Maggy let her expression fall. "Oh, dear. If you have

to be a rancher's wife, I suppose that excludes me at present, doesn't it, darling?" She peered up at Edward.

"We have allowed fiancées in the past."

Turning back to Mrs. Druitt, she brightened. "Have you?"

"I'll need to speak to my vice president and secretary first, but…" The woman let her words hang there. "I believe we might be able to issue you an invitation to join us."

Maggy smiled. "How gracious. I would love to be a part of your club."

The four of them exited the inn, and she and Edward bid the Druitts good night. After settling on the buggy seat, she looped her arm through Edward's once more, maintaining appearances as they drove away from the inn.

"We did it!" she said quietly, though she wanted to shout it to the twilight sky. "I'm as good as in the club already."

Edward turned to her and laughed. "We did well." He faced forward again. "You did well."

"So did you." Not just in engaging Mr. Druitt and the other ranchers in conversation throughout the meal but also in how he'd help calm her nerves. "Thanks for coming to my rescue at the beginning."

His look conveyed understanding. "Being a detective doesn't make you impervious to fear, I imagine."

"No," Maggy said with a chuckle. "It certainly doesn't. My first mission I was so scared I thought I might be sick all over the floor of the train." She'd never admitted that to anyone, not even to James at the office. "What about you? What unnerves you?"

He appeared to think her question over. "Losing my ranch." The lines around his eyes and mouth tightened.

"You aren't going to lose it, Edward. Because I will do everything in my power to stop that from happening." She nudged his shoulder. "Besides, don't forget that—"

"You always get your man," he finished, his gray eyes sparking with amusement.

Maggy grinned. "Yes, I do. Now let me see if I can remember who is who tonight."

She reviewed each of the ranchers, what she'd observed about them, who of those were married, and the names and personality traits she'd noted of their wives. The evening, though tense at the beginning, had been successful. And she felt confident they'd been convincing in their role as an engaged couple.

It wasn't until they reached the ranch sometime later that Maggy discovered her arm was still linked with Edward's, her knee nearly touching his. She tugged her arm free and pretended to tuck a stray hair into her coiffure. But instead of feeling upset at having ridden so far in such a fashion, seated close to a man, she realized she didn't mind so much this time.

Chapter Seven

The dream felt so real, as if Maggy were reliving that fatal night all over again. She could feel the sharpness of the early March air in her lungs and the brush of the shawl around her shoulders as she walked the street to her and Jeb's cabin. She kept her chin low, to avoid being recognized, as the loneliness and despair nibbled away inside her.

Up ahead she heard someone shout, "Fire! There's a fire."

Maggy lifted her head to see for herself. Only then did she notice the glow against the dusky sky. And it was coming from the direction of her cabin.

She began to run, panic throbbing along with her feet as her shoes smacked against the dirt. Was Jeb all right? He'd come home inebriated—again. But unlike the other nights since the beginning of the latest miners' strike, she hadn't stuck around to coax him out of his foul mood with a good meal and plenty of platitudes that they'd be all right. No, tonight she'd gone for a walk, Jeb's hollering nipping at her heels as she'd left.

The sight of her own cabin in flames stopped her

cold. What little she and Jeb owned was inside, except for the money she'd slipped into her pocket before leaving on her walk. She'd feared in her absence that Jeb might find her secret hiding place where she'd stashed the small amount of cash. And where was her husband?

"Maggy, where's Jeb?" one of her neighbors asked.

She shook her head. "I—I don't know. I went for a walk… Jeb was deep in the bottle…but…"

"There may be someone still in there," she heard someone shout as the fire brigade appeared.

No! She couldn't stop shaking her head, couldn't stop shaking all over. "Jeb? Where's Jeb?" She pushed through the crowd toward the cabin door. He wasn't still in there, was he? He would have gotten out, wouldn't he? Except if he'd passed out on the bed like he usually did…

Arms restrained her from drawing any closer. The heat of the fire burned her cheeks. She reached up to touch them and realized she was crying. But that wasn't possible—she never cried. She hadn't shed tears in front of another person since she was seven.

"Jeb!" she screamed, her fear so strong she could hardly see straight. She had to rescue her husband. He would be furious if she didn't at least try. Fighting against those who held her back, though, proved futile. "Jeb!"

The roof collapsed, sending sparks leaping toward the darkening sky. Kind hands steered her away from the fire and wrapped a blanket around her shoulders. Maggy crumpled to the hard ground. Her chest hurt something fierce and every breath she drew in was laced with smoke. A pounding had begun inside her head, too…

With a great gulp of air, Maggy sat up, her heart racing. She wasn't in Colorado and it wasn't the night of the fire that had claimed Jeb. A peek at the window anchored her chaotic thoughts and harried emotions. It was morning, judging by the sunlight on the other side of the lace curtains, and she was in Wyoming, in Edward Kent's guest house.

The pounding she'd heard was real, though. Someone was knocking on her door. She took a moment to lock away the feelings of fear and loss that always accompanied that dream. Then exiting her bed, she threw a dressing gown over her nightdress and hurried across the room. She opened the door to find Edward standing there.

"What is it?" she asked, holding her robe closed. "Did something else happen on the ranch?"

Edward eyed her in obvious confusion. "No. It's Sunday."

"Yes, I know." That's why she'd slept in.

He took in her attire with a bewildered frown. "You're not ready to go."

"Go?" She briefly shut her eyes, wishing she could crawl back under the covers. Maybe she could get some more sleep, sans the nightmare this time. "Go where, Edward? Don't horse thieves and ranch vandals take Sundays off, too?"

His warm laughter rumbled in her ears. "I can't say for certain. But here at the Running W, we attend church on the Sabbath."

If he expected her to go to church, he would be sadly disappointed. "Then have a lovely time." She gave him what she hoped looked like a sweet smile as she scrambled for an excuse. "I'll gladly watch over the ranch while you're gone. It wouldn't do to leave the place unguarded, even on the Sabbath."

She started to turn, but he stopped her retreat by taking her elbow in hand. He was entirely too proficient with that move.

"I've already made arrangements for two of the wranglers to stay behind and keep watch."

"Then I can keep them company?" she asked hopefully.

She could think of plenty of other things she would rather do today than attend church services. She hadn't been inside a church since she'd been a girl at her mother's funeral. That was the last time Maggy had been allowed to go to worship services, even though she'd begged and pleaded for a whole month afterward for her father to take her as her mother had. But he'd refused—with more anger at each request, and she came to learn it was safer not to ask. Eventually she'd come to believe there was truth in her father's rants about God. That He didn't care about them, about Maggy.

"As my fiancée," Edward said, his words cutting through the painful memories, "it would appear quite strange if you don't accompany me to church while you're here."

Maggy pushed out a sigh. He had a point. And if attending church together would help her solve this case, and hopefully snag her promotion, then that's what she would do.

"Fine." She pushed him out the door. "Give me a few minutes."

His incredulous chuckle echoed in her ears as she shut the door. She would show him how quickly she could get ready. She hastily traded her nightgown for her other new dress and twisted her hair into a knot. After anchoring the coiffure with hairpins, she donned gloves and a hat. She breezed out the door to find Edward standing beside the buggy. The startled look on his face was well worth her harried pace.

"You weren't exaggerating about the time." In the yard, Mr. McCall and Mrs. Harvey shared a seat on the wagon, while the wranglers had squeezed into the back. Most of them were watching her and Edward.

Maggy smiled. "I hardly ever exaggerate, especially when it comes to my skills."

"True." His rich laughter greeted her as she stepped off the porch and approached the waiting carriage. "But I've never known a woman to devote less than an hour to dressing for any occasion."

"Sounds like a great waste of time to me."

"Agreed." He joined her on the opposite side of the buggy and handed her onto the seat.

Her stomach grumbled with hunger as she arranged her skirt, making her blush. She would've liked to grab a little something to eat before leaving.

"I have some breakfast for you," Edward said as though reading her thoughts. Or perhaps he'd heard the rumbling in her middle. He grabbed a tin plate from the back of the buggy and passed it to her.

Maggy stared in surprise at the two pieces of toast. "That was kind of Mrs. Harvey."

"I knew you hadn't eaten…"

She paused, the toast halfway to her mouth, as he sat next to her. "You did this?"

"It was a combined effort." He looked uncomfortable. "Mrs. Harvey made breakfast. I simply asked if she could put together a little something for you."

Not once in all her twenty-seven years of life could Maggy recall a similar gesture, a time when someone showed consideration for her needs in such a way. "Thank you," she murmured before biting into the toast.

He gave her an answering nod and drove the buggy down the drive. The wagon followed behind them.

He's likely just keeping up appearances, she reminded herself as she chewed. Looking after his fiancée would reflect well on Edward and the state of their betrothal, especially with nearly all of his staff watching them.

Still, the gesture was kind, whatever the motive. And the toast was the perfect remedy to her hungry albeit nervous stomach. She nibbled it daintily as much to keep the crumbs off her new gown as to appear decorous to any passerby.

"Aren't we driving into Sheridan?" she asked when Edward turned toward the mountains instead of in the opposite direction.

He shook his head. "We attend services in Big Horn."

She felt a bit of excitement push against her uneasiness. Unlike Sheridan, she hadn't yet explored the nearby small town. After placing the emptied tin plate in the back of the buggy, Maggy brushed specks of toast from her gloves and dress. She tried to focus on the landscape they passed instead of the feeling of foreboding that lingered inside her. Would she be welcome at Edward's church? Or would those in attendance somehow sense her hidden doubts and feelings of unworthiness?

In a short time, they reached Big Horn. The town

boasted a newspaper office, two mercantiles, a hotel, a couple saloons and a livery stable. The absence of trees helped the place look far less like the mining town where she'd once lived, to Maggy's relief. But when Edward parked the buggy in front of the wooden church, she felt a renewed spike in her anxiety.

Edward helped her down and wrapped her hand over his arm. Did he sense her reluctance or was he merely playing a part? They joined the small crowd moving toward the church's front doors. Maggy's feet felt heavier the closer they drew to the steps. Her heart beat a heavy staccato beneath her muslin bodice.

How ironic that she'd once risked her father's wrath to beg him to go to church. Now, all these years later, she wanted to bolt the other way.

After they entered the church, they were stopped by several people who looked pointedly at Maggy, curiosity flashing in their gazes. Edward politely introduced her. Maggy did her best to smile and be charming, but unlike at the dinner the night before, she couldn't recall a single name after it was shared with her.

Edward guided her to one of the wooden benches in the center of the church's main room, where Mrs. Harvey and the rest of the staff had already taken their seats. Maggy entered the pew and sat next to the housekeeper. She attempted to take calm, even breaths. Would she remember what to do and when? She felt at a complete disadvantage here, nothing like the confident detective she was supposed to be.

"I promise you the minister won't bite," Mrs. Harvey whispered, patting Maggy's gloved hand.

She threw the older woman a grimace. "Do I look that terrified?"

"Not so much that anyone else would notice, love."

Maggy didn't know whether to feel comforted or concerned that Mrs. Harvey had noticed. It was one thing to play the role of Edward's fiancée—it was another matter entirely to play the role of his fiancée inside a church. But she could do this. She had to do this.

It's no different than the dinner last night, she chided herself. If she could pull that off with self-possession, she could do the same here.

She let herself relax a bit as she studied the people around her, including Edward. His attention remained fixed toward the front of the chapel. Not in a self-righteous way but in an interested, earnest way. She couldn't recall ever meeting someone whose religion so naturally worked itself in and through the fabric of their daily life. And yet, that was exactly what she'd discovered about Edward over the past six days.

He hadn't wanted to lie about their engagement, so he'd proposed to her. His prayers at mealtimes were sincere, too, nothing rote, and he'd seemed genuinely happy about attending church this morning. He didn't push his faith on her, either. It simply was there.

Had her mother been that way? She had so few memories left of her mother. Most of them had been crowded out and squashed by fresher, more unpleasant ones that had followed after her death. A shudder ran through Maggy at the realization, causing Edward to glance at her with mild concern in his gaze. She attempted a smile to reassure him, though she let it drop the moment he faced forward again.

She wouldn't think about her father. Rather she would pull what wispy recollections she had of her mother to the forefront of her mind. She remembered her mother's auburn hair and her kind eyes. They weren't blue like Maggy's but green and full of warmth and tenderness. But their light had dimmed with pain near the end of her illness.

"Please don't die, Mama. Please."

The memory of her seven-year-old words, full of pleading, startled her with their sudden appearance and clarity. Why hadn't she remembered them before?

"Are you frightened, Maggy?"

"Yes." Tears burned her throat before leaking out her eyes.

Her mother traced a trembling finger across Maggy's cheek. "I'm a little frightened, too, dearest. Not to die but to leave you." Her voice cracked. "I want to stay and see my Maggy girl grow up."

"I want you to stay, too, Mama." She clung to her mother's hand.

There were tears in her mother's eyes now. "I can't do that, dearest. Not anymore. This pain is my last to endure on this earth. But you won't be alone, Maggy."

"I know. Pa will still be here."

The lines around her mouth tightened. "Yes, but I'm speaking of someone else."

"Who?"

Her mother tugged her forward so they were almost nose to nose. "Remember how I taught you to pray?" When she nodded, her mother went on. "God will be with you. Every single moment. But sometimes it's hard to see Him. You have to look for His hand in the small things and the big things, Maggy. Look for His hand."

Moisture stung Maggy's eyes and she bit down on her tongue to dissipate it. She wasn't sure why she'd suddenly been able to recall this memory, especially

in its entirety. Maybe it had to do with being in church
again—a place her mother had loved. A place Maggy
had longed to go back to after her mother's death. But
her father had refused, even became enraged at the
idea. She could remember weeping bitterly to herself
behind the pine tree near their cabin when she finally
made the decision to stop asking him.

Where was God's hand then? she wondered. Where
was His hand each time her father had lifted his hand
to strike her? Or when he'd been too inebriated to care
for her, so she'd had to stop attending school to cook
and clean for the two of them?

She squirmed against the hard bench, her breath
coming faster, the tears growing harder to fight. She
didn't want to remember; she didn't want to relive the
same feeling of abandonment from God that she'd felt
from her father and from Jeb. Had her mother been
wrong? Did God only love others but not Maggy?
Could she find some evidence, any evidence, of His
hand in her life since that awful day her mother had
died?

Edward shifted beside her, accidentally bumping
her with his shoulder. He smiled in apology, but the
simple contact gave her an anchor amidst the swirl-
ing storm of emotions and memories. His kindness
and friendship had been unexpected. He could have
turned out to be arrogant or a tyrant, and instead, he'd
proven himself trustworthy and kind nearly from their
first meeting. If he hadn't, Maggy never would have
suggested playing the role of his fiancée or been able
to keep it up so effectively.

Was this evidence of God's hand in her life? Her

mother had said it wouldn't just be in the big things; it would be in the small ones too.

The question felt too weighty to consider for long, but Maggy noticed she felt far less troubled and nervous than she had earlier. She no longer had to battle tears, either. Her breath came out in a whoosh as she attempted to find a more comfortable position on the pew. That was something else she could suddenly recall from her girlhood—feeling ready for the services to end long before they actually did.

On the bench ahead of theirs, a little boy also moved restlessly, twisting to look one way, then the other. His mother raised an eyebrow at him, which prompted him to sit still. But after another minute, he was back to shifting and gazing about the room. When he glanced over his shoulder, Maggy smiled at him. His eyes widened before he hurried to face forward.

Only a few seconds passed before he peeked at her again. This time she winked. The boy eyed her a moment, then he winked back. Maggy pressed her lips over a giggle. He didn't turn around after that, but he did seem less fidgety the remainder of the meeting. The exchange, however small, cheered her immensely and allayed the rest of her discomfort.

"God will be with you. Every single moment." She let her mother's words repeat through her mind. This time they didn't prick with pain; they felt almost hopeful. *"Sometimes it's hard to see Him. You have to look for His hand in the small things and the big things, Maggy. Look for His hand."*

Later, talking about the meeting with Edward over lunch, she couldn't recall a single word of the sermon or what hymns they'd sung. But she no longer felt as anxious at the prospect of returning the following Sunday. If nothing else, she felt a little closer to her mother while there. She might even remember more of the happy, tender memories. And maybe it was time to take her mother's long-ago challenge to heart—about looking for God's hand in her life, however big or small. After all, she wasn't one to back down from a challenge.

Edward leaned his forearms on the top rung of the pasture fence, his gaze wandering over the herd of horses. The two wranglers who'd stayed behind from church had reported no suspicious activity. He'd been relieved to hear the news. It had added to the already pleasant day.

He'd been uneasy about attending church with Maggy as his fiancée. Though he wasn't any less worried than she'd been, judging by her abnormally tight grip on his arm as they'd walked inside and her restlessness throughout the early part of the meeting. Thankfully he'd been able to ease his own concerns with the reminder that, for all intents and purposes, she was his fiancée. He wasn't lying to God or to anyone. There'd even been moments during the service, as there'd been last night at dinner, when he'd felt content—even proud—to have her seated beside him.

Our arrangement is only temporary, he reminded himself. He couldn't imagine loving a woman again, not after Beatrice's betrayal. Besides, did he even know what real love looked and felt like? Not that it mattered with Maggy. She had a career she treasured and wasn't likely to give up to become someone's wife. They might be friends, but that was all.

A pinprick of sadness filled him at the thought, but Edward stifled it. He lowered his arms to his sides and started to turn away from the pasture when a flash of movement across the way caught his eye. Whirling back, he tried to look between the grazing horses to see what had captured his notice. Then he saw it. Someone in a cowboy hat was creeping away from the pasture, half bent over.

"Hey," Edward shouted. "You there!"

The man whipped around, but he was too far away, his hat pulled too low, for Edward to see his face. Turning forward again, the man ran faster.

Edward broke into a run, too, moving parallel with the fence. When he circled the corner, he pushed his pace faster. But the man had too much of a head start on him. By the time Edward reached the spot where he'd first spotted the man, he was nowhere in sight.

Breathing hard, Edward studied the surrounding landscape. No horse and rider appeared. Anger and suspicion boiled within him. The man had been up to something. But what? Edward moved back toward the fence. A gunnysack lay forgotten in the grass. He picked it up, feeling confused. What had been inside? Had the man dropped it by mistake?

A high-pitched whinny jerked his attention from the sack to the horses. Several reared in terror and bolted for the opposite side of the pasture.

"What in the world—"

Lowering his gaze to the pasture grass, he saw a snake, coiled and ready to strike. The realization crashed into him with all the force of a hoof to his chest—the man had released a snake into the field to frighten the horses. And a couple of spooked horses could cause the entire herd to stampede, possibly injuring themselves or destroying a fence.

Dropping the sack to the grass, Edward raced toward the main barn. His hat flew off as he ran, but he left it where it landed. He had to get rid of the snake and calm the horses.

"McCall," he yelled as he skidded through the open barn doors. His foreman, thankfully, joined him in his mad rush to the tack room. "Get all the boys and run the horses in the east pasture into the corral. Someone let a snake loose."

The grim look on McCall's face surely matched the one on Edward's. He trusted his foreman to follow through. Edward grabbed a shovel and a pair of gloves from the tack room and sprinted back outside. His lungs burned. But he had to hurry if he wanted to keep his horses safe.

When he reached the spot where the snake still sat, he pulled on the gloves, hopped over the fence, and brandished the shovel. Most of the horses were running nervously about at the other end of the pasture. Edward gripped the shovel and brought it down on the head of the snake. After several more strikes, the serpent lay dead.

Edward sagged against the shovel to catch his breath. To his relief, he spied McCall and the wranglers leading the horses through the pasture fence and toward the corral.

"That was close," he said, half to himself, half in prayer. "Too close."

If he hadn't been standing near the pasture, he wouldn't have seen the man and real damage might have occurred. Probably just as the culprit wanted.

Fury mounted anew inside him as he tossed the shovel aside and picked up the lifeless serpent. He stuffed it back in the gunnysack and took off toward the hill where he'd last seen the man.

Perhaps Maggy had spied the intruder while on her ride, though Edward doubted it, given that she and Persimmon had headed off in the opposite direction. Maggy had been quieter than normal since leaving church, though not in a despondent way—more in a thoughtful way. Edward had almost gone riding with her, but he'd sensed she wished for time to herself. Now he was glad he'd stayed behind.

He reached the top of the knoll, but he couldn't see any movement. There were no hoof prints in the grass either, which meant the man had either walked to the Running W or stowed his horse somewhere farther away.

Scowling, Edward dumped the dead snake onto the grass. He'd keep the gunnysack, though with no markings or distinctive features, he wasn't sure it would provide any clues as to its owner. He marched back toward the ranch. Frustration—directed at the saboteurs and at himself—dogged his heels. There hadn't been any new acts against him since before Maggy's arrival. Foolishly he'd believed the vandalism might have stopped for the time being. But that illusion had been shattered. He and the Running W were still targets.

"Edward!"

He lifted his head from glaring at the ground to find Maggy striding toward him. She'd changed out of her Sunday dress into her men's clothes for her ride, and yet, she still moved with a determined grace whatever her outfit.

She waved toward the commotion near the corral. "Why are McCall and the others moving those horses?"

"Because someone let a snake loose in the pasture," he answered, hoisting the empty gunnysack for her to see. Fresh resentment snarled inside him. "I saw a man on the other side of the pasture, but he ran before I could get a proper look at his face. Then one of the horses reared and I realized the visitor had left us a gift."

She slowly shook her head, her blue eyes full of concern. "It was meant to frighten and possibly harm the horses, wasn't it? Are they all right?"

"I believe so." He started walking again, the sack strangled in his fist. "I killed the snake while the men moved the horses into the corral."

Reaching out, she rested her hand lightly on his arm, where his sleeves had been rolled back. Her fingers felt welcomingly cool. "We're going to solve this, Edward. I give you my word."

Instead of comforting him, though, her statement grated against his frustration. "How, Maggy?" he countered. "In the past six days, all we've uncovered is who *isn't* orchestrating the sabotage." He shook the sack in the air as proof. "Not who is."

"It takes time to solve a complex case like this." A frown formed on her lips as she crossed her arms.

He glanced back at the now-empty pasture. "Time is not something I have in abundance right now."

"What does that mean?"

Should he tell her about the Cavalry? He hadn't told anyone else, except for McCall. But perhaps if Maggy knew, it might help her understand his urgency. "I've been in contact with a gentleman employed with the

British Cavalry. They've heard great things about the horses bred in this part of the world and are considering securing a large shipment of animals from here for their soldiers."

"That's wonderful, Edward."

He acknowledged her compliment with a nod. "You can see now why I need this case over and solved. I won't let all my hard work be laid to waste right before my eyes. I will not fail." He hadn't meant to add the latter—it had simply slipped out on a tide of anger.

"You're not just talking about supplying horses to the Cavalry," she said perceptively and with annoying calm. "Damage to your property or even your horses wouldn't mean you've failed. Look at what you've accomplished here." She swept her arm in an arc.

But if it was all taken from him by some unknown assailant... The thought brought all the inadequacies he'd felt growing up roaring to new life inside him. *He wasn't needed; his parents already had an heir and a spare. He was less than his brothers, a fixture largely forgotten in the great house. His success at university, his prowess with horses, none of that had been enough for his family, for Beatrice...for himself.*

With a slight growl, he stalked forward again, tossing over his shoulder, "You don't know what you're talking about."

"Oh?" Maggy irritatingly kept pace with him. "Maybe that's true. But I wasn't born into a life of ease and luxury like you were, Edward. With education and possibilities right there for the taking. With parents who didn't..."

He wheeled around, his breath coming as harried

now as it had when he'd been running earlier. "Who didn't what?"

"Never mind." Her expression became instantly shuttered. "I told you we'd solve your case, and I meant it. But I won't stand here and let you browbeat me with your fears of failure."

With that she strode away. Edward blew out a long breath. Anger at his attackers was reasonable, but it wasn't right for him to direct it toward Maggy. Sending a quick prayer of apology heavenward, he walked swiftly after her.

"Maggy, wait. Please."

She slowed to a stop, though she didn't turn around. Her arms were defensively folded against him once more.

"I'm sorry," he said, stopping behind her. "That was unkind and unfair. You've done nothing but help since you've arrived. And in return, I unjustly turned my frustration on you."

Her shoulders relaxed slightly as she turned to face him. "Why do you feel the need to prove yourself?" Leave it to Maggy to cut straight to the heart of the matter.

"You were right about my life growing up." He glanced down at the sack in his hand, so he wouldn't see the potential derision in her gaze. "I did have everything I could possibly ask for, except…" Edward cleared his throat. "Except for a real place in my family. I never felt like I had much purpose in life. Until I came here."

When he lifted his head, he found her watching him, not with scorn but with a mixture of understanding and mild surprise. "That's how I felt when I became a detective."

"Ah." He ventured a smile—so she did understand. "Again, I apologize for my rudeness earlier."

"Apology accepted." She pointed toward the stable. "I still need to brush down Persimmon."

"I'm headed to the house."

They stepped at the same time, to head in opposite directions, and ended up colliding. Instinctively Edward dropped the sack and clasped Maggy's arms to keep her from stumbling.

"Sorry about that," he said.

He gave a self-deprecating laugh, which faded the moment he realized how close they were standing. Closer than they ever had before. Her hands had come to rest against his chest and her eyes were twice as large as normal and deeply blue. And her lips... Why had he never noticed their perfect shade of rose?

"Sorry," he murmured again, though he couldn't say why he was apologizing.

Those pink lips parted. "You already said that."

The most irrational thought entered his mind—he wanted to kiss her, to hold her face between his hands, and gently explore the feel of her lips with his own. He'd shared a piece of himself by telling her of his private fears, and now he very much wanted to share a kiss. Would Maggy allow it, though?

Before he could think on it further, the sound of carriage wheels reached his ears. He and Maggy both looked toward the drive. A woman in a buggy was headed for the house. She didn't appear to have seen them yet.

"I think that's Mrs. Winchester," Maggy said in a slightly breathless voice.

Edward studied the other woman's face. "I believe you're right."

"And look what I'm wearing." Her face blanched as she glanced down at her clothes. "I'd better go change."

"I'll stall her while you go around the back of the house to the guest cottage."

She nodded, her gaze locked on his for another moment. Almost as if she didn't want to leave. His heart gave a leap at that thought. Then without another word, Maggy took a step back, breaking his hold, and sprinted toward the house.

As he watched her go, aware of his empty hands, Edward wondered how one could feel the loss of something one didn't truly have in the first place.

Chapter Eight

Maggy concluded two things within five minutes of Mrs. Winchester's visit, which had apparently been mandated by Mrs. Druitt to deliver a handwritten invitation to join the wives' club. First, she would need to stop wearing her favorite clothes, even for riding. Now that she was an official member of the club, female visitors might descend upon the ranch at any moment and Maggy didn't relish another mad dash to the guest house to change. Second, Winchester's wife had no knowledge of her husband's involvement—however large or small—with the attacks on the ranch.

If Lola Winchester had been privy to Mr. Winchester's nefarious behavior, she wouldn't have held back from saying so. The woman, who was likely ten years older than Maggy, acted nervous and that meant she talked and talked and talked. Maggy wasn't sure if Lola was anxious about making a good impression or about the report she'd need to give to madam president about how the visit had gone. Either way, the woman jabbered on about anything and everything—her children, husband, neighbors, the club, the weather and

Maggy's dress. If Lola had information that linked her husband with what was happening against the Running W, surely it would have spilled out, too.

Maggy did her best to listen, in order to pick up any useful information from Lola's chatter. But her thoughts kept drifting back to Edward's apology and those tense but pleasant minutes right before the woman's arrival.

Not once in her life could she recall a man apologizing to her or taking responsibility for his anger as Edward had. She'd even considered brushing off his words and the shock she'd felt at hearing them with a cynical remark, but the sincere and somber look in his eyes and voice had stopped her. Instead she'd asked what he was trying to prove. To her further amazement, he'd answered her question with honesty and openness.

Then his gaze had moved from her eyes to her lips, and Maggy had thought her heart might skip right out of her chest. She'd feared his kiss, but at the same time, she'd been disappointed and confused when it hadn't come. Now she didn't know what to make of those terrifying yet exhilarating seconds they'd shared, standing so close she'd felt his own heartbeat beneath her hands.

"Miss Worthwright, are you feeling well? You look rather flushed. I hope you don't have a fever. Summer illnesses are positively the worst…"

Maggy blushed deeper. "It's a little warm in here," she managed to interject when Lola paused. "I'll just open the window."

She set aside the tea that Mrs. Harvey had brought them and stood. Crossing to the window, she jiggled the frame until she was able to wrench it upward. A welcome breeze cooled her warm face. Someone walked into her periphery view. It was Edward. Her pulse tumbled at the sight of him and the memory of his muscled forearm beneath her hand.

He saw her at the window and waved. She offered a small wave back, then turned away. Lola continued to converse with herself. Settling once again in the armchair, Maggy mulled over her conflicting emotions. It was only natural that she'd feel friendship toward Edward. He was honorable, honest and kind. And yet friendship wasn't what she'd felt when she thought he might kiss her. That feeling had stemmed from something deeper.

Maggy frowned as she took another sip of tea. She was likely experiencing the natural feelings that followed being his fiancée, even temporarily. There would surely be moments when the line between what was real and what was temporary became blurred as she performed that role. It wasn't as if she and Edward were actually planning to marry.

The thought of being married again made her shudder. She'd thought Jeb was an affable person before their marriage. Two weeks later she discovered that was only one side of him—a side she rarely saw when they were alone. She'd gone from feeling hopeful and in love to hollow and numb. It wasn't until she'd completed her first mission for Pinkerton's that she found herself once more and vowed she'd never go back to that half life again.

"So you'll come?" Lola gazed at her expectantly.

Maggy tried to recall the last thing she'd heard the other woman say. Something about the club's next meeting. "I'm sorry. I think the warm day is catching up to me. When is the tea?"

"Tomorrow."

She forced a smile. "I'll be there. Thank you for inviting me into your club."

"Well, it isn't my club," Lola said, standing. "It's Dolphina's, I suppose. I'm only the secretary."

Did Maggy detect some envy there? "Secretary is still an important job. Look at how you drove all the way out here."

"Yes." The woman looked thoughtful. "It is an important job. Thank you, Miss Worthwright."

Maggy walked Lola to the door and bid her good day. Tomorrow would begin her real work among the ranchers' wives. And she very much hoped it would be productive.

Edward's words—*In the past six days, all we've uncovered is who* isn't *orchestrating the sabotage. Not who is*—repeated through her mind, reaffirming her determination to solve this case. Not just for her possible promotion either, but for Edward, too.

After his evening ritual of discussing the day with McCall, Edward returned to the house. Had Maggy turned in already? he wondered. She'd been more talkative at supper than she had at lunch, but he sensed her heart wasn't in the conversation, that she was using it as a way to avoid any quiet between them. He wasn't sure why. Perhaps she'd realized he had wanted to kiss her earlier and wasn't happy about the prospect. If that were true, he could only imagine what her reaction would have been if he really had kissed her.

Women are complicated creatures, he reminded himself as he stepped through the front door. *Maggy, most of all.*

He needed to stop trying to riddle her out. Instead he would focus on playing his role as her fiancé and do all in his power to solve the mystery of who wanted him gone.

Resolved, he strode down the hall. A casual peek into the parlor had him slowing to a stop. Maggy had fallen asleep on the sofa while reading, her eyes closed and her expression relaxed. Any man would be blessed to be the one to see her like this every day.

He didn't want to disturb her, but it wouldn't bode well for either of them if she didn't retire to the cottage soon. It wouldn't do if anyone caught wind of Maggy sleeping inside the main house.

As he entered the room, the floor creaked beneath him and Maggy sat up, wide-eyed and visibly startled. The book she'd been reading tumbled to the rug. "Edward."

"You fell asleep."

She reached down to retrieve her book. "I did. It's been a rather…eventful day."

"That it has." He took a seat at the other end of the sofa, keeping a respectable distance between them. "What are you reading?"

Maggy tucked her finger into the book and lifted it for him to see the title. To his surprise, it was one of his equestrian volumes. "I…wanted to better understand horses and what you do here."

The thoughtfulness behind her selection filled him with gratitude—and guilt. He'd chastised her about the maddening delay in his case, but it wasn't due to her lack of effort or expertise.

"You don't have to read that…"

She lowered her gaze and the book. "I know. I'm hoping it might help me solve your case sooner."

"Maggy." He waited for her to look up before he continued. "I was wrong about what I said earlier. I understand that finding out who isn't behind what's happened is the only way to narrow down who is behind it. And you've done a phenomenal job of that in only six days."

Her cheeks turned an attractive shade of pink. "I believe that's the fourth time you've apologized."

"And it likely won't be the last." They shared a chuckle. "Did the book put you to sleep? Or were you overly tired?"

She made a face, which drew another laugh from him. This time their conversation didn't feel forced; it had, thankfully, returned to its normal ease. "If I said I fell asleep just because I was tired, I'd be lying."

"Those aren't the most thrilling of books, I'm afraid." He offered her an understanding smile. "Mrs. Harvey is always trying to get me to read the dime novels she adores."

"You should write a horse book."

Edward smirked. "Me?"

"Why not?" She sat up straighter. "Yours would be far more interesting to read than this one."

He'd never considered writing a book before, though he had to admit the idea held some appeal. There might be other equestrian enthusiasts who would enjoy reading about his experience building a horse ranch. "Perhaps when this business with the sabotage is fully resolved."

"Thank you for saying *when*, not *if*." Maggy shot him a smile, one that didn't look feigned and infused him with hope. "I've been thinking about the snake incident."

He frowned. So much for feeling hopeful. "I wish I'd been able to see the man's face. He looked about my height, though slightly heavier in build."

"Do you still have the gunnysack he dropped?"

"Yes. But there weren't any markings on it."

Maggy set her book on the side table and rose to her feet. "I'd still like to see it."

"I put it in the stable." Edward stood as well, and followed her outside. Blue twilight smeared the sky and the nightly chorus of insects was in full swing. Before the threats to the ranch had started, this had been his favorite time of day. A time of quiet and reflection.

Inside the stable, he lifted the gunnysack off the tack table and handed it to Maggy. She examined it, her bottom lip caught beneath her teeth.

"Can I see your feed sacks?" she asked after a minute or two.

Edward led her to where several sacks of grain sat. Loosely crossing his arms, he watched as she inspected the other gunnysacks.

"The one that held the snake is new." She pointed to one of the feed sacks. "See how this one has frayed along the opening, while the one the man dropped hasn't."

He raised his eyebrows, impressed. "What does that tell us?"

"It tells us that this bag is too new and too large to have been used already. The man had to remove a much larger portion of whatever was inside in order to use it for the snake." Maggy flipped the gunnysack inside out, her expression focused. "But what was removed?"

She studied the inside folds of the hem, then ran her finger along the edges. "Ah-ha!" She lifted her finger and grinned in triumph. "This sack held sugar."

"And that explains what exactly?"

Maggy stepped closer to him, her excitement palpable. "Whoever used this sack had to transfer all of the sugar into some other container. And such a large sack of sugar isn't something a bachelor would have on hand."

"So the culprit is likely married," Edward concluded.

She nodded. "Which also means there's one rather annoyed wife out there who might be prodded into spilling her frustration about her husband at the tea tomorrow."

"Excellent discovery."

Another pretty blush filled her cheeks. "I wouldn't have been able to figure it out if you hadn't kept the sack."

"We make a good team then."

She regarded him with those lovely blue eyes. "Yes, we do." He had a sudden longing to breach the narrow distance between them as he had when they'd collided in the yard earlier. But instead of lingering, Maggy handed back the gunnysack and took a step backward. "I think we're much closer to figuring out who our snake-wielding culprit is now."

"Agreed," he said, returning the sack to the tack table. They exited the stable and moved in silence toward the house.

Near the porch, Maggy stopped. "I think I'll head to bed now."

"That really was brilliant." He motioned toward the

stable. "I never would have deduced all that from one ordinary sack."

"I wouldn't have either, before becoming a Pinkerton agent," she admitted with a chuckle. "Now those are the moments I live for—when things click and a piece of the muddied picture becomes suddenly clear."

He wanted to ask if there were other moments she lived for as well, but he didn't want to disturb the open, happy quality of her expression. "I'm glad you're here, Maggy." And he meant it. He hadn't anticipated how skilled she'd be at her job or the friendship he'd come to appreciate between them.

"Me, too." The words were hardly more than a whisper, and she walked away the second they escaped her lips. But he'd heard them.

"Good night," he called after her.

She turned back to throw him another genuine smile. "Good night, Edward."

After picking up the rest of her dresses from Ms. Glasen, Maggy strolled into the ladies' parlor at the Sheridan Inn a few minutes before the tea meeting would officially start. The hum of conversation matched the hum inside her stomach, though she was far less nervous today than she'd been before her first dinner. A quick sweep of the room revealed there were eleven women present, ranging in age from early twenties to mid-sixties.

She couldn't recall a time when she'd been in a room with so many women. The realization nibbled at her confidence, until she reminded herself that she wasn't here as just another participant. She was also a detective. And today her light green-and-lavender-striped dress, perfectly pinned chignon, and approachable smile were her disguise as she used her honed skills to further crack Edward's case.

His words from the night before, about being glad she was at the ranch, filled her with fresh happiness and restored her self-assurance. Somewhere over the past seven days, this mission had become more than a means to furthering her career; it was about helping someone who'd become a friend. And that meant a stellar performance was needed at her first club meeting.

She greeted Lola Winchester and Dolphina Druitt, thanking the older woman for allowing her admittance into the club. Mrs. Druitt nodded regally, then offered to introduce Maggy to anyone she didn't yet know. All but two of the women she'd met at the dinner on Saturday night or at church yesterday. One of the strangers was Gunther Bertram's sister Josephine Preston. She appeared to be about Maggy's age, but a constantly furrowed brow made her look older.

The other woman Maggy hadn't met was Vienna Howe, who looked to be the youngest member of the group. Vienna's hair was light blond and she seemed incredibly shy. Her green eyes darted to Maggy's for only a moment before she lowered them.

"Pleased to meet you, Miss Worthwright," she said softly.

Maggy felt a surprising wave of compassion for the girl who reminded her of herself as a young bride. "You, too, Mrs. Howe. Have you been married long?"

"Two years."

"And she'll be a mother in another six months," Mrs. Druitt interjected with an approving smile. "Isn't that right, Vienna?"

The young woman's cheeks went scarlet. "Yes."

"Congratulations." Maggy could tell Vienna felt uncomfortable, though she wasn't sure if it was because of Mrs. Druitt's nosiness or for another reason.

Mrs. Druitt called the meeting to order and asked everyone to take their seats. Uneasiness still radiated from Vienna as she sat at the far end of the table. Her discomfort prompted Maggy to sit beside her. Relating to other women had never been her strong suit, but she could recognize another human being in need. There was no reason she couldn't be friendly as well as smart in using the meeting to investigate.

A waiter poured the tea for each guest. Maggy tried not to grimace as she brought the porcelain cup to her lips. Why did tea—especially warm tea—have to signify refinement?

"Do tell us how you and Mr. Kent met," a woman named Matilda Kitt said in a dreamy tone. Choruses of "yes" echoed around the table.

Maggy dabbed at her mouth with her napkin and affected a wistful air to her voice as she conveyed the same details she'd already shared with Mrs. Druitt and Lola. Most of the women sighed happily when she finished.

Matilda leaned forward in eagerness. "You've snagged yourself quite a catch, Miss Worthwright. A handsome man with a prosperous ranch." Her expression reflected longing. "Oh, to return to those early days of marriage."

"Young love is all well and good," Bertram's sister Josephine said sourly, "but those early days require a great deal of work, too. Don't be forgetting that,

Matilda. You'll fill Miss Worthwright's head with fanciful, unrealistic dreams."

Lola frowned and set down her cup. "Now, Josephine, you're only going to depress her with all your pessimistic talk."

"No, no," Maggy interjected. "I would very much appreciate any advice you can give me."

The women needed no further urging. All of them, except for Vienna, threw out their tidbits of counsel. Maggy paid less attention to the actual words and more to what subjects they felt strongly about.

"Any advice on housekeeping?" she asked when the hubbub wound down. It was time to see who had a bee in their bonnet over a certain sack of sugar. "Mrs. Harvey will still be in charge of the cooking, but I may want to try my hand at things in the kitchen now and then."

There were plenty of comments about cooking Edward's favorite meals and letting him know the kitchen was her territory. But to Maggy's disappointment, no one made any mention of a husband emptying out a perfectly good sack of sugar. The only remark that came close to touching on the topic was Josephine's.

"Don't let him rattle around in there alone," the cross woman stated. "He's likely to upend your organization that way."

Was it Josephine's husband who'd emptied the sack? Or her brother? No, Bertram wasn't married. So was it someone else entirely? Maggy swallowed some tea to hide her frown. Movement to her left caused her to look at Vienna. The younger woman hadn't said a word since sitting down. And Maggy wasn't the only one to notice.

"Vienna," Mrs. Druitt said, clearly attempting to bring the girl into the conversation. "You've been married the shortest amount of time—those first days of marriage are still fresh in your memory. What advice do you have for Miss Worthwright?"

The girl's face turned pink as she cleared her throat. "I don't believe I could add anything to the excellent advice that's already been given."

Mrs. Druitt beamed as if she were the sole provider of such "excellent" advice. "Very good. Then let us turn our attention to the annual summer ball. It's still four weeks away, but the event will be upon us before we know it."

Maggy tuned out the planning talk and instead glanced at Vienna. The young woman still looked flushed and she kept dabbing at her forehead with her napkin.

"The tea is a bit warm for my tastes," Maggy said, throwing Vienna a grimace. "What I wouldn't give for a tall glass of ice-cold lemonade."

A brief smile perked up Vienna's mouth. "That does sound lovely." She set down her napkin, but it slipped from the table to the rug. Vienna leaned down to pick up the cloth, causing her sleeve to rise above her wrist for a brief moment. It was long enough, though, for Maggy to see a fading bruise there.

Vienna caught her staring. Blushing again, the young woman hurried to right herself in her chair, while tugging her sleeve back into place. The reality of what she'd seen had Maggy struggling to draw a full breath. It was little wonder Vienna hadn't been interested in hearing the story of Maggy's courtship with Edward or in dispensing marital advice. The girl's hesitation about her pregnancy made sudden sense, too.

Vienna was living a life similar to Maggy's with Jeb.

She attempted to drink more tea. However, the tepid liquid and the realization this woman bore identical bruises to those Maggy had once worn had the room feeling hotter than a stove in July. Pushing her teacup aside, she noticed Vienna mopping her forehead again.

"Do you need some air?" Maggy asked. "Because I'd like to step out for a moment."

The relief on Vienna's face was as much an answer as her quick nod. "I would, yes."

"Ladies." Maggy pushed back her chair. "Vienna is noticeably warm and I, myself, could use some air. We'll dash out to the porch for a sit and return shortly."

Mrs. Druitt's expression conveyed her annoyance at the interruption, but she nevertheless nodded her permission. "We'll decide which parts of the ball you two may wish to handle."

"That would be wonderful." Maggy motioned for Vienna to go ahead of her, then she followed the younger woman out of the parlor, across the lobby, and outside. Several of the chairs were occupied, but Maggy spied two rockers at one end of the porch that stood empty.

"Much better," Vienna murmured, after she and Maggy sat down. She shut her eyes, obviously enjoying the breeze.

Maggy did the same—not as a way to relish the cooler temperature but to give herself a chance to think. Vienna's situation incited a swell of compassion in her. The girl might look differently than Maggy, with a far less openly spirited personality, and yet, she recognized in Vienna the same wide-eyed innocence, fear and hopelessness she'd felt soon after becoming a bride. Was there anything she could say or do to help? Would Vienna even welcome her attempts?

She thought back to those awful few years as Jeb's wife. If someone had tried to help her, would she have welcomed it? She couldn't say for sure, but she hated the thought of seeing another woman suffering in a similar way and doing nothing.

Opening her eyes, she kept her face pointed forward—as much to give herself space and privacy as Vienna. "I was married once before, though I'm a widow now." She didn't know this young woman, and yet like Edward, she sensed she could trust her.

"You were?" There was no disguising the shock in Vienna's voice.

Maggy nodded, pushing the rocker into motion with the toe of her shoe. Every one of her twenty-seven years, and then some, weighed upon her.

"I was young when we wed. And thought I was in love." She rocked a little faster. "It was only a few weeks after my wedding that I realized everything I'd hoped and dreamed about beforehand wasn't going to be mine after all."

She had to push the rest of her words past her dry throat. "No matter how many good meals I cooked or words of encouragement I offered or affection I gave, it would never be enough." Emotion rose painfully into her chest, but Maggy willed it back down. "And yet, more days than I can count, I kept trying to do just that. I couldn't let go of the notion that if I kept trying, kept working, it would make all the fear and hurt disappear..." She cast a meaningful look at Vienna. "That it would make the bruises and scars go away."

The girl's face went white and she tugged at her sleeve again. "I..." She visibly swallowed, then faced forward as Maggy had done. "I want to be a good wife. I want to love him, Miss Worthwright. Chance means well. He didn't have it easy growing up."

Hearing some of her own rationale repeated back to her in Vienna's pleading tone brought a feeling of nausea to Maggy's stomach. She'd told herself these same things—over and over again—up until the day Jeb was killed in the fire.

"I know," she said softly.

Tears glittered in Vienna's green eyes. "I think I'll go home now. I've been feeling poorly of late." She rested her hand against her middle. "And probably should've stayed home."

"I'm glad you didn't." And Maggy meant it. She could relate to and understand Vienna, and for the first time in ages, she hoped to make a real friend.

They both climbed to their feet, and as they did, something inside Maggy nudged her to offer one last piece of counsel. "Just remember, no matter what Chance says, you're not worthless, Vienna. You're somebody of value, too."

Vienna brushed at her wet eyes with her finger. "Thank you," she whispered. Then in a stronger voice, she added, "Will you please give my farewell to Mrs. Druitt and the others?"

"Of course."

Maggy returned inside to the ladies' parlor and gave Vienna's regards and regrets to the group. But she could no longer concentrate on the inane conversa-

tions or the plans for the ball. She accepted an assign-
ment to be part of the decorating committee, thanked
everyone for the lovely tea, then excused herself.

On the drive back to the ranch, her mind was an
endless jetty of thoughts. Had she missed an opportunity for sleuthing by focusing on Vienna? She hoped
not, but she didn't regret talking to the younger girl.
Especially when she felt the truth of her own words to
Vienna about not being worthless. She'd told herself
the same, again and again, since Jeb's death, but saying those words out loud in an effort to help someone
else had made the statements resound more powerfully
within her. Hopefully Vienna would know she had an
ally—a friend—in Maggy.

She only wished she'd been able to discover whose
husband had emptied the sugar sack. Josephine's might
be the culprit; she was the only one to mention anything
about a man upsetting the organization in the kitchen.
Or was she the only one? Maggy sat up straighter. Vienna's husband could very well be the wrongdoer, and
the girl wouldn't have said anything out of fear.

Urging the horse faster, Maggy found herself hum-
ming a song they'd sung in church the day before. She'd
likely made a friend today and narrowed down the
snake perpetrator to two possible suspects. Her first
tea meeting with the wives' club had proven to be a
success, and she couldn't wait to tell Edward about it.

Chapter Nine

Edward trudged toward the house, feeling every one of his sore muscles. It had been some time since he'd performed all the tasks the wranglers typically handled. But after assigning another man to guard the pastures throughout the day, he felt it only right that he make up the shortage in help himself.

The smell of Mrs. Harvey's cooking greeted him as he entered through the front door. He would change, then he and Maggy could eat supper. Afterward, he would read or perhaps work more on the notes he'd written, in hopes of seeing if he had enough material to write a book of his own as Maggy had suggested.

He paused beside the entry table to leaf through the waiting stack of mail. There was another letter from his mother and one from the man at the British Cavalry. Edward had written back some weeks ago, expressing his confidence once again in the quality of horseflesh he could supply them. Were they ready to purchase his horses? Excitement crowded out some of his fatigue.

Tearing open the envelope, he extracted the letter and unfolded it. They were still interested, yes. But by the time he reached the end of the missive, his eagerness had faded. The number of horses they required was far greater than Edward alone could supply. They were asking him to secure other ranchers in the area who would also be willing to sell their horses to the Cavalry.

Edward folded the letter, replaced it in the envelope, and hung his hat on the hall tree. Disappointment peppered his exhaustion. Without knowing who wanted him gone, he didn't know who he could trust with this new and lucrative business venture. He didn't want to unknowingly take on as a partner the person attempting to sabotage him. Still, if he wanted to keep the Cavalry's interest, he would have to find others to join him—and soon.

He started for the stairs, but before he reached them, Maggy came barreling out of the parlor. "You're late, Edward."

"Late?" He scrubbed at his face with his free hand, trying to recall what appointment he'd forgotten. "Late for what?"

She looked slightly irked. "You're supposed to eat dinner with the other ranchers tonight, remember?"

"Right." Edward hefted a sigh and threw a look of longing toward his own dining room. He didn't want to ride into Sheridan or make conversation—he simply wanted a quiet evening at home, especially after his long day and the troubling news in the letter he still held.

I sound quite like an old married man, he thought with a wry shake of his head.

"You are going, aren't you?" Maggy frowned at him, as if she could riddle out his thoughts. Being a detective, she probably could. "We need your interactions with the ranchers to round out our investigation."

Yes, they did. He might loathe the reality of someone trying to ruin him, but it *was* his reality nonetheless. And the sooner they narrowed down the list of suspects, the better. Then he could determine who to approach about the Cavalry's offer. Maggy had done an excellent job of gathering information at the women's meeting two days ago—now it was his turn.

He started up the stairs, calling back, "Yes, Maggy. I'm going." Her smug sniff brought a quick smile, even though he didn't relish the task before him.

After choosing one of his suits, Edward hurried to change. He didn't want to miss the food, not with how hungry he felt. He finished tying his tie as he returned downstairs. Not surprisingly, Maggy waited for him beside the door.

"Now be sure to speak with Josephine's husband," she said as she reached up to adjust his tie. "And Vienna's."

"Who?"

She brushed the shoulders of his suit coat. "Mr. Preston and Mr. Howe. Remember, one of them is likely the person who captured the snake and set it loose in the field."

"Preston and Howe, got it."

Stepping back, she eyed him up and down, then dipped her head in a satisfied nod. "You look successful but approachable."

"Rich but poor," he quipped.

Maggy shook her head, but he caught the amused sparkle in her blue eyes. It struck him right then that this was how things would likely be between them if they were married—her double-checking his attire and throwing out reminders, him submitting to her ministrations and bantering back and forth.

Was this how his life would have been with Beatrice? Edward knew the answer at once. No, Beatrice might have fussed over how he looked, but she wouldn't have teased or cajoled him in the same good-natured way that Maggy did.

Still, this is temporary. He couldn't get too comfortable with the ways things were between them. His case would hopefully be solved soon, and then he would go back to the way his life had been before Maggy had burst into it. The thought left him feeling sad.

"Ready?" she asked, her eyebrows rising.

He clapped his dressier bowler hat onto his head. "Yes."

"Just act natural."

He chuckled as they stepped out the front door together and onto the porch. "No outright questions regarding their nefarious activities?"

"Edward…" Her voice held a note of exasperation.

Walking backward, he tipped his hat to her. "I understand my role, Maggy. You've taught me well."

"Good." She lifted her hand in a wave. "Have a nice time."

"Catching a crook?"

With a low growl, she spun back toward the house. But Edward didn't miss the impish smile that had alighted on her mouth, if only for a moment. She appreciated his teasing as much as he did.

He'd always liked making people laugh, especially his sister. At some point, though, he'd stopped trying. Had it been after Liza's death or Beatrice's rejection?

He couldn't say for sure, but he wanted to hold on to this lighthearted part of himself—even after Maggy left.

To save time, he chose to ride Napoleon instead of hitching up the buggy. The ride to Sheridan passed uneventfully. When he reached the inn, he tied his horse to one of the posts out front.

The dining room was only half-full of ranchers tonight. Edward studied those in attendance and felt disappointment that Chance Howe wasn't among them. Still, Preston was and so were Bertram and Winchester. Another gentleman, seated next to Nevil Druitt, looked vaguely familiar, but Edward couldn't place him. The man wasn't among the regular social crowd at the inn.

Winchester waved Edward over to his table. "Kent, good to see you again."

"You, as well," Edward returned evenly. He couldn't help thinking the man seemed overly affable and friendly—decidedly more so than usual. Taking the empty seat, he exchanged greetings with the other men at the table, which included Preston. "Who is that sitting next to Druitt?"

Preston glanced at the other table. "That's his son-in-law, Felix Jensen."

That's why Edward had recognized the fellow. Each summer Jensen and his wife, Lavina, the Druitts' only child, came to visit.

A waiter set a full plate of food in front of Edward. The smell alone resurrected his earlier hunger. After thanking the man, he began to eat.

"Doesn't Jensen own a store in Buffalo?" Winchester asked.

Nodding, Preston gave a snort of contempt. "I still

don't get why he doesn't up and start a ranch here like Druitt hints at every time the man visits."

"Perhaps because he's already established as a store owner," Edward interjected, watching Preston and Winchester closely. "It takes a lot of work to make a ranch successful. He likely doesn't want to start over, not when he's already worked so hard at a different profession."

Preston threw another scornful look at the shop owner, but Winchester dropped his gaze to his nearly empty plate, his ready smile drooping along with his mustache. Had Edward's words struck a guilty chord in him?

Edward returned his focus to his meal, though he paid attention to the conversation that soon began again among those at his table. There were no veiled hints that he could decipher. Preston remained his usual disparaging self, which made him less of a suspect in the snake caper in Edward's mind. Winchester, on the other hand, returned to acting cheerful. Other than the one slip in his demeanor, nothing appeared out of sorts with him, either.

When he finished his dinner, Edward attempted to add to the small talk about the weather, the new horses some of the men were breaking in, and when the inn's part owner Buffalo Bill Cody might audition more people for his Wild West show. He couldn't shake his frustration, though, at not learning anything that put him closer to solving his case. Perhaps he'd be more successful if he changed tables. After Preston and Winchester left, he took the empty seat next to Bertram.

"Howdy, Kent," the man said, a little too loudly.

Edward nodded. "Evening, Bertram. How'd you like dinner?"

"Good. Real good. Beats eating mess food, that's for sure."

"You could hire a housekeeper."

"Naw. I'm trying to save money to get more horses. Druitt's promised me a real nice deal…" His voice trailed to silence as he threw a stricken look at the older man.

Druitt turned from speaking to his son-in-law to look at Bertram. "What did you say, son?"

"Nothin'. Just talking horses."

Edward watched Bertram closely. Why would he look troubled about buying horses from a neighbor? It wasn't as if the other ranchers hadn't purchased horses from each other. Unless… Bertram had been promised a good deal on Edward's stolen horses. The man's behavior struck him as suspicious once again. Bertram hadn't always acted so uncomfortable in Edward's presence.

"Kent," Druitt said, commandeering the silence. "You remember my son-in-law Felix Jensen, don't you?"

"I do." Edward extended his hand and Jensen shook it. "You still own a store, correct?"

Jensen's face lit up. "That I do."

"Do you find it hard to get away?" Edward asked, as much to make conversation as to know the answer. He imagined the younger man wouldn't relish leaving his store, even to make a visit to his wife's parents.

Jensen folded his arms on top of the tablecloth, his expression relaxed. "My brother runs it for me whenever Lavina and I come here. But I don't like to be away for too long." He shot his father-in-law a quick glance. "Though it's worth the sacrifice to come visit."

"And we hope to make those visits more permanent, don't we, son?" Druitt smiled at Jensen, then at Edward. He didn't seem to catch Jensen's frown or he was ignoring it.

Edward leaned back in his chair. Preston's earlier remarks about Jensen and Druitt repeated through his mind. "Are you thinking of relocating to Sheridan?" he directed the question at Jensen.

"Well, I don't rightly know for certain. Maybe one of these—"

Druitt clapped his hand onto Jensen's shoulder. "Dolphina and I are hopeful we can convince these kids to move here and run a ranch like us. Lavina does pine for her family, doesn't she, son? And when the grandchildren finally come along, what's better than having grandparents close by?"

Jensen flushed, then ducked his chin. Edward felt sorry for the man. Clearly he enjoyed operating his store, but the Druitts had their own plan for their daughter and son-in-law and they weren't ones to give up easily.

"Do you have an interest in ranching?" Edward inquired.

The man looked like an animal caught in a trap. "I… uh…don't really know much about horses. Running a store is what I've always wanted to do."

"And that's where other ranchers like myself can step in to teach you everything you need to know," Druitt said, releasing the man's shoulder. An awkward quiet settled over the table. Bertram cleared his throat, while Jensen and the two other ranchers seated next to him looked everywhere but at Druitt.

After a moment, the older man said in a less boisterous tone, "I do so miss watching my baby girl ride. You don't think when they're younger that someday they'll grow up and move far away." He glanced at Edward, his smile sad. "Keep that in mind when you become a father, Kent."

"Are you married now?" Jensen looked relieved at having the focus of the conversation no longer on him.

Edward shook his head. "Not yet, but I am engaged."

"To a real sophisticated lady. Not unlike those Brits back home, right, Kent?" Smiling, Druitt rested his hands on his ample belly. "Wouldn't be surprised if she decides this place isn't as exciting as the big city."

A desire to defend Maggy rose inside Edward. "She's adapting quite well, actually."

"Just like my Dolphina."

He inwardly cringed at hearing Maggy compared to Druitt's wife. He felt more than ready to take his leave. The thought of talking things over with Maggy back at the ranch sounded far more enjoyable than remaining here with his so-called friends, even if he'd enjoyed talking with Jensen. The younger man appeared to be honest and hardworking.

"Gentlemen." Edward scraped back his chair. "I'm going to head home. It was nice to see you again, Jensen."

The man gave a quick nod. "Likewise, Kent. Congratulations on your engagement."

"Thank you." Edward left the inn and rode home. To his delight, he saw a light shining in the parlor. Had Maggy waited up for him? He brushed Napoleon down quickly, fed the horse and gave it a farewell rub on the nose before he headed inside.

Maggy sat in the parlor, though she wasn't alone. Mrs. Harvey was seated in one of the armchairs, doing some mending. Both women looked up as he entered.

"How did it go?" Maggy asked, rushing to her feet, her expression expectant.

Mrs. Harvey gathered up her sewing things before Edward could answer. "I'll duck into the kitchen, sir, and take some tea while I finish my mending. Would you care for a cup?"

"No, thank you, Mrs. Harvey." Edward threw her a grateful smile, knowing she was giving him and Maggy privacy to talk about the evening.

The moment the housekeeper left the room, Maggy pounced again. "So?" She trailed him to the sofa where he sank down. "Were Howe and Preston there? Did any of them say anything suspicious?"

"Howe wasn't in attendance." Edward removed his tie and tossed his hat on the low table. "Preston was there, along with Bertram and Winchester."

Maggy dropped onto the other end of the sofa, making the entire thing bounce. "Did Preston act differently?"

"Unfortunately, no." He leaned back against the sofa. "He was his usual cynical self. Winchester still seemed overly friendly and Bertram was acting strange again."

Drawing her feet up beneath her long skirt, she placed her elbow on the back of the sofa. Her entire demeanor spoke of how comfortable she'd come to feel inside his home. And reminded Edward how comfortable he felt at having her here. "My guess is Howe must have been the one behind the snake incident. But even if Bertram and Winchester wouldn't stoop so low as to deliberately spook your horses with a snake, they sound as if they know something, possibly more than writing those notes." She lifted the stack off the table. "Otherwise they wouldn't still be acting strangely."

"Fair point." He waved to the notes in her hand. "Were you looking at them again?"

Maggy nodded. "Trying to see if I missed something."

"And?"

She pursed her lips, causing her nose to scrunch in dismay. The childlike expression was rather charming, but he knew better than to say so. It would likely sound too personal, too familiar. "I didn't find anything new."

"Nevil Druitt's daughter and son-in-law are in town." He couldn't recall any other interesting bits of news from the dinner. "The son-in-law runs a successful store in Buffalo."

"Do the Druitts have any other children?"

Edward rubbed at his tired eyes. Now that he wasn't moving or trying to be a detective himself, the fatigue he'd felt earlier stole over him again. "No, they only have the one now. If I remember right, there was a son who died as a child."

"How sad."

Nodding, he twisted to face Maggy on the sofa. "Apparently Druitt is desperate to have his daughter living closer."

"What do you mean?" she asked as she stifled a yawn.

"He keeps hinting to his son-in-law that Jensen needs to move here and start his own ranch."

She rested her cheek on her arm. "Does Jensen want to run a ranch?"

"No." Edward shook his head. "He sounds quite proud of his store, and says he doesn't know the first thing about ranching. I certainly don't envy him. Druitt and his wife aren't the type to back down anytime soon."

"Poor man." Maggy made a face, then yawned again.

It was time they both turned in. He stood and gathered up his hat. "I'm sorry I don't have more to report, Maggy." He held out his hand to help her up.

"It's all right," she murmured, staring at his hand. "As you said the other day, narrowing down who isn't a suspect, such as Preston, helps us get closer to knowing who *is* a suspect."

He nearly dropped his hand to his side, guessing she didn't want his help, but then she pressed her fingers against his palm. Their smoothness derailed his thoughts for a moment before he realized he was supposed to assist her in standing. Edward tugged her onto her feet.

"Thank you for remembering the dinner tonight," he said with sincerity. He might not have wanted to go, but he also felt the need to do his part in their investigation. And, he had to admit, he liked knowing Maggy had confidence in his sleuthing abilities, however untrained they might be.

She glanced at their joined hands, then slowly pulled hers free. "You're welcome."

More than his fingers mourned the sudden absence of her touch.

He pushed away the ridiculous thought as he accompanied her outside and bid her good night. As he waited for her to enter the guest cottage and shut the door, he realized that once his case was solved his life would be as empty as his hand had been moments ago—empty of Maggy's presence. A keen sadness he couldn't fully explain or understand filled him. Things would never be quite the same, not after a certain brilliant and beautiful female detective left the Running W for good.

Chapter Ten

Maggy felt far less nervous before her and Edward's second dinner than she had before their first. It was nice to have already established themselves as an engaged couple. She chose to wear a rich brown brocade dress. Like her other new dresses, this one fit well and wasn't uncomfortable.

She didn't feel right about taking these clothes with her when she left, but a small part of her wanted to keep them. It was a notion she didn't plan to share with anyone, especially not Edward or her supervisor at the Denver office.

Unlike their last dinner, she and Edward were early this time, and yet, the tables were nearly full already. Maggy didn't see the Howes among those seated or standing. She hoped Vienna and her husband arrived soon. Not only did she want to observe Chance Howe, but the idea of talking to Vienna sounded more pleasant than conversing with some of the other women.

"Miss Worthwright," Mrs. Druitt called out, rising to her feet.

Maggy forced her lips up in a magnanimous smile. "Mrs. Druitt."

"I'll get us a seat," Edward said before untucking her arm from his.

She'd grown accustomed to having him take her by the arm or the elbow. Or the hand as he had last night. But helping her stand up from the sofa hadn't been a necessary gesture as it had at other times.

Last night her heart had lurched, though not unpleasantly, when Edward had extended his hand. The feel of his fingers gently closing over hers had only increased the rapidity of her pulse. And frightened her.

She couldn't get too comfortable with Edward or their temporary arrangement. This was a mission; it wasn't as if she was truly engaged. It would be unwise to read too much into Edward's actions. After all, he was a gentleman. Helping her stand, even with no one present, was the same automatic courtesy he showed when others were watching.

Mrs. Druitt approached Maggy with a young woman in tow. "Miss Worthwright, I'd like you to meet my daughter, Lavina Druitt Jensen."

"It's lovely to meet you, Mrs. Jensen."

The brunette nodded. "And you, Miss—"

"Lavina and her husband will be here for a few weeks." The older woman smiled at her daughter, then at Maggy. "Isn't that wonderful? We never see them enough, although I still hope to persuade them to come live in Sheridan."

"That would be nice, Mother. But Felix's store—"

Mrs. Druitt interrupted again. "I know all about Felix's store, my dear. After all, your father and I helped finance it in the beginning." Lavina's cheeks turned red with obvious embarrassment at her mother's wagging tongue. "But land and ranching are still wise investments. And to think, if you lived back in Sheridan, you would only be a short buggy ride away."

Maggy recalled what Edward had said the night before about Mr. Druitt trying a similar tactic with his son-in-law. The older couple had helped finance Jensen's store, too. It was an interesting bit of information to tuck away.

The older woman kept talking, extolling her daughter's virtues and talents, which apparently included being an exceptional rider. Lavina stood silent and visibly uncomfortable. Clearly mother and daughter were very different in temperament. While Lavina didn't strike Maggy as being as shy as Vienna, the Druitts' daughter didn't possess the same domineering personality as Dolphina, either.

She did feel the tiniest prick of envy at the pair. If her mother were still living, what would she say about her daughter? Would she be proud of the woman Maggy had become or disappointed? She hoped her mother would be pleased at how she'd taken charge of her life after Jeb's death and had become a detective.

"Lavina will be helping with the summer ball and attending our weekly tea meetings while she's here," Mrs. Druitt said, yanking Maggy back to the present.

She managed a quick smile. "I look forward to getting to know you better, Mrs. Jensen."

"The same to you, Miss Worthwright."

Everyone, except for the three of them, had taken their seats. Maggy looked for Edward. He was sitting at a table with the Prestons and Matilda Kitt and her husband. Why hadn't he tried to sit at the table with the Winchesters and Bertram? she wondered with a frown.

Edward saw her walking toward him and stood to pull out her chair.

"You didn't want to sit at the table with the Winchesters?" she asked in a whisper.

He shook his head. "I was hoping that if the Howes came they would sit with us."

She'd shared with him the other day about how she'd gotten to know Vienna a little, though she hadn't told him the painful bond she shared with the young woman.

"And now they'll have to," he added, "since our table is the only one with two empty chairs."

A quick glance at the other tables confirmed his words. Maggy gave him an apologetic smile. "That was a risky move, but apparently I'm not the only brilliant one around here."

"So pleased you've finally noticed."

With a laugh, she sat down and allowed him to push in her chair. She would miss bantering with Edward. The truth of that thought snuffed out some of her merriment. Edward wasn't just another client whose case she was solving; he'd become a good friend.

"I remember when you used to tease me like that, when we were courting," Matilda said, bumping her shoulder lightly against her husband's.

Douglas Kitt started to smile, then covered it by coughing. "That was a long time ago."

"But it doesn't have to be."

Maggy shifted uncomfortably in her chair, as did the Prestons. She couldn't relate to Matilda's romantic sensibilities and hopes. Or maybe she could. Before marrying Jeb, she'd felt much like Matilda about life and love, and look where and who she'd ended up with as a result?

Still, she let herself relax as she came to a conclusion about the Kitts. They weren't likely to be part of the group trying to sabotage Edward—not with the open way they interacted together and with others. The Prestons had been ruled out as well, which made tonight's dinner far more pleasant. All she had to do was listen and see if anything suspect came up...

"Howdy, folks." A sandy-haired young man with a grin strode up to their table. Maggy realized it was Vienna's husband only when she saw the man held the younger woman's hand, though she lagged a few steps behind him.

The men greeted Howe as he dropped Vienna's hand and settled into his seat. Vienna wordlessly slipped into the remaining empty chair beside Maggy.

"How are you, Vienna?"

The young woman glanced at her husband. "I'm doing fine, Miss Worthwright."

"Please. Call me Maggy."

A brief smile appeared. "Then you'd best call me Vienna."

"So, Kent," Howe said loudly as the food was served. "This is your bride-to-be, huh? She's not from around here, is she?"

Maggy fisted the fingers of her gloved hand beneath the tablecloth, hating the way he talked around her as if she weren't there. "I have a name. It's Maggy Worthwright. And, no, I'm not from around here. I'm from Colorado."

"Plucky, aren't you?" Howe sized her up, but Maggy

maintained a level gaze. She was no longer a novice when it came to handling boorish men like him.

Vienna flushed. "Chance," she murmured.

"What?" he countered with a frown. "I haven't said somethin' wrong, now have I, Maggy?" He turned his steely gaze toward her.

She responded with a cool smile. "Would you be so kind as to call me Miss Worthwright, *Mr. Howe*?"

From the corner of her eye, she could see the discomfort on the faces of the Kitts and the Prestons, but she didn't care. She was tired of men like Howe and Jeb thinking they could railroad anyone, particularly a woman...

"My Maggy might be from the city," Edward interjected flawlessly as he placed his arm along the back of her chair, "but she's quite the horsewoman. We went riding the other day, and she bested me in a race."

She twisted to face him, doing her best to hide her surprise. First, he'd called her *his* Maggy. The endearment repeated softly through her mind like the ripples of a quiet pond. Second, he'd told everyone at the table that she'd beat him in their horse race when it had been a tie.

"You were not an easy opponent." Maggy smiled fully at him. She hoped he understood how grateful she felt for him coming to her defense.

Chuckles echoed around the table, breaking the earlier tension. They all started eating their food. Maggy felt Howe's eyes on her, but she ignored him. After a few minutes, he began talking to Mr. Preston about a new colt.

When she felt certain everyone was occupied with

eating or conversing, she glanced at Edward. "Thank you," she mouthed quietly.

His answering smile filled her head to toe with warmth, along with the delicious feeling of being safe. "My pleasure," he murmured back.

She listened to the conversations moving about the table, on the hunt for any interesting tidbits that might help Edward's case, until she realized Vienna hadn't spoken for some time. Memories long forgotten surfaced in her mind of times as Jeb's wife when she'd sat in a group, feeling invisible. A tug of compassion had Maggy turning toward the young woman.

"Are you from here, Vienna?"

She looked momentarily startled that someone was addressing her. Then she dabbed her mouth with her napkin and shook her head. "Not originally. My family moved to Sheridan when I was eleven."

"Does your family still live here?"

Her green eyes filled with unmistakable sadness. "No. My parents passed away six years ago. I lived with my aunt and uncle, the Druitts, until Chance and I were married."

"The Druitts are your relatives?" Maggy couldn't conceal her shock. The interactions between Vienna and Mrs. Druitt hadn't come across as warm and friendly as she expected family might act. Then again, what did she know about warm, friendly family relations?

Vienna nodded, and to Maggy's further surprise, she laughed softly. "You're not the first to find that unexpected. My mother and Uncle Nevil are siblings."

That might explain why Dolphina Druitt wasn't as

doting on Vienna as she was toward her own daughter. "Then you and Lavina are cousins?"

"Yes." Vienna took another bite of food.

Maggy cast a glance at the table where Lavina and her husband sat with her parents. "Are you two close?"

"Somewhat," Vienna admitted. "Lavina is three years older than me. I did enjoy her company for about a year before she married and moved away." She studied her plate as she added, "It wasn't so easy living on the Druitt ranch once she was gone."

Maggy could believe that. "Do you enjoy riding as much as your cousin does?"

"Not really. I like gardening and working with my hands." Vienna's expression blossomed as she spoke of what she loved doing. "I can ride, but it isn't something I enjoy doing as much as other things. What about you? Do you enjoy riding?"

The recollection of racing Edward made Maggy smile. "Yes, very much."

"Are there other things you enjoy, as well?"

Maggy pushed at the remaining food on her plate with her fork as she tried to think how best to word her answer. "I also like to…work out riddles…and solve puzzles."

"That's an unusual talent," Vienna said.

She heard Edward cough as if covering a laugh. "Very unusual indeed." He spoke low enough that Maggy was certain she alone heard him.

"So I've been told," she replied, glancing at Edward. He coughed again and she hurried to smother her own laughter by taking another bite.

Feeling someone watching her, she looked up to find Howe scowling in her direction. Maggy met his surly look with a strong one of her own. She wouldn't be intimidated by him or any other man ever again.

If only she could share some of that strength with Vienna…

She glanced at the young woman again and felt renewed determination rise inside her. As long as she was here, she would do all she could to help not only Edward but Vienna, too.

Edward led Maggy out the front door of the inn. The sun had set, leaving the sky a purplish blue. The dinner had gone well—except for the tense moment between Maggy and Howe. Edward had been upset by the other rancher's condescending tone and words, but he'd been equally as angry at the others seated at their table who'd simply let Howe carry on in such a rude fashion.

"You and Vienna seem to get along well," he said as they stepped off the porch.

Maggy smiled. "We do." After a moment, she added in a subdued voice, "She reminds me a bit of myself at that age."

"Now you're jesting," he said with a chuckle.

Her expression instantly changed from open to steely. "Why would you say that?"

"Well, because…" He stopped walking and glanced around to make sure no one was close enough to hear. "I don't think two women could be more different. Vienna is shy and often timid. And you…" He waved a hand at her, trying to convey what seemed so obvious to him.

Maggy's eyebrows rose haughtily. "I'm what, Edward?"

"You aren't shy or timid," he countered with a hint of annoyance. Surely she knew what he meant. "You're strong and determined and you met Howe's insolence with poise."

He started forward, only to be tugged back when Maggy didn't move. "You thought I handled his behavior with poise?" The uncertainty and hopefulness in her tone erased his irritation.

"Yes, Maggy, you did." He covered her hand where it lay against his sleeve. "I couldn't have been more proud."

Her cheeks filled with an attractive blush. "Thank you...for saying so." She began walking toward the buggy, pulling him along this time. "You're right in a way about Vienna and me. I'm not like her—not now. But there was a time when I was far more like her than you may realize."

"Really?" He cut a glance at her, still not able to imagine Maggy as anything close to shy or timid. Except... Moments of observation, which he hadn't thought about for some time, floated through his mind. Times when she'd looked vulnerable or frightened, such as the first time he touched her hand. "Will you tell me why?"

Her pause felt heavy with unvoiced thoughts and possibly painful recollections. "Not yet. Maybe one of these days."

He didn't know how many more of these days they would have, but he sensed it was better not to point that out. Things felt comfortable and familiar between them tonight, and he didn't want to disrupt that with more questions or reminders about their time together ending.

"Did you conclude anything new this evening?" he asked, when they stopped beside the buggy.

Maggy brightened as she did whenever she talked about investigating. He recalled what she'd shared with Vienna, about liking to work out riddles and solve puzzles, and smiled. Of course she hadn't been able to tell the other young woman that she was a detective, but he'd thought her explanation amusing and fitting.

"I think we can safely rule out the Kitts," she said quietly. "Both of them seem too caught up in romance and each other to do anything nefarious. I agree with your conclusion about the Prestons, as well. They're naturally sullen about everything and everyone but with no particular vendettas or enemies."

He nodded in agreement. "And the Howes?"

"If Howe is a coconspirator, I doubt that Vienna would know it. Even if she did, she wouldn't share or question it."

"Why not?"

Maggy peered at something in the distance. "Please just trust me on this one."

"All right," he said without hesitation. Over the twelve days that had passed since Maggy's arrival at the ranch, he truly had come to trust her, her skills, and her judgment. He saw no reason to begin doubting any of those now.

He went to hand her up onto the seat, but she didn't move. Instead she stood staring at the horse.

"What is that?" she asked, pointing with her free hand. "There's something tucked into the horse's bridle."

The white slip of paper was familiar and had the

power to make Edward's jaw tighten. "I believe I can guess."

Releasing her hand, he pulled the note from its perch. He unfolded the paper, already certain he'd find some ominous message written there.

"What does it say?" Maggy moved closer and peeked over his shoulder.

He didn't recognize the handwriting, but the words were every bit as threatening as they'd been on the other notes.

When are you going take a hint, Brit? You aren't wanted here. And if you don't start heeding the warnings you've been given already, you risk not only your ranch and your horses but your fiancée, too.

"A new note," Maggy declared.

The excitement in her voice grated on his darkening mood. "That isn't something to celebrate, Maggy," he said, turning to face her. "They're trying to threaten you, too."

"I know, but I'm not afraid." Her blue eyes glowed with resolve. "And this is a significant clue, Edward."

He fisted the note, even though he knew they'd need if for reference later. "How is it significant?"

"Because whoever placed it there arrived after we did or at least waited until we were inside the inn before leaving the note." She paused as if waiting for him to say something, but Edward wasn't sure how to reply. "If it was left by another rancher," she continued when he remained silent, "and I firmly believe it was, then he must have come into dinner after you and I did."

Edward rubbed at his chin with his other hand. "The only one who arrived after we did was... Howe."

"Yes," Maggy said with a smile.

Smiling wasn't what he wanted to do right now. He wanted to find Howe and land a good punch to the arrogant rancher's face. It had been years since Edward had tussled with his brothers, but he remembered enough that he felt certain he could hold his own.

"I'm going back in there and confronting him." He fell back a step, the muscles in his jaw clenched tighter. "He already offended you once. I won't stand by and let him threaten you, too."

The enthusiasm on her face drained away. "No, Edward, please don't." As if she feared her words wouldn't be enough to stop him—and he wasn't sure they would have been—she placed her hand against his chest, her blue eyes entreating him to stay. "I appreciate you wanting to protect me and my honor, but we don't have solid proof."

"But you just said—"

She hurried to add, "I know what I said and I stand by it. I firmly believe it was Howe who left the note. But we don't want to reveal how much we know just yet. We're much closer to solving the mystery with this clue, but we need evidence, not just accusations."

He wanted to argue with her, and he still wanted to show Howe exactly what he thought of him by using a good right jab. But Edward knew deep down that Maggy was right. They needed hard facts.

"Fine." He let his shoulders slump. "I won't get into fisticuffs with Howe."

One corner of her mouth lifted. "You would get into fisticuffs for me?"

He sensed she meant it in a teasing way, but he couldn't bring himself to jest about something he felt strongly about. "Yes, Maggy." He placed his hand over hers where it still rested near his heart—just as it had the other day when they'd stumbled into each other. "I would."

Her eyes widened as she regarded him. A longing to show her precisely how he felt about her—with a firm kiss—filled him to near distraction. But it wouldn't be right. She wasn't staying and he wasn't sure there was much left of his heart to give to anyone.

"Let's head home then," he said after clearing his throat.

Maggy nodded, her earlier fervor replaced by somber determination. And a slight bit of disappointment? He shook his head as he helped her onto the seat. He was likely reading into things.

After they were both settled in the buggy and he drove away from the inn, he kept hearing her question repeat inside his head—*you would get into fisticuffs for me?*

He'd been honest when he'd told her that he would. It wasn't solely about protecting her honor from boars like Howe, either. He would protect Maggy, too, as long as she would let him.

Chapter Eleven

Maggy had been at the ranch for almost four weeks now, and she could finally admit she didn't mind attending services on Sundays. There were still long minutes when she found it hard to concentrate, but the same restless boy sat in front of them each week, and she entertained them both by winking at him whenever he turned around.

The pastor had also said something this morning that she'd been mulling over ever since. In his sermon, he'd told the congregation that God loved them and knew them by name. He'd quoted a scripture in Romans and reminded them they were each His child and that made them enough.

Maggy decided to look up the verse after church, but only when Edward was out talking with McCall. She didn't want him to know yet that she'd been reading the Bible in short snatches the last couple weeks whenever she had a private moment. While she trusted Edward not to tease her about it, matters of faith and how much her father and Jeb had affected those still felt too private to share.

Tracing her finger beneath the words, she read the verse softly to herself. *The Spirit itself beareth witness with our spirit, that we are the children of God.*

She'd believed that as a child, before her mother's death, but did she still? It was hard to imagine a loving Father who thought her good enough to be His child when her own father hadn't. And neither had Jeb.

The pastor seemed so sure, though, and so had her mother. Even Edward, who'd lost a sister to death, believed in a loving God—Maggy could tell each time he prayed. So what helped them continue on in faith?

She lowered her gaze back to the open page of the Bible and decided to keep reading where she'd left off. There were other verses she read that she liked, but nothing else resonated with her until she reached the last two verses of the chapter.

For I am persuaded, that neither death, nor life, nor angels, nor principalities, nor powers, nor things present, nor things to come,

Nor height, nor depth, nor any other creature, shall be able to separate us from the love of God, which is in Christ Jesus our Lord.

Her heart began to race but not in a frightening way. She read the words through a second time, then a third. If nothing could separate her from God's love, including any other creature, then why had she felt abandoned by Him for so many years?

A flow of thoughts, quiet yet penetrating in truth, entered her mind. *It's because I stopped looking like Mama told me to do. I stopped searching for Him, stopped praying to Him. He didn't move or change... or stop loving me.* She blinked back the sudden blur of tears in her eyes. *I was the one who stepped away.*

The beauty and peace that accompanied her realization lasted a few moments more before the old doubts and insecurities resurfaced to blot them out. *See, you are worthless—you turned your back on God.* These weren't words Jeb had spoken to her, but she heard them inside her head in his caustic voice anyway.

Fear pecked mercilessly at the harmony she'd just experienced, freezing her in place on the sofa and tightening her lungs. Would she ever truly be free of the dread, of the feelings of worthlessness...

A thought surged forward in her mind, a reminder of what she'd told Vienna the other week about being of worth, of being somebody. It was what the pastor had also confidently declared during his sermon. And while Maggy might have stepped away from God, that didn't make her worthless. Regretful, yes, but not worthless.

A tear broke loose and slipped down her cheek. Maggy brushed it away, embarrassed, even though no one was in the room. That was another travesty from her experiences with her father and Jeb. She could not bear to let anyone see her cry—tears had been a sign of weakness to them. And she'd wanted to be strong. To prove to them, to everyone, that she wasn't weak.

"Is that what I'm doing?" she murmured out loud.

Was she trying to prove something to two men who weren't even living on this earth anymore?

Maybe...in part.

She did love her job as a detective, though, and she was skilled at it. Did God see that? No sooner had she thought the question, then a feeling of warmth spread through her. It called to her memory an experience from her girlhood. She'd been caught outside in a rainstorm and was soaking wet when she arrived home. Her mother had her change into dry clothes before wrapping Maggy in a blanket and holding her on her lap. She'd felt cocooned in warmth and love that day. That was how she felt now.

After ensuring the house still echoed with quiet, she clasped her hands together and shut her eyes. "Heavenly Father…" It surprised her how easily she began her prayer, as if she hadn't stopped petitioning Him years ago. "Thank You for helping me see things more clearly. I'm sorry for stepping away. There's a lot I still don't understand, but I want to learn. I'm grateful for this job and for the friends I've made." She thought of Edward, Vienna and Mrs. Harvey, and even the nameless boy at church. "Please bless them. And bless me and Edward to solve his case. In the name of Thy Son. Amen."

Maggy whipped her chin up, half expecting someone to be watching. There was no one in the open doorway, though, and she was still alone in the parlor. A relieved chuckle escaped her lips as she stood and put the Bible back in its designated spot.

She felt lighter and stronger and clearer in thought than she had in a long time. She wasn't alone—and that knowledge in and of itself made her want to sing.

Smiling to herself, she strode outside into the sunshine. She'd heard Edward pray over his case, but after today, he wouldn't be the only one doing so.

The following afternoon Maggy climbed onto the buggy seat to drive herself to another tea meeting, while Edward held the horse he'd hitched to the vehicle. "I'll be back in a few hours."

"No rush," he said. "I know how riveting these tea meetings can be." His gray eyes were lit with humor.

This would be her fourth tea meeting with the wives' club. She'd also attended an additional meeting at the inn the week before for those women assigned to decorate the city hall building for the upcoming summer ball. To Maggy's relief, Vienna had also been assigned to the decorating committee, along with Matilda Kitt, whom Maggy had come to enjoy talking with, as well.

"Very funny," she remarked, shaking her head in feigned annoyance. In truth, she loved bantering with Edward. And talking with him. And the way his gray eyes darkened with protectiveness whenever they talked about that last threatening note. She had no doubt he would've marched back into the inn that night two weeks ago and defended her against Howe if she hadn't persuaded him to stop. "Thanks for hitching up the horse."

"You're welcome." He let go of the animal's bridle and stepped back. "See you in a few hours."

She tapped the horse with the reins and waved to Edward as she drove past. No further action had been taken against the ranch since that last menacing note. And while Maggy itched to find more clues to solve the case and secure her promotion, she hadn't minded the respite, either. There were moments—when she was reading in the parlor with Edward seated nearby, outlining his equestrian book, or Mrs. Harvey let her help with the cooking, or she, Vienna and Matilda got to talking—when she felt as if she really was Edward's fiancée and not simply on a mission.

Guiding the horse and buggy down the drive and beneath the Running W's arch, she realized how familiar and pleasant the sprawling land and tidy buildings had become to her. It would take time to adjust to living back in a city again, once she left here. The thought of leaving—Edward, the ranch and everything behind— tightened her throat with emotion, and she hurried to clear it away with a cough. She wasn't finished here yet, so there was no need to prematurely dwell on the inevitable goodbyes.

The buggy wheels rattled over the stones of the bridge as Maggy drove over it. The sunshine had won out over the earlier cloudy skies, making her grateful for her hat. Though it was one of her new ones, it provided considerably more shade than the one she had worn when she'd traveled here.

Her thoughts returned to Edward, as they often did when they were apart these days. She loved how his brow and mouth pursed when he was concentrating and the way his eyes lit when he was amused or excited. She loved how his gentle, strong hands could soothe a horse and how those same hands touched the small of her back or helped her rise from the sofa.

She looked forward to seeing him at mealtimes or around the ranch or during their occasional horseback rides. And though he hadn't taken her back to the rock pile, she still cherished the fact that he'd trusted her enough to show her such a significant spot.

Maggy suddenly realized she'd kept the horse at a plodding place as she'd been woolgathering. If they didn't hurry, she'd be late for the meeting. She moved to increase the horse's speed, but a sudden thought entered her mind: *Stop!* The impression was so clear and firm that she jerked back on the reins, bringing the horse to a halt.

Was there something in the road? She rose to her feet to look around, but the lane stood void of any other people, carriages or animals. Confused, Maggy sat back down. Had she conjured up the thought from her own imagination?

Frowning, she slapped the horse lightly with the reins. But the thought returned: *Stop! Don't keep driving.*

She stopped the horse a second time, more than a little baffled. What should she do now? Maggy eyed the road again as well as the back of the horse, but she couldn't see anything amiss. Maybe things would become clearer if she got out of the buggy.

Rising to her feet, she climbed out of the vehicle. She surveyed the horse, though nothing appeared wrong with it. The animal simply watched her with what she imagined was a bit of confusion, too.

"I don't understand it either, boy," she murmured as she retraced her steps back to the side of the buggy.

The vehicle looked to be as sound as it had been when they'd driven it to church the day before. Was she missing something? Maggy moved closer to examine the buggy's rear exterior and side. Her careful perusal at last paid off when she reached the right wheel. There was a large crack in the axle that hadn't been there before—a crack Maggy suspected was deliberately made and not an accident.

The reality of what might have happened had the horse begun to trot slammed into her with such force she sagged against the side of the buggy, gripping it with both hands to remain on her feet.

If the horse had quickened its pace, the axle would have broken completely, causing the wheel to fall and likely throwing Maggy from the vehicle. She could have been seriously injured if she hadn't heeded that warning thought.

Some of the peace she'd felt yesterday afternoon returned, soothing the shakiness in the pit of her stomach. Someone had been looking out for her. *Look for His hand in the small things and the big things, Maggy. Look for His hand.* If she wanted to know that God knew her individually, here was evidence.

She needed to let Edward know what had happened—and that their reprieve had come to an end. Taking the horse's bridle in hand, she guided the animal to the side of the road. Once she had the buggy out of the way, she unhitched the horse and walked it back toward the ranch. Thankfully she didn't have far to go. Her trembling softened a little more with each step, while at the same time her resolve grew stronger.

The culprit here was someone who knew her schedule, at least well enough to know she always took the buggy out on Mondays to attend tea meetings. The awareness of being watched sent a ripple of fear up her spine. She glanced around but saw no one lurking about.

As she drew closer to the house, she saw Edward exit the stable, leading Napoleon behind him. His eyes widened in surprise when he saw her. "Did you change your mind about going?"

"Not exactly." Maggy waited to say more until she reached his side. Even then, she glanced around to ensure no one was nearby before continuing. "The buggy is broken down past the bridge and before the road to go to Sheridan."

He frowned. "What happened? It was fine yesterday."

"Someone tampered with the right-wheel axle. It would've broken completely if I hadn't stopped driving when I did."

She could tell the moment he understood the implications of what she was saying. His face drained of color. "Someone knew you would be driving the buggy to the tea meeting."

Maggy nodded. "I came to the same conclusion."

"Are you all right? Were you hurt?" His gaze swept her from head to toe.

"No. I'm a little shaken but fine."

Before she could say anything more, he dropped the reins of his horse and pulled her to him in a tight embrace. The action surprised her—she hadn't been this close to him in several weeks—but she didn't stiffen in fear or discomfort this time. Instead she wrapped her arms around Edward's waist, feeling secure and cared for within his arms. The moment felt all the more precious because his action wasn't about convincing an audience they were engaged. Edward's gesture was surely one of genuine worry for her, and she welcomed it, even if there was nothing more to his embrace than kindness.

At least that was what she told herself, in spite of the way her stomach quivered with delight as he continued to hold her.

"You might have been seriously hurt, Maggy." He whispered the words, but she didn't miss the fear and concern that underscored them.

She shut her eyes and pressed her cheek to his shirt,

knowing she would have felt the same had it been him driving the damaged buggy. "I know."

"Did you notice something wrong with the wheel while you were driving?"

Maggy recognized what he was really asking—how had she known to stop? Could she share her experience with him? Did she trust him enough to tell him something so personal? She didn't have to search for the answer; she already knew it.

Blowing out her breath, she responded simply, "I had a thought—it came twice, actually—that I needed to stop driving. It was only after I examined the buggy that I found the crack in the axle."

"You were protected."

He didn't state it as a question, but she felt the need to nod anyway. If only to show that she also recognized the import of her impression.

She eased back, though she didn't want to, until he released her. "I still need to get to the tea meeting. It will take too long to hitch the horses to the wagon, but if we saddle—"

"No." His eyes looked as dark as thunderheads. "Someone is trying to hurt you, Maggy. To get at me through you. It's not safe for you to go to the meeting today."

She placed her hand on his arm. "I'm not afraid, Edward. And we need to show that to whoever did this."

He didn't know whether to shout or take Maggy into his arms again—possibly both. Couldn't she see how close she'd come to being injured? He couldn't shake the panicked feeling in his gut over what could have happened.

Or the realization of how natural, how right, how wonderful it had been to hold her close and have her hand resting against his arm like this.

He wasn't open to letting another woman into his life, though, especially one who was only here to do a job. He liked Maggy—she was smart, beautiful, matter-of-fact, kind. She didn't play coy or manipulate, either. Best of all, she accepted him, not because he was successful or the son of an earl, but because he was himself. And yet she wouldn't be staying, and he knew all too well the painful regret of giving his heart to a woman and watching her discard it before walking away.

"You really think you should still go?" He didn't like the idea, but he could see her determination. It was another quality he admired about her.

She lowered her hand to her side, bringing a sting of disappointment to him. "Yes, absolutely."

"All right. Then I'll ride with you."

Her brow pinched with a frown. "Edward, that isn't necessary. I'm perfectly fine. I wasn't harmed. And I can take care…"

Her speech ended on a squeak when he lifted his hands and cupped her beautiful face between them. He wanted to secure her undivided attention for what he had to say. And, judging by her wide eyes and parted lips, he'd been successful. Except the feel of her soft cheeks beneath his fingertips was more than a bit distracting. He had to clear his throat in order to be able to speak.

"I know you can take care of yourself," he said in a low, slightly gruff tone. "What I'm asking is if you'll please indulge me in seeing that my fiancée gets to this meeting safely?"

She studied him, her expression radiating strength, grace and trust. Could she see that his question stemmed from more than a gentlemanly need to protect those in his care? In spite of his own resistance, he'd come to care a great deal about Maggy. And not simply as a friend, if his desire to kiss her in this moment was any indication. Only he feared breaking her trust if he did so.

"All right," she whispered back.

What had they been talking about? "All right?" he repeated.

"You can ride with me." She shook her head in mild exasperation, but she was smiling.

With much reluctance, he lowered his hands and stepped back. "Thank you."

It didn't take long to saddle the horse for her. Since Edward didn't own a sidesaddle, Maggy had to straddle the animal, but she had enough profusion of skirt to keep her looking modest. Though he wasn't sure how they would explain to anyone who asked why she'd ridden into town astride a horse instead of in the buggy this time.

They set out, riding down the drive and across the bridge. When they reached the buggy, Edward stopped to examine the axle. The large crack in it incited his anger and concern all over again.

Who had done this? he wondered as he remounted. How had they sneaked onto the ranch without anyone seeing?

The recent lull in acts against the Running W or ominous notes had been a welcome break for all of them, though he'd still had his wranglers rotating guard duty. If the sabotage now included people slinking onto his property undetected, he might need all of his staff to serve as guards instead of managing the ranch. But if he took that step, what would become of his horses or the Cavalry's interest then?

Edward cut a look at Maggy riding beside him. She'd been protected earlier, when she'd had the thought to stop driving. And he had no doubt where the impression had come from. God was watching out for her, and that meant Edward needed to continue to trust her and the Lord, too.

Yes, his property and horses had been tampered with, and yet, not one person in his employ, including himself, had been physically harmed. They'd all been safe so far.

"That's what made this time different," he suddenly declared, renewed energy coursing through him.

Maggy turned in her saddle. "What did you say?"

"What happened back there with the buggy? It was different."

"Different how?"

He sat up straighter. "None of the other 'accidents' were designed to hurt a person. Until now. Even those notes, however threatening, weren't followed up by acts of violence that would harm someone. Property, yes, and possibly the horses, but not another human being."

She nodded slowly, then faster with understanding. "You're right. This last act isn't in keeping with the others."

"Which means?"

Her bright laughter drew a smile from him. "You

tell me. You saw something I didn't. What do *you* think it means?"

He considered her question carefully before answering. "Perhaps whoever is behind all of this is growing desperate. After all, like that last note implied, I haven't heeded any of the warnings."

"True, and I've seen firsthand how desperation can drive others to drastic measures."

For the first time, he wondered what she had witnessed during her career as a detective. Surely it was a darker side of humanity.

"Could there be another possibility?" he asked as he adjusted his hat.

"Most likely." She threw him an impish smile. "And you wouldn't excel at your newfound detective skills if you didn't ask yourself what other possibilities might exist."

He chuckled, grateful for her confidence in him but feeling no less stumped. "I don't know. There's something a bit off-kilter—no pun intended—about this last action. It's more aggressive and seems less aimed at the ranch and more at me personally. Could it be that the person's motives have changed?"

"Could be." Maggy's face scrunched in concentration. Far from being unattractive, Edward found it endearing. "I agree that what happened today, or what might have happened, is far more aggressive than anything else that's been done."

A reflective silence settled between them for a few minutes before she spoke again. "If the man who left that last note was Howe, as we suspect, then maybe the damage to the buggy means he has more of a grievance against you than just wanting you to leave."

"Possibly, though I don't know what the cause for his vendetta could be," Edward replied honestly. "I've not interacted with him personally beyond a handful of conversations over the last couple years."

"Did you know he's the nephew-in-law to the Druitts?"

He glanced at Maggy in disbelief. Why hadn't he known that? Howe had only been around the area less than a year before he and Vienna had married, but Edward hadn't known the girl's relation to the Druitts. "So Vienna is their niece?"

"Yes, and it isn't a surprise that you don't know. Both sides seem content to keep the fact quiet." She glanced forward once more. "I can understand why Vienna would do that, but I'm not sure why the Druitts aren't more doting toward their niece."

Edward's thoughts returned to Howe and why the man would hate him enough to hurt his ranch and Maggy. Nothing new came to mind. He wasn't even sure Howe had been to the Running W before. Like so many aspects of his case, the perpetrator's motive still remained a frustrating mystery.

The ride to Sheridan passed uneventfully, to Edward's immense relief. He might have been overly concerned for Maggy's safety, but he was still grateful to see her to the inn and know she'd arrived without incident.

Douglas Kitt was helping his wife down from their wagon when Edward and Maggy rode up and dismounted. Thankfully neither of them seemed to notice or care that Maggy was riding horseback in a nice dress and wasn't driving the buggy as usual.

"Howdy," Kitt called to them.

Edward lifted his hand in greeting before turning to Maggy. "I can stay in town until the meeting is over."

"No." She shook her head. "I'll be fine." When he raised his eyebrows in challenge, she laughed. "I will."

He didn't like the idea of her riding home alone and unprotected. But he did need to return to the ranch. Plus he wanted to see if he could find footprints or any other clues near the stable. "I'll head home then," he conceded.

"I'll be back soon." She leaned in and, to his astonishment, pressed a quick kiss to his cheek.

The gesture was over and done with in just a few seconds. But the soft brush of her lips lingered on his jaw, even after she'd moved toward the porch where Vienna stood waiting for her and Matilda. The three women entered the inn together.

"You're putting us to shame, Kent," Kitt muttered, but his expression didn't match his surly tone as he watched his wife disappear inside.

Edward cleared his throat and tried to push Maggy's kiss to the back of his thoughts. She'd likely done it because others were watching them. Still, that didn't erase his strong wish to march after her and show her what a real kiss between them ought to be. A wish that had nothing to do with being observed or not.

It took another moment for him to remember what Kitt had said. "I'm afraid I don't know what you mean."

"All this courting stuff between you and your fiancée." Kitt waved his hand in the air. "It's got Matilda all dreamy-eyed and insisting she and I act like we're sweethearts again."

Edward couldn't help chuckling. "That isn't to your liking?"

"I wouldn't say that. It's been kind of nice." The other rancher turned red, though there was a genuine grin on his face. "I'd forgotten how crazy in love I was with that woman when I first met her."

Had Edward been *crazy in love* with Beatrice? He'd thought so, but looking back, he'd felt more relieved than in love at having someone like Beatrice interested in him—the third, oft-overlooked son. Believing he had the affection of a beautiful, charming, wealthy woman had made him feel enough. In truth, they hadn't shared the easy camaraderie he'd always hoped to have with the woman he intended to marry.

Had Beatrice felt the absence of genuine friendship in their relationship? he wondered. Had she found that with his brother?

The questions prompted a flicker of compassion for the woman he'd once believed he adored. Of course he still wished she'd been honest with him and hadn't gone behind his back to pursue his oldest brother. But maybe Beatrice had recognized something was missing between them. He even found himself hoping she'd found more than financial gain in her union with his brother. He hoped she'd been able to find real companionship and love, too.

A stray thought entered his head, chipping away at his magnanimous mood. Had Maggy ever been in love in the way Kitt had described? Edward frowned. He wasn't sure why the idea of her loving another man didn't sit right with him, but it didn't.

Kitt spoke again, pulling Edward's thoughts to the present. "I'd forgotten what it's like to be friends and sweethearts like we were in the early days. Like how you and Miss Worthwright are right now."

Edward swallowed the argument that settled on the tip of his tongue. True, he and Maggy were friends. But they weren't sweethearts—not in a real sense. Instead of feeling proud that they'd convinced the Kitts of the validity of their temporary engagement, though, he felt sadness.

If there was a woman out there for him, one he could truly open his heart to and trust, it would be someone like Maggy. Someone of strength, cleverness, and tenacity. Someone with whom he could laugh, race horses, share his faith.

He'd caught sight of Maggy reading the Bible during the past few weeks and it had made him smile each time. She still let him say the mealtime prayers, but he sensed a softening, a relaxing, to the awkwardness his praying had once trudged up.

These characteristics were different than the ones he'd envisioned wanting when he'd met Beatrice. And yet, he feared this new list of qualities would only ever bear one face—and that was Maggy's.

"Before I go, there's something I need to tell you." Kitt's expression held none of its earlier lightheartedness.

Edward nodded, feeling wary. "What is it?"

Kitt looked around, then motioned for Edward to join him on the other side of his carriage. "Howe was talking to me yesterday." He kept his voice low.

The mention of Howe set Edward on edge. "What did he say?" Would Kitt reveal something that would provide more clues?

"He seems to have taken a disliking to his wife and your fiancée being friends." Kitt shook his head as if he thought Howe's sentiment absurd. "Says he doesn't want her being a bad influence on Vienna."

Edward frowned. "How has Maggy been a bad influence on her?" He'd seen the way Vienna brightened whenever Maggy spoke with her during the Saturday dinners. Howe's accusation made no sense. If the man had written that last hostile note, was that why the wording had included Maggy? Did Howe have such an aversion to Maggy that he'd orchestrated the potential buggy accident, too?

"I don't know what he meant." Kitt shrugged. "Thought it best to warn you, though. Might want to mention it to Miss Worthwright, too."

"Thank you."

Perhaps it would be wise if Maggy interacted less with Vienna. Edward suspected she wouldn't fancy the suggestion. She seemed more at ease conversing with Howe's wife than with any other woman, except for Mrs. Harvey.

"I think I'll head on over to the general store while I'm waiting for Matilda." Kitt slapped the side of his carriage. "You wanna come?"

"No, I need to head back." On sudden impulse or inspiration, he added, "I have a business idea I'd like to run by you, though." He respected Kitt and had been relieved when Maggy had dismissed the other rancher and his wife as possible suspects. That respect and trust had only increased today with Kitt's willingness to share with him what Howe was saying. Kitt would be a good one to join the Cavalry venture.

"What sort of business idea?" Kitt asked with mild interest.

After glancing around to ensure they wouldn't be

overheard, Edward continued. "I've been in contact with the British Cavalry, and they are very interested in buying horses from this area."

"The British Cavalry?" Kitt's tone sounded a bit dubious, though he did look impressed. "How'd they find you?"

"An acquaintance of my father is employed there. I contacted him earlier this year about the possibility of them purchasing horses from here."

Kitt rubbed at his clean-shaven chin. "And they liked the idea?"

"Very much so," Edward answered with a genuine smile. "They're going to need far more horses than I can provide, though. Which leads me to my question. Would you be interested in contracting with them for your horses?"

The fellow rancher grinned. "Course I would. Have you talked to any of the others?"

"I haven't." And he hoped Kitt wouldn't, either. "It's not a guarantee, but I believe the Cavalry's interest is genuine. Still, I'll ask you to keep this between us for now."

Kitt looked him straight in the eye. "I can do that." Then he gave a disbelieving shake of his head as he chuckled. "This could be huge. Thanks for thinking of me, Kent."

"You're welcome." Edward decided to hazard one more question. "Other than Howe's upset over Maggy befriending his wife, no one else has voiced a complaint against me or anyone else at the Running W, have they?"

"Not that I've heard." The confusion on Kitt's face brought as much relief to Edward as the man's words.

They also confirmed again that Kitt wasn't involved in trying to ruin Edward's ranch. "Got a reason to think otherwise?"

Edward had plenty, and though he trusted Kitt, he didn't think it wise to share those reasons yet. Not when he and Maggy still had more suspicions than tangible proof. "Just want to know my neighbors feel I'm contributing to the community."

"I got no complaints about you," Kitt said with another shrug. "You're honest and hardworking, have been since you got here. Even Druitt seems to have changed his mind about you."

Druitt? Edward felt on the brink of learning something significant, but he kept his expression impassive to ask casually, "Druitt had complaint against me?"

"Not you personally. It's just that he hoped to buy up that spot of land that's yours now, but at the time, he didn't have enough cash on hand." Kitt loosely folded his arms. "You know how he's always trying to convince his son-in-law to quit storekeeping and be a rancher? Well, I guess Druitt hoped to sway him by buying the spread where the Running W now sits."

Druitt had once wanted the property that Edward now owned. Did the man still want it? Badly enough to threaten the current owner to try to make him leave? Excitement coursed through him at the new information. Perhaps this was what Maggy felt when something finally clicked with a case.

Maggy! He needed to tell her—right now—that he'd found not only another suspect but someone with a real motive, too. And motives were things they'd been hard-pressed to figure out lately.

"Good talking with you, Kitt."

Kitt dipped his head in a nod. "You, too, Kent. See you Saturday, if not before." He waved and climbed into his carriage.

Edward waited until the man had turned his vehicle around and was headed down the street before he jogged toward the inn's front door. There was a great deal to tell Maggy, and he couldn't wait another minute to do so.

Chapter Twelve

What had compelled her to kiss Edward's cheek earlier? Maggy asked herself for the umpteenth time as she drank more tea she didn't taste and listened to conversation she didn't really hear. His protective look had been one reason. But she'd also acted without thinking. One moment she'd been listening to him voice his concern for her, and the next she'd leaned forward and brushed her lips against his jaw. What had seemed so natural, and wonderful, in the moment now felt awkward and overly bold.

She tried to remind herself that Edward would likely think she'd kissed him like that as a public show of their role as a couple. At least she hoped he would think that. She wouldn't allow herself to consider what he would think if he knew the truth.

And what is the truth, Maggy?

The truth was…she'd come to care for Edward. A great deal, actually. As far more than just a friend.

She resisted the urge to plunk her forehead against the tablecloth and groan out loud. How could she have let herself come to care for a man she'd never see again when her job here was done? That was her real reason for being in Wyoming—to do a job. Not even the reprieve of the past few weeks could change the fact that someone was still trying to ruin and hurt Edward, and it was Maggy's mission to figure out who and why.

"Maggy?" Vienna murmured from the chair at her left. "Maggy?"

She lifted her chin, pulling her gaze from the nearly full plate in front of her. "Hmm?"

"I believe someone wishes to speak to you."

Maggy frowned. She was in no mood for guessing games. "What?"

"It's Edward." Vienna smiled at her. "He's waiting over there by the door."

Swiveling, she glanced in that direction. Sure enough, Edward stood in the doorway of the parlor, his gaze on her. The sight of his familiar, handsome face disrupted the rhythm of her pulse as if it had been days instead of minutes since she'd last seen him.

Was he here to ask her about her kiss? Her stomach lurched at the thought, making her grateful she'd only nibbled at the finger food. He didn't look angry, though. If anything, he looked excited.

He motioned for her to join him at the door. Keeping her head high, she set down her teacup and pushed back her chair. "Excuse me for a moment, ladies."

"He just can't bear to say goodbye," Matilda murmured in a dreamy tone.

Ignoring her, Maggy willed back a flush of embarrassment as she strode across the room. She could feel the eyes of the other women on her back with every step.

At last she reached the door...and Edward. "What are you doing here?"

"I have something to tell you and it can't wait another moment."

He took her elbow in his hand—making her heart thrum even faster—and steered her away from the ladies' parlor to a secluded corner. When he stopped, though, he simply stood there, watching her.

"Edward, what is it?"

The corners of his mouth rose. "Did you know that dress is the exact same shade of blue as your eyes?"

"Is that…" She had to swallow past her suddenly dry throat to finish her question. "Is that what you came here to tell me?"

He seemed to collect himself. "Uh…no." Shaking his head, he lowered his hand from her arm. "I just learned the most fascinating bit of information from Kitt."

Ah, the mission. That was why he was here. Not to tell her that he'd noticed her dress and eyes matched. She forced a smile. "What did he tell you?"

"Before I bought the land for the Running W, Druitt wanted to purchase it." He leaned forward, his anticipation palpable. "That way his daughter and son-in-law would have no excuse not to move here and set up their own ranch."

Despite her conflicting emotions where Edward was concerned, Maggy couldn't be happier at this news. "That might still be a strong enough motive for getting you to leave now, especially with the ranch doing as well as it is." She ruminated on that before adding, "If he could scare you off and you tried to sell the place in a hurry, he'd likely get it for less than it's worth. He could gift Lavina and Felix with a fully operational ranch at a bargain price."

"My thoughts exactly," he said, pocketing his hands.

A triumphant smile lit his face and reminded Maggy of what she'd thought of him her first day here. She'd wondered what he would look like if he were to smile or laugh with abandon. That was no longer a mystery to her; she knew and cherished every one of his open, unabashed smiles as well as his deep, rumbling laughter. And she would miss both when she left.

"This is pivotal information, Edward," she said as she pushed back against her other thoughts. She must focus on his case and only that. "Excellent job."

His smile turned to a boyish grin. "As I've said more than once, any investigative skills I've garnered are only a credit to your own."

Maggy hoped her cheeks didn't look as red as they felt. "Thank you. I'd better return to the meeting." She fell back a step. "I'll pay more attention to what Mrs. Druitt says. Especially any more hints about Lavina moving back."

"Wait. There's one more thing." His expression was no longer eager but subdued.

Had something else happened at the ranch? She quickly dismissed the idea—Edward hadn't even gone back home yet. "What?"

"Howe has been talking to Kitt."

A knot tightened in Maggy's middle at the mention of Vienna's husband. "And?" she asked with wariness.

"Apparently he doesn't fancy the idea of you and Vienna being friends." Edward glanced away as if embarrassed to relay more, but he continued. "He believes you're a negative influence on his wife."

She folded her arms against the anger rising inside her. Of course Howe would feel threatened by her—

she was strong and so was Vienna, though the young woman hadn't fully realized it yet. That hadn't stopped Maggy, though, from looking for opportunities to remind Vienna that every woman was of worth and not an afterthought of a person to be pushed around. Little wonder a bully like Chance Howe didn't appreciate someone putting that idea in his wife's head.

"Kitt thinks it might be best to distance yourself some from Vienna, at least until Howe simmers down." His gray eyes shone with compassion and concern. "After what happened today with the buggy, I'm afraid I am in agreement, Maggy." He stated the words with a measure of apology, but they irritated her nonetheless.

"Are you asking me to ignore someone who has become my friend—someone who might still prove useful to our investigation, I might add—because her scoundrel of a husband is unhappy?" She drew herself up to full height, though it still didn't mean she was as tall as him. "Besides, I'm the detective here. I can decide for myself who to talk to and who to befriend."

The lines around Edward's mouth relaxed. "I'm not making an edict here. And I know this isn't something you wish to do. I simply want to keep you safe. Please trust me in that."

She wanted to argue further, if only to rid herself of the warmth his words inspired deep inside her. It wasn't as if he meant anything more by them than gentlemanly concern. But she also sensed what he hadn't said—that Edward cared about her. Even if it was only in the capacity of a dear friend, she felt a wash of gratitude. She hadn't suspected in the beginning that they would get along so well.

"I'll try," she said after releasing a long breath. "I

don't want Vienna to think I'm slighting her, but I'll try to be equally as chatty with everyone."

He smiled. "Thank you."

"I'd also like to see if I can gather any more information about the Druitts wanting your land."

With a nod, Edward followed her back toward the entrance to the ladies' parlor. "You were right, you know," he said in a low voice when they stopped.

"I can't say I don't like the sound of that." If she kept things light, then perhaps it wouldn't hurt so much when she had to say goodbye.

He chuckled, though the merriment faded after a moment as he studied her in a way that made her heart leap once more. "You were right about solving this case and the time it takes. We're on the right path. I can feel it. So thank you, Maggy, for not giving up and walking out on me that first day when I was so convinced you should."

"I would never…" She hurried to swallow what she'd been about to say—that she would never walk out on him. It would sound far too familiar and hint at her deeper feelings for him. "I would never walk out on a case, even if the client turns out to be a bit conceited and obstinate."

His eyebrows rose, though the gleam in his gray eyes hinted at his amusement. "Are we talking about the client or the detective now?"

"Ha." She reached out to poke him in the ribs in feigned indignation, but he captured her hand.

His fingers slowly stroked hers, robbing Maggy of breath. "I suppose you ought to return to the meeting."

She nodded, though neither of them moved.

"Miss Worthwright?" Mrs. Druitt's voice carried

out the open door. "We're going to be breaking into our committees soon. We must have everything ready for the ball this Saturday."

Lowering her gaze, Maggy pulled her hand free and stepped toward the door. "I'd better get in there."

"Right." Was it her imagination or did he appear disappointed? "I'll see you back at the ranch in a while."

She clasped her hands together, still feeling the touch of his fingers. "Thank you again, Edward. For coming to share the news."

"You're welcome." A full smile lifted his mouth before he turned to go.

Maggy entered the room and returned to her seat. But her thoughts and feelings weren't any less snarled than they'd been earlier—if anything they were more tangled. She felt elated at this significant turn in Edward's case, sad at the prospect of speaking less with Vienna, and confused about her blossoming emotions for Edward.

Forgetting her tea was now cold, she drank a sip and nearly spewed out her mouthful. The memory of Edward doing just that on her first day had her smiling to herself. She'd been annoyed at his reluctance to agree to her engagement plan, then terrified about actually pulling it off successfully. Now, being his fiancée felt like the most natural thing in the world.

And given this new information, she would not need to fulfill that role for much longer. The smile fled her lips at the thought, her amusement now replaced by a sharp ache.

"Maggy, are you all right?" Vienna asked quietly as they moved to one side of the parlor to meet with the rest of the decorations committee.

She barely managed a nod. "I'll be fine."

"You sure?" The young woman's expression furrowed with perceptiveness.

Forcing a quick smile, Maggy settled onto one end of the sofa. "Yes, thank you." Then remembering her commitment to Edward, she turned to the rest of the women and asked, "What do we have left to gather up for the decorations, ladies?"

By the time the committee finally finished their discussion—including the latest debate on whether yellow or soft blue was a more appropriate color for the décor—Maggy had a headache. It hadn't helped that she'd needed to appear as if she were conversing with everyone, while also surreptitiously asking Lavina questions about her husband's store and the possibility of them moving to Sheridan. Away from her mother, the young woman chatted more easily about how much she enjoyed working in the store and living in Buffalo.

Despite her parents pushing, it didn't seem like Lavina and her husband were as willing to give up that life as the Druitts wanted to believe. Were they hoping to entice their daughter with more than property as Maggy had guessed earlier? A beautiful house and ranch might be enough to sway the girl, especially if the gift came with a heaping amount of parental pressure, too.

She felt more than frustrated as she exited the inn at the conclusion of the meeting. There were still too many questions without answers. If Howe was still their primary suspect for the snake and the sabotage to the buggy, which she believed, where did his motive and the Druitts' align? Or did they? Were they unknowingly working independent of each other?

"Maggy?"

Hearing Vienna call after her, she turned and pasted on a smile. "You heading home, too?"

"Soon." Her expression looked troubled, which elicited Maggy's compassion. But she couldn't be seen talking so freely with Vienna.

"I'll see you on Saturday to set up the decorations."

She turned to go, but Vienna said in a rush, "Can I ask you something?"

"If it's whether I like the yellow or the blue," she said, facing the girl again, "I'm afraid I still don't have an answer."

Instead of prompting a smile as she'd hoped, Vienna glanced downward. "It isn't about the decorations. It's about…" She lifted her chin, giving Maggy a glimpse at her watery green eyes. "Chance would be furious if he knew I'd bullied you into talking to me again."

"Is that what he said?" Anger had her clenching her jaw. "That you're bullying me into talking to you?"

Vienna's face flushed. "I haven't meant to, truly. I've just found that talking with you is very helpful…"

"I've enjoyed every one of our conversations," Maggy said with confidence and honesty. "And I would welcome another right now."

She linked her arm with Vienna's and steered her toward the far end of the porch. A seedling of doubt attempted to sprout inside her. After all, she'd committed to trying to spend less time talking with Vienna. But she wouldn't stand by and let this girl's husband convince her yet again that she was the one in the wrong, that she was the bully.

They sat in the same rockers they had the first afternoon they'd met. Only this time, Vienna hesitated only a moment before asking her question. "What did you do after your husband died?" Maggy had told her the other week about Jeb being killed in the fire. "I mean...how did you go from being more like me to... well, being like you are now?"

Maggy was tempted to laugh at the wording of the question, but she didn't. She wouldn't belittle Vienna's courage to ask something so personal, for Maggy and for herself. And while she couldn't tell her the part about deciding to become a detective, there were other things she could share.

"The biggest thing was time," she answered as she set her rocker into motion. The back-and-forth rhythm helped her stay calm, in spite of the memories that would come to mind as she talked.

Vienna sighed, her hand rising to her stomach as it often did. "I don't feel like I have time. Not with this little one on the way. I so want him or her to have a happy, loving home." Maggy heard the silent plea behind her words—*is that possible?*

"I felt so lost after Jeb was killed. So scared." She remembered the irony of those feelings. She'd felt them nearly every day while Jeb had been alive, and yet, they'd remained a constant inside her even after his death. "It took me several weeks to realize those feelings were mine, not something Jeb had put in me. I could keep feeling and living in fear and emptiness, or I could choose to feel something else."

She paused, reliving that pivotal day in her mind. "And did you?" Vienna prompted. "Did you choose to feel something else?"

"Yes and no."

Vienna shook her head in obvious confusion, making Maggy chuckle.

"I let go of feeling scared all the time," she explained, "but I didn't know what to replace it with. It took more time before I realized I could feel...free."

"Free," Vienna echoed in a half whisper. The awestruck quality of her voice reminded Maggy so much of herself that tears burned in her eyes.

She willed them back. "I was free of Jeb's unkindness, both in word and deed, but I still needed to be free of the ugliness I'd let those things create inside me. So every morning the first thing I did was tell myself that I wasn't worthless. That I was somebody."

"Did you believe it?"

Maggy gave her a grim smile. "Not at first. There were days I had to tell myself over and over again, almost every hour, that I was worth something." Her voice cracked with emotion at the memory, but she didn't feel embarrassed. Vienna wouldn't judge her. "The more and more I told myself that, the more I came to believe it. It was only then that I could see Jeb's actions clearly and how my own fear had me making excuses—to myself and to him."

"I've started to see some things differently, too," Vienna admitted.

Maggy wasn't surprised. Howe's dander was up about more than Vienna talking with her. She guessed he'd gotten a glimpse of Vienna's inner strength and it frightened him.

"Anything else that helped you while you were with him?"

Her real question rang in the air between them as if

Vienna had shouted it. She was asking if things might get better if she stayed.

Maggy took her time answering; she couldn't know what Vienna needed to do for her situation. Only Vienna could. But she hoped to offer some insight. "I needed that separation from Jeb for me to really see him and myself. Maybe it will be different for you, Vienna. Had I known and believed I was worth something back when he was living, I like to think I would have stood up for myself. And yet I don't think we would have lasted too long that way. Jeb needed me weak and doubting. It was the only way for him to feel like he was enough himself."

Her last declaration reverberated through her, clearly and powerfully, in a way that told her what she'd said was the truth. By the look on Vienna's face, the young woman had been as affected by the words as Maggy.

If this understanding, this ability to see her past so clearly, was the result of sharing her experience with Vienna, then she wished she'd shared it sooner and with more people. Maybe the more she did so, the less she would feel those old anxieties.

As if reading her thoughts, Vienna asked, "Do you ever feel scared now? Being engaged to another man like you are?" She fiddled with the cuff of her sleeve, making Maggy wonder if she were hiding new bruises. "Do you ever worry Mr. Kent will end up being like your late husband?"

"No," Maggy replied without hesitation and with full conviction. "Because I know Mr. Kent is different. He's kinder and doesn't feel challenged by my strength." He was also handsome and smart and had a dry sense of humor that Maggy had come to admire.

If there ever was a man she might consider marrying, it would be Edward. She felt safe with him, and equally as important, she felt valued by him. Her thoughts and feelings mattered to Edward, and not just in how they related to his case. He seemed genuinely interested to know her.

But she wasn't staying. She had the possibility of a wonderful new job waiting for her. For the first time, though, she didn't feel the usual flicker of excitement at the thought of being promoted to head female detective.

"There are times I still feel scared." She wanted to be as honest as she could with Vienna. "Flashbacks of memory will bring up all those old words and feelings. Even with someone as kind as Edward." Maggy recalled how he'd found her in the middle of an episode that first day and how terrified she'd been when he'd held her wrist that first time.

Vienna dipped her head in a slow, thoughtful nod. There was no censure or pity in the gesture. "I could see that happening to me, too."

"I wish I could tell you what to do." Maggy reached out and gave the girl's hand a quick squeeze. "But that has to be your decision, Vienna. Even if someone had shared all of this with me, when I was married to Jeb, I don't know that I would've listened. So the fact that you're asking and listening says a lot about your strength."

New tears glistened in Vienna's eyes. "Thank you. I do feel stronger each time we talk."

Which explained Howe's anger.

Had he been the one to tamper with the buggy? If so, would Maggy incur his wrath all the more after talking with Vienna today? She didn't want anything happening to Edward or the ranch because of her.

Concern chewed at her peace of mind, until she reminded herself that Howe's main quarrel seemed to be with her, and if he did try something, that would be his choice. Just as talking with Vienna had been her choice—one she was glad she'd made. Seeing the return of strength and hope in Vienna's green eyes solidified Maggy's resolve to face whatever outcomes came of her decision.

"I'd better go," Vienna said, climbing to her feet. "Thanks again for talking with me and answering my questions."

Maggy stood up from her rocker too. "You're more than welcome." On sudden impulse, she gave the young woman a quick hug. If she'd been blessed to have a sister, she liked to think the girl might have been a lot like Vienna. "I'll see you Saturday."

With a wave goodbye, she turned and headed toward the hitching post where she'd left her horse. Except the animal wasn't there.

Maggy studied the other tethered mounts, but none of them were hers. Fury followed quickly on the heels of her concern. Hands on her hips, she surveyed the occupants of the porch and those moving about in the street. She didn't recognize anyone, though.

She resisted the urge to kick one of the porch columns. First the buggy and now her horse. Her only consolation was that she hadn't ridden Persimmon into town. She could hire another horse and carriage, but it felt like a waste of money, especially since she or Edward would need to pay to fix the broken one.

"It appears I will be walking," she muttered to herself.

Keeping her chin high, she marched into the street. She'd certainly experienced far worse than a seven-mile trek on a summer day.

She hadn't gotten far when she heard someone call her name. "Miss Worthwright."

"Mrs. Druitt," Maggy said, dipping her head as if on a social call.

The woman looked around. "Did you...walk to town today?"

"Uh...no." She couldn't reveal that her horse had been stolen. Not when she didn't yet know if this woman was an accomplice to the deed or not. "Edward was kind enough to convey me." Which was true. "But he was needed back at the ranch, so he was unable to wait until our meeting ended." Also true.

Mrs. Druitt's expression revealed only genuine pity. "If you aren't opposed to walking the last mile or so, I can drive you that far."

It took a great deal of effort for Maggy to hide her surprise and her happiness at her good fortune. That the very woman she hadn't been able to converse with earlier was now offering her a ride back was more than fortuitous.

"That would be wonderful. Thank you." She climbed onto the seat and arranged her skirt, feeling grateful she didn't have to straddle the horse in her dress again. It wasn't that she cared how she looked, but more the questions of why she wasn't using the buggy that might come up.

As Mrs. Druitt headed south, Maggy settled in for a good, long chat. Hopefully one that would give her and Edward some definitive answers. She started out by asking the older woman about the history behind the upcoming ball. Mrs. Druitt, as Maggy well knew, loved talking about anything to do with the wives' club and their events. After a while, Maggy steered the conversation from the club to questions about the woman's early years in the area.

She learned the Druitts were among Sheridan's founding families, a fact Mrs. Druitt clearly took pride in. However, each time she asked about the best ranches in the area or what Lavina and her husband would do if they did move here, her efforts were thwarted. Mrs. Druitt would reply with noncommittal answers such as "Oh, I couldn't say."

Frustration, born of the continuous dead ends in the conversation and the rising temperature, had Maggy feeling overly warm. She fanned her cheeks with her gloved hand, attempting to cool down. Her lapse into silence ironically produced an even greater talkative streak from her seat companion. Mrs. Druitt chattered away about the Fourth of July activities coming up next month and about some social occasions in the fall.

"They're lovely events," she said. "If you're still here, I think you'll quite enjoy them, Miss Worthwright."

Maggy froze, her hand still in front of her face. A tingle ran up her spine. Had the woman actually said *If you're still here*? Pasting on a neutral expression, though inside she was crowing with triumph, she lowered her hand to her lap. "I'm sorry. I think I misheard you. Did you say *if* I'm still here I'll enjoy the events?"

"Is that what I said?" Mrs. Druitt laughed a bit too robustly and shifted nervously on the seat.

From the corner of her eye, Maggy could see that the woman's face resembled a tomato in color. "Is there some reason I wouldn't be here next month or this autumn?"

"No, of course not. It's just that…well…" Maggy watched her visibly squirm. "Sometimes, unfortunately, things don't work out between a couple. Nevil and I once thought Lavina would fancy one of the local ranchers, but then she became smitten with Felix." Mrs. Druitt threw her a tight smile. "I only meant it would be a pity if things didn't work out for you and Mr. Kent. We would certainly miss you."

Maggy returned her smile—it wasn't hard to do, given how victorious she felt. "I appreciate you saying so, Mrs. Druitt. Although…" She let her lips droop into a frown. "I don't think everyone shares your opinion of me."

"Oh?" The woman's tone suggested confusion.

She pushed out a fabricated sigh. "Yes, someone meddled with my rented buggy today." Maggy needed to see Mrs. Druitt's reaction to this information, so she could test the theory she'd been thinking about since the near disaster. "If I'd kept driving, I would have likely been seriously injured." She feigned a shudder. "It's all rather frightening, especially since whoever did this had to know it was me who'd be driving the buggy today."

Mrs. Druitt jerked back on the reins so quickly that Maggy had to grab the side of the carriage to keep from pitching forward. "I… I…just remembered I promised to be home early. May I let you off here?" Her face now looked as white as flour.

"Oh, of course. Thank you for the ride, Mrs. Druitt."

Maggy hopped down to the ground and waved enthusiastically as the woman drove off, none too slowly, either. There were still about two miles to go before she reached the ranch, but she didn't mind the walk. It would give her time to think and align these new bits of information with what she and Edward had already gathered.

Because, at long last, Get-Her-Man Maggy was one giant step closer to solving the case.

Chapter Thirteen

Edward glanced in the direction of the drive for the tenth time in so many minutes. His concentration on the accounts book he balanced on his knee was waning. Where was Maggy? He'd expected her much sooner, but there was still no sign of her and her horse. Had something happened? Perhaps the person who'd damaged the buggy had figured out his failure and had attempted to finish the job. His gut tightened at the possibility.

There had been no footprints near the stable, and he'd found nothing amiss inside the building, either. Whoever had perpetrated the damage to the buggy had been as thorough in concealing their work afterward as they had been in nearly splitting the axle.

He frowned at the number next to his pencil, trying to remember what he'd been adding. If there hadn't been things that required his attention here—such as the finances and overseeing the training of a couple horses—he could've stayed in town and ridden back with Maggy. Though she might have taken that as evidence that he didn't trust her to look after herself, which wasn't true. He trusted her; it was Howe and anyone involved in the sabotage whom he didn't trust.

Tossing aside the pencil and book, he stood. It was pointless to keep calculating the same sums over and over again. He'd walk to the bridge to see if Maggy was coming.

He strode down the drive, his gaze lifting to the top of the arch. Each time he glimpsed the Running W brand—his brand—prominently displayed there, he felt a measure of satisfaction. He loved every square inch of this place, most of which he'd helped clear and construct with his own two hands. The same two hands that had known little physical labor five years ago.

Now he couldn't imagine a life where he didn't work and sweat and dream of the fruits of his efforts. He didn't plan to give up such a life without a fight, either. And a fight was something he felt that he and Maggy were almost ready for.

After crossing over the bridge, Edward started up the road. The buggy still sat where Maggy had left it earlier that afternoon. He sent a prayer of gratitude heavenward, though it wasn't his first today, that she'd been protected.

"Edward!"

He shifted his gaze to the road and felt his concerns ebb away when he saw Maggy strolling toward him, one gloved hand lifted in a wave. She'd unpinned her hat and was using it to fan her face. Her auburn hair had come loose, as it often did, from its pins, so that it tumbled past her shoulders. She looked tired but as beautiful and confident as ever. The sight of her made his heart jump inside his chest—and it wasn't just because she was safe.

Only then did it register in his mind that she was walking, not riding a horse. A flicker of uneasiness disrupted his relief. "Did something happen to the horse?" he called out as she drew closer.

She nodded, though she didn't offer any further explanation until she reached his side. "Someone took it," she said between labored breaths. "When I went to ride back, the horse was gone."

"Stolen, you mean." Edward ran a hand over his chin, wishing he had a good fence post to topple at the moment. "Do you know who?"

"No. My guess is Howe, but I don't know for sure."

When he noticed her flushed cheeks and dusty dress hem, his frustration gave way to chagrin. "Did you walk all the way from Sheridan?"

Thankfully she shook her head. He hated to think she'd walked the entire seven miles back to the ranch.

"I should have stayed in town," he said, feeling guilty.

To his surprise, Maggy smiled. "If you had, then Mrs. Druitt wouldn't have given me a ride after Vienna and I finished talking."

"You and Vienna were talking?" His jaw tightened as annoyance crowded out his guilt. Hadn't she agreed to keep her distance from Howe's wife?

Color flooded her cheeks. "Yes, but it wasn't like that, Edward. I made sure I talked with everyone during the meeting. It was only afterward that she asked me something…"

"Do you honestly think her husband will care that you were only conversing after the meeting?"

He pulled off his hat and slapped it against his leg. How could he protect Maggy if she needlessly put herself in harm's way? She'd told him one thing, only to turn around and do exactly what she wished to do regardless of the consequences. *Just like Beatrice did.* The comparison filled him with dread—and fresh anger.

"You may have put yourself or me or the ranch in danger by doing what you said you wouldn't do, Maggy. And I don't know which I can't abide more. Your negligence or your dishonesty."

Her eyes flashed with blue fire. "Since you've already made up your mind about the situation, then there's nothing more to say. If you'll excuse me." She marched past him toward the bridge, her chin thrust out.

Edward glared hard at the road as he crossed his arms. Maggy's blatant disregard for what he'd said to her earlier cut deeply. More so than it ought, given she was just a detective he had hired, nothing more. An irksome thought told him that he was the one being dishonest now.

Maggy was so much more than a detective to him. She'd become his good friend and confidante. The person he looked forward to seeing each morning and spending time with each evening. She was the reason he laughed and smiled more—a change both Mrs. Harvey and McCall had commented on.

She'd become the woman who'd successfully breached the walls around his scarred heart.

This last realization had him jerking his gaze from the dirt to the distant hills. How had that happened? He gave a rueful shake of his head, already knowing the answer. Maggy had been pushing her way past his defenses since her first afternoon here. And though he was still upset she hadn't taken his warning about Howe more seriously, he shouldn't have compared her to Beatrice or accused her of dishonesty. He should've listened to her reasons for doing what she'd done before reacting.

"Edward."

He whirled around to find her standing nearby, her eyes deep blue with what appeared to be regret. "Maggy, I'm—"

"Please." She held up her hand. "Let me go first." When he obliged by keeping silent, she continued. "You were right. I did say I wouldn't talk as much with Vienna. And I'm very sorry for not abiding by that. Your trust means…" Her voice hitched with emotion, making him wish to take her into his arms as he had earlier that day. But he wasn't sure she'd welcome his touch just yet, so he busied himself with putting his hat back on. "Your trust means a great deal to me. I don't want you to mistrust me. And I certainly don't want anything to happen to the ranch…and especially not to you."

He couldn't resist the urge to comfort her any longer. Reaching out, he swept aside a strand of her hair. "I must apologize, too. I'll admit I was surprised to hear you spoke with Vienna, but I'd like to hear your reasons for doing so. Because the truth is, Maggy, I do still trust you."

The tangible relief on her lovely face mirrored the same emotion stirring in his heart. "There's something else I need to tell you."

"Yes?" he asked calmly, though his gut tightened. Had she been hiding something from him—as Beatrice once had?

Help me listen to her, Lord.

Maggy squared her shoulders as Edward steeled himself for what she was about to reveal. "Vienna asked for my advice because…" Her gaze lowered, then rose to meet his directly. "Because Howe's temperament is a lot like my late husband's."

"Y-your late husband's?" He couldn't hide the shock that leaked into his voice. His thought from earlier about her loving another man filled his head and stabbed through his chest. "But you were never engaged before?"

She nodded. "That's true. Jeb asked me to be his wife only two days before our wedding. We were married for a few years. Then he was killed and I became a detective."

Those were the facts, but they gave no indication of her feelings. Did she love this Jeb still? Edward wanted to ask, and yet, he sensed her reluctance to discuss the topic further.

"I did keep a little more distance through the meeting," she said, her tone almost pleading. "When Vienna wanted to talk to me afterward, I couldn't refuse, Edward. She's struggling and I just couldn't…walk away…" Her chin dropped. Edward could see it was trembling.

He placed his hands lightly on her shoulders and waited for her to lift her head. "Of course you couldn't. That would be a hard decision. And I believe you made the right one."

"You really think so?" She sounded far less self-assured than she normally did, making him wonder again who or what had caused her to doubt herself in the past.

Giving her shoulders a gentle squeeze, he released her. "I mean it. You care about Vienna and aren't allowing Howe's threats to change that."

"I just hope he doesn't get it in his head to hurt something more than a buggy." She turned and began walking toward the ranch again.

He fell into step beside her. "How far did Mrs. Druitt drive you?"

"All but the last two miles." Her expression became suddenly elated. "That's what else I wanted to tell you. She and her husband are definitely behind some of the acts against the Running W."

Edward stopped her progress with a hand to her elbow, his heart kicking up at the news. "How do you know? What did you find out?"

"It's more what slipped out," she replied with a laugh. Her blue eyes were dancing with delight. "Do you mind if I tell you while we walk back, though? I need at least one glass of water and to change into a dress that isn't covered in dust and sweat."

He couldn't help laughing as he released her arm. Only Maggy would be frank enough to mention sweat in mixed company. "All right. We'll walk while you talk."

They started forward once more. "I tried to get Mrs. Druitt to admit to wanting to buy your land five years ago, but she dodged every attempt. Then just when I was sure the time with her had been a waste, she started talking about upcoming events in town. About how, if I were still here, I would enjoy them."

"*If* you were still here?" Edward repeated with a stunned shake of his head. "Did she actually let that slip out?"

Maggy grinned. "She did. I could hardly believe it myself. Only then..."

She paused, ratcheting up his curiosity even more. Which was likely her intent. It took a great deal of effort on his part not to comment or slow his pace.

"Don't you want to know what happened next?" she finally asked, her eyebrows raised.

Edward shrugged. "If you want to share it. Otherwise, I'm content to simply walk."

"You're impossible." She nudged his shoulder, but she was laughing.

"I'm not the one drawing out the suspense."

"True." She gave him a saucy grin before continuing. "After she said that, I asked her what she meant. Mrs. Druitt babbled on about how engagements don't work out sometimes and how she'd miss me if I left, but she was definitely flustered and nervous. I told her I didn't think everyone shared her opinion about me being welcome here."

He thought he could see where she was going with that bit of information. "That was clever."

"Thank you." She swung her hat in a carefree manner at her side as if she hadn't already walked quite a ways. "Then I brought up the buggy accident."

He frowned in confusion, unclear why she'd shared that information. "Do you think that was wise?"

"I wanted to see her reaction," Maggy explained. "And it was exactly as I suspected it would be. She went white, Edward. Completely white."

"Which means?" he asked, trying to draw his own conclusion but coming up empty.

Maggy looked more animated than he'd ever seen her. "It means that Mrs. Druitt wasn't involved in what happened to the buggy. The person who did that had to be acting independently of her and her husband."

"You still think they're the ones behind the notes and the other damage?"

She put her hat to her head and lifted it as if tipping it to him. "Yes. My theory is they were hoping to scare you away so they could finally buy the ranch and give it to Lavina and Felix."

"What about Howe, though?" Her reasoning made sense, except for how Vienna's husband was involved. "Where do the buggy and that last threatening note come in?"

"My suspicion is that while Howe gave you that note on their orders, the buggy was his own doing. I think his vendetta turned from the ranch to me. Which is why Mrs. Druitt was not only shocked to hear about the incident but seemed appalled too. I don't think the Druitts intended to physically harm anyone to get what they want."

Edward nodded slowly as he considered her theory. It was sound and plausible. "Why would Howe or anyone else help them, though? What's in it for the others?"

"That I don't know—yet."

Which didn't bother him. They had far more information now than they'd ever had.

A part of him wanted to pull her close and kiss her in triumph. His case was nearly solved. And yet, another part of him wanted to go back, to the moment he'd brushed her hair from her cheek as they'd stood in the road. That way her departure would be less soon in coming.

"What do we do now? Confront the Druitts?"

Maggy shook her head. "No. The theory is solid, but we can't actually prove it. We have to time this right. Otherwise they'll just deny it. We need to coax a confession out of them."

"And how do we do that?"

She pursed her lips in thought, drawing his attention to them. "I'd like to wait until the ball on Saturday. Let them think we don't suspect them of anything. My guess is that there won't be any more threats, at least not until after the event. They'll hope this incident with the buggy has died down by then."

"So we wait?" He wasn't keen on the idea, especially since Howe was still out there. "What about Vienna's husband?"

Maggy frowned, revealing a crack in her enthusiasm and sureness. "If he took my horse today, he'll likely lay low for the next week, too. Horse rustling is a serious crime."

"Which the Druitts may also be guilty of," he pointed out.

"Agreed, but since we don't know if they were the actual ones who took those horses and changed the brand, it's your word against theirs. At least until we can get a full confession or other proof from them."

He conceded to her reasoning with a sigh. "You're right. We'll wait until the ball and seek a full confession then."

"I'm confident we'll get one, Edward."

Her reassuring smile did more than ease his concern. It went straight through his chest and set his heart galloping like a runaway horse. And yet it wasn't just with pleasure; it was with a measure of sadness, too. Because come Saturday, he had no idea how much longer Maggy and her brilliant smiles would remain in his life.

A rapping at the front door drew Maggy's head up from the book she'd been reading. She threw a puzzled glance at Mrs. Harvey who was engrossed in one of her beloved dime novels. Judging by the worn edges of the pages, it was one she'd read several times before.

"Who would be coming around now?" the housekeeper asked, echoing Maggy's thoughts.

They hadn't had visitors to the ranch for several weeks, and Edward wasn't home tonight, either. After yesterday's occurrence with the buggy, which he and Maggy had slowly conveyed to Big Horn for repair that morning, Edward had decided to dine at the inn and see if there was any talk among the other ranchers about the near accident.

Setting aside her book, Maggy stood. "I'll see who it is."

The person on the porch knocked again before she could reach the door, the sound more insistent this time. She didn't imagine Howe or anyone else would be brazen enough to come knocking, but caution had her opening the door only an inch to see who stood there.

Vienna's tearstained face, disheveled hair, and dusty dress met Maggy's gaze. She threw open the door at once. "Vienna. Are you all right? What's wrong?"

"Oh, Maggy." She threw a wary glance over her shoulder. A saddled horse, its reins wrapped around the porch rail, stood there patiently. "I left him," she burst out as she turned back to face Maggy. "And… this was the only place I could think of where I knew I'd be welcome."

Maggy quickly recovered from her shock—both at Vienna's sudden appearance and her words. "Of course you're welcome here. Come in, come in."

"What about the horse?"

She opened the door farther. "I'll see to it in a bit."

With a distracted nod, Vienna entered the house. She clutched a valise in one hand, which reinforced her earlier announcement. "Thank you. I... I don't want to impose."

"It's no imposition," Mrs. Harvey said, exiting the parlor. "If you're a friend of Maggy's, you're welcome in Mr. Kent's home. And that's a fact."

Vienna blushed, but it didn't hide the red mark on one of her cheeks. Maggy felt certain she knew who was responsible for it. "Is Mr. Kent home?"

"No." Maggy linked her arm with Vienna's. "He'll be home later. But Mrs. Harvey is right. You can stay here as long as you like."

Instead of the comfort she'd hoped to inspire, Maggy watched as Vienna's expression crumpled. She covered her mouth with her free hand as a sob leaked from her lips.

"Mrs. Harvey, would you mind getting us some tea?" Maggy exchanged a meaningful glance with the housekeeper. Vienna needed to talk and she was likely reluctant to do so in front of a stranger.

The older woman gave an understanding nod. "Of course. Make yourselves comfortable in the parlor and I'll have nice cups of tea for the both of you in no time."

Maggy mouthed a "thank you," then led the young woman into the parlor. When she released her comforting grip on Vienna, the girl sank onto the sofa. Her entire body trembled, but Maggy wasn't sure if it was from fear or intense relief. Remembering those first days after losing Jeb, Maggy realized it was possibly both.

"What happened?" she asked gently as she took a seat on the other end of the sofa.

Vienna rubbed at her eyes with her hand. A bitter laugh escaped her mouth. "I finally stood up for myself. Chance was angry and shouting, but I told him that he needed to stop talking to me in such a way."

Maggy waited for her to go on, though she'd already guessed the rest of the story.

"He didn't like that one bit," Vienna said with a shake of her head. "And he told me so before giving me this." She gingerly touched her cheek. "Then something just snapped inside me. I told him that I was through, that I wouldn't stay another moment in a house with someone who treated me as less than his precious horses."

Her expression now radiated strength. "He raged for a while longer, then he left. Probably for the saloon. But he didn't hit me again, Maggy. And I think I know why."

"He was scared," Maggy concluded.

Vienna shot her a grim smile. "Yes. I don't think he really expects me to be gone when he comes back, either. But I knew I had to leave right then or I'd lose my nerve. So I packed a bag, then saddled a horse and rode here."

"I'm so proud of you, Vienna." Emotion filled her throat at the girl's courage.

"I couldn't have done it without you."

Maggy glanced down. "I don't see why not."

"Because…" Vienna didn't speak until Maggy

looked up again. "It was you who helped me remember that I'm somebody. That I'm not worthless. I wouldn't have been brave enough to actually leave him if you hadn't helped me believe in myself again."

Had she done the right thing? Maggy wondered. She'd chosen to talk with Vienna again and now the girl was here, on the ranch. This would enrage Howe, and she had no way of knowing how much. It could be dangerous—for her, for Edward and for everyone at the Running W.

And yet, how could she regret what'd she'd said and done? She'd helped Vienna, yes, but she'd helped herself, too. Each time she'd reminded the young woman that she was of worth, Maggy had been reminded of that truth for herself.

"I know I can't stay here indefinitely," Vienna said, squaring her shoulders. "But a few days would be wonderful, if you don't think Mr. Kent will mind."

Maggy wasn't sure what Edward would say at first, but she felt confident at how he'd respond once he'd heard the whole story about Vienna. "You can stay as long as you like."

Even after Maggy left, there would surely be work here for Vienna to do. Maybe the girl could help Mrs. Harvey with cooking for the wranglers.

After she left... The reminder brought a physical ache to Maggy's chest, which she hurried to set aside. Right now she needed to concentrate on helping Vienna, not on the pain of leaving those who'd become dear to her. *Especially Edward.*

"Do you think Chance will look for you here?" She hated to voice the question, given Vienna's relative calm at the moment, but she wanted to be prepared.

A visible shudder ran through the young woman. "I don't know. He may. But I don't imagine it'll be tonight. He'll likely come home too drunk to notice much of anything."

Her words inspired more compassion inside Maggy, along with painful memories of nights when her father or Jeb had come home in a similar state of inebriation. "Let's get you set up in a room upstairs, then have that tea."

She'd likely need to move into the main house herself with Vienna here. That would be the most proper thing to do, wouldn't it? She'd ask Mrs. Harvey.

Maggy rose to go into the kitchen, and Vienna hopped up, too. "Can I come with you?"

"Of course." She reassured the girl with a smile, guessing Vienna didn't want to be alone right now. "We'll ask Mrs. Harvey which room to give you."

Vienna trailed her to the kitchen. Any more reticence on her part seemed to evaporate like the steam coming from the kettle, when Mrs. Harvey extoled the joys of having a third woman about the ranch. The housekeeper also agreed with Maggy's idea about moving out of the guest quarters and into the main house.

After some tea and quiet conversation, the three of them carted Maggy's things from the guest house to a room upstairs and across the hall from Vienna's. They'd just finished hanging Maggy's dresses in the wardrobe when someone started hollering outside.

Maggy crossed to the window that faced the front of the house. Her heart jumped into her throat when she recognized the figure stumbling off his horse—it was Howe. Before she could warn Vienna, the man shouted his wife's name.

"Vienna! I know you're here."

The girl's face went gray, her hand rising to her throat. She stumbled backward and dropped onto Maggy's bed. "He came."

"It's all right, love." Mrs. Harvey patted Vienna's hand. While the young woman hadn't revealed a great deal of her circumstances to the housekeeper over tea, she had shared that Howe mistreated her. "You don't have to go down."

As if in challenge to the housekeeper's words, Howe shouted again. "Vienna, you come out here—now. Or I'm coming in. I know Kent ain't here. I saw his horse in town."

Apprehension knotted Maggy's stomach. While McCall and the wranglers were around, they might not hear Howe from the bunkhouse. Or Maggy, if she yelled for help.

Please help us, Father. We need Thy protection.

A portion of peace settled within her. Not enough to drive out the fear completely, but she did feel stronger. "I'm going down there."

"Maggy, no," Vienna cried, shaking her head. Fresh tears trickled down her cheeks.

She squared her shoulders. "I won't go unarmed. But someone needs to send him on his way." With that she bent and pulled her gun from her trunk. "Stay here, and lock the door."

Vienna looked too stricken to answer, but Mrs. Harvey nodded. "God go with you, love."

Slipping into the hall, Maggy forced her shaky legs to descend the stairs. She could do this. After all, she was a detective and had been in far more precarious situations than dealing with an angry, abusive bully. That didn't mean her heart didn't continue to beat wildly inside her chest, though, as she reached the front door and opened it.

Howe was leaning against one of the porch columns, but he whirled around when he heard her step outside. The movement threw him off balance and he had to brace himself against the other column to keep from falling down.

"You," he spat out. "Where's Vienna?"

Maggy leveled him with her most imperious look, while keeping the gun out of sight for now against the folds of her dress. "You're trespassing on private property, Mr. Howe. So I'm going to ask you to leave."

"Not without my wife. She ran off, the thankless fool." A few curse words spewed from his mouth, but Maggy refused to be intimidated. "Where is she? Is she staying in that guest house over there?"

She took a commanding step forward. "No. I've been staying in the guest house. And Vienna doesn't have to go anywhere she doesn't choose. She's welcome here. It's you who needs to leave."

"I said not without my wife and I mean it." He pointed his finger at her, his eyes full of hatred. "Don't think I don't know what you've been saying to her. Filling her brainless head with all them stupid, nonsensical ideas."

Maggy clenched her free hand into a fist. "She isn't brainless, and those stupid, nonsensical ideas are facts, Mr. Howe."

He swatted her words away as if they were pesky insects. "You let me see her or I'm going for the sheriff."

"By all means, go for the sheriff and tell him you're threatening a pair of women who won't allow you to keep your wife a prisoner." She raised her eyebrows in challenge at him. "Except who would he say was breaking the law in this situation?"

His face mottled with anger. "You can't keep me from my wife!"

"I'm not," Maggy replied in an icy tone. "You managed to do that all on your own with every slur and every hit."

Howe's eyes widened for a moment, then ducked away. "I don't know what you're talking about, woman."

"Don't you?" She marched another step forward, her breath coming faster with her own fury. "I know all about men like you, Mr. Howe. With your sweet, charming words that trap a woman like a fly in honey. And then…then you show your true nature." Her fingernails dug into her palm as an onslaught of recollections crashed over her. "You hurt again and again to assuage the pain roaring inside your own heart. But it never goes away, not for long. And so you inflict that pain on this person you swore before men and God that you would love and cherish."

He paled, but the reaction was short-lived. "Enough," he hollered as he took a teetering step toward her. "You send Vienna out right now."

"She won't come." Maggy adjusted her grip on the weapon in her hand. "She meant it when she said she wouldn't live with someone who treats her so poorly."

If she'd thought his gaze hate-filled before, it was nothing to the rage in it now. "You listen up and listen good," he sneered. "You think you're so high and mighty with your fine clothes and nice ranch. But deep down, you're nothin', *Maggy*. Nothin' but a weak woman with a mind for stirring up trouble."

It wasn't Howe's voice that thundered in her ears now. It was Jeb's. *You're nothin', Maggy. Nothin'.* Her lungs began to squeeze tighter and tighter. The hand holding the gun started to tremble, and bits of light danced in front of her eyes. She couldn't pass out, not now.

Please, she prayed, her eyes locked on Howe's triumphant expression.

Then from deep within her, a rolling wave of strength rose up. She wasn't nothing. She, Maggy Worthing, was someone of worth.

"You've said your piece, and now I need *you* to listen, Mr. Howe." She brought the gun into sight and barely managed to swallow back her satisfied smile when the man's eyes went wide again. "It's time for you to leave. And do not come back."

Over the man's shoulder, Maggy spotted McCall and two of the wranglers moving toward the porch. All three of them held drawn guns in their hands. She wasn't sure what had alerted them to the trouble, but she felt weak-kneed relief that they were there.

Howe scowled at her, obviously ready to challenge her authority. But McCall spoke up from behind him. "You heard the lady," the foreman barked in the coldest voice Maggy had ever heard him use. "Take your horse and get outta here, Howe."

Whirling around, Vienna's husband glared at the three newcomers, but he was outnumbered and seemed to know it. "I'll be takin' both horses."

He stumbled a bit as he untied the reins of Vienna's horse and attempted to climb into the saddle of his own. Eventually he got himself situated. Maggy kept her gun trained on him until he threw one last scathing look her way before trotting off down the drive, leading the other horse. Only then did she lower her arm. Her muscles felt shaky as she sagged against the porch column.

"You okay, Miss Worthwright?" McCall asked as he approached.

Maggy nodded. "I will be. Thank you…for your help."

"You're welcome. Though you did a mighty fine job of standing up to him yourself." The wranglers murmured their agreement.

She tried to smile, but it felt more like a grimace. "Still, I'm glad you came when you did."

"I thought I heard someone yelling," the foreman confessed, pushing up the brim of his hat. "And I had this nagging thought I needed to get up to the main house right quick."

This time she managed an actual smile. The Lord had been looking out for her—and Vienna—again. "I'm very grateful you paid attention to that thought. I think my gun might have persuaded him to leave, but it certainly helped to have three more aimed at him."

He glanced past her toward the house. "Is Vienna really here then?"

"She is," Maggy answered. The familiar way the foreman said the girl's first name made her wonder if they knew each other. "I'm guessing she'll be here for some time."

His taunt expression relaxed a little. "Probably wise. And if you'd like, we'll wait out here until Mr. Kent comes back."

Hearing Edward's name, Maggy felt a needling of worry. Would he be angry at her for letting Vienna stay? Or for her part, however indirect, in the girl's choice to leave her husband? Maggy recalled his humility the day before and felt a glimmer of reassurance. Still, it would be best if Edward heard of the evening's events from her instead of his foreman.

"If you'll stay out here until I can make sure Mrs. Howe is all right, then I'll wait for Mr. Kent."

McCall frowned. "You sure?"

"Yes, though if one of you wouldn't mind sticking close to the house tonight, that would be wonderful." She didn't think Howe would come back, but it wouldn't hurt to have another man on guard.

"Will do, ma'am."

After thanking all three of them again, Maggy went inside. She felt suddenly bone tired as she moved toward the stairs. But she also felt profoundly satisfied—just as she did whenever she solved a case. Only, she had to admit, this was better.

Vienna Howe was safe—she would never have to return to her bully of a husband if she didn't wish to—and Maggy had been a small part of that. That realization flooded her with new energy and had her taking the stairs two at a time.

Chapter Fourteen

It wasn't full dark but close to it by the time Edward returned from dinner in town. He saw to his horse, then exited the stable.

He walked toward the house, noting with approval one of the night guards patrolling near the house. As he drew closer to the porch, he noticed Maggy seated in the rocker—fast asleep. The temperature was pleasant tonight, but he wasn't sure why she'd chosen to wait for him outside instead of in the parlor as usual. He stepped onto the porch. Even in the dying light, he could clearly see her face. Unlike the time he'd caught her dozing while reading, her expression now appeared troubled.

"Maggy," he called softly.

She didn't rouse.

"Maggy." He stopped in front of the rocker. "You can't stay out here all night," he said as he placed his hand on her shoulder.

She jerked awake at once, scrambling onto her feet. "Is it Howe?" Her wide gaze frantically swept the yard. "Did he come back?"

Only then did Edward notice she was gripping a gun in one hand. His heart banged against his ribs. "Howe was here?"

She nodded. "He came to get Vienna. And you weren't here and I thought it would be all right if she stayed." Her statements tumbled over each other, barely giving Edward time to register them. "I didn't know that what I'd said yesterday would make her leave him, Edward. Honest. And then he was yelling..."

He carefully took the gun from her, set it on the porch railing, then cupped her shoulders in his hands. To his surprise, he could feel her trembling. "Start at the beginning, please. Why did Vienna come here?" He tried to tell himself that he didn't need to fear for Maggy's safety—she was clearly all right—but the panicked note in her tone had concern bleeding through him.

"She came because..." Maggy glanced away. "Because she refuses to stay with Chance another minute. He treats her horribly—worse than ever lately, since she's starting to stand up for herself. You have to believe me, Edward. I was only trying to help remind her that she's every bit as strong and of worth as anyone else."

He gave her shoulders a gentle squeeze. "Of course I believe you. So Vienna came here?"

"Yes. I told her that she could stay as long as she needed. Which I hope was all right." She waited for his nod before continuing. "Mrs. Harvey and I got her to calm down with some tea. And then we'd just moved my things and hers into rooms upstairs when Howe came."

The name alone had him clenching his jaw. "What did he do? Did he harm you?"

"No." She shook her head. "He yelled a lot and demanded Vienna return home with him. But I told him she didn't have to. That he was the one who needed to go."

He sensed there was more to the encounter. "Did he leave peacefully?"

Maggy lowered her chin. "Not exactly. I drew my gun on him, but it wasn't until McCall and two of the wranglers showed up, also armed, that he finally took off."

Relief coursed through him, though he did wish he could have been here himself. He would've liked to help Maggy and to see what he imagined was a very strong performance by her at standing up to the tyrant.

"You did the right thing. Vienna is welcome here on the ranch for as long as she needs."

The words didn't inspire the happiness he'd expected. Instead, Maggy seemed to grow more morose. Something was still bothering her.

"Did Howe try to hurt you, Maggy?" He barely managed to get the question past his gritted teeth. If the other rancher had so much as placed a finger on her…

Thankfully she replied with a soft, "No."

"What is it then?" He tried to peer into her eyes, but she refused to meet his. "Did he say something?" He could easily recall Howe's brashness.

Her cheeks went white at his question and the shaking of her shoulders increased. "How did he know?" she whispered, her voice strangled.

"Know what?" Edward countered with more bite

than he intended, but the dread inside him was growing louder and more insistent.

A plaintive sob leaked from her lips before she covered her face with her hands. He'd never seen her so distraught.

Edward pulled her to him and wrapped his arms securely around her. He stroked her hair as she wept, his own heart near breaking at the sound.

"What did Howe say?" he asked after a few minutes. He needed to know as much as he sensed Maggy needed to share.

She shuddered and pressed her cheek tighter to his suit coat. If the moment hadn't been so raw, Edward would have felt true contentment at holding her close. Now and for the rest of his life.

That last thought had him tightening his embrace and wishing he had a true claim on her affections. But he didn't. Reluctantly he released her to arm's length.

"Maggy," he beseeched. "Please tell me what else happened."

She lifted her head, her eyes deep pools of pain. "I don't know how he knew what things Jeb used to say to wound me or maybe it was coincidence. It wasn't even Howe's voice I heard after a while. It was Jeb's."

Her late husband. Edward's chest constricted as it had yesterday when she'd told him that she had been married before. "What did you hear Jeb say?"

"The same cutting words." Maggy wet her lips and stepped away from him. "That I'm worthless, that I'm nothing." Her voice was devoid of emotion.

Before he could argue the absurdity of her late husband's claims, she went on, "I couldn't breathe and I started to shake. Just like when I've had these episodes in the past. I thought I might pass out, right there in front of Howe."

Edward suddenly remembered how she'd looked the day he'd met her—upset, disheveled, pale. "Is that what happened that first day when I found you coming up the drive?"

Maggy nodded as she turned and gripped the railing with both hands. Her knuckles looked as white as the wood. "Your little cabin reminded me too much of the one I lived in with my father...and the one I later shared with Jeb." Another visible shudder ran through her. "Most of the time I can forget all of that, but tonight when Howe started yelling the same things Jeb used to..."

An overwhelming desire to smash a fist into Jeb's face and then Howe's had Edward breathing hard himself. Then a thought pushed its way through his rising anger.

"You said yesterday that Howe and your late husband share a similar temperament. And he's been mistreating Vienna." He swallowed hard as Maggy's past life, and what she had endured, became clear. "Jeb mistreated you, didn't he?"

He heard her sharp intake of breath. "Yes," she whispered in a voice wracked with hurt. "He hit me when he was drunk, which happened more frequently when there was a strike or trouble at the mine."

Edward shut his eyes, his fury white-hot. How could any man justify raising a hand to a woman? Especially his Maggy?

His Maggy.

Opening his eyes, he studied her bent head. When had he come to think of her as *his*? He couldn't pinpoint the exact moment; he only knew a deep bond had been forged during these weeks together.

"Will you tell me…what it was like?" He knew her answers would likely infuriate him, but he needed to know what she'd experienced.

"Jeb was meaner than my father," Maggy began. "My father could be angry and belittling, but he didn't start drinking and knocking me around until after my mother died. I believe something died inside him after her funeral. She'd always taken me to church, but afterward he refused to let me go, and a year or so later, I quit school. There were too many days when he'd do nothing but lie around inebriated or asleep." Her voice cracked and she gave a light cough. "Jeb was drunk the night he died. I don't know why I didn't try to coax him out of his bad mood like I usually did. Instead I chose to go for a walk. I think he must have knocked over the lantern. By the time I returned, the entire cabin was on fire." She threw him a sad look. "I like to think he was so drunk he didn't suffer."

The pain emitting from her was calling to Edward to help in some way. Unsure what to do, he stepped behind her and placed his hands on her forearms, hoping the contact would be comforting. After a long moment, she leaned back against him. He needed no other invitation to encircle her in his arms.

"I'm so very sorry, Maggy." The words seemed so paltry in comparison to the horrors she'd lived through, but he hoped they would convey the deep sadness, compassion and outrage he felt. "There is no excuse for such despicable behavior. None. That two men, whom you cared for, treated you in such a fashion is deplorable."

Her hands curled over his where they held her. He recognized her touch was as much a reassurance to him as a silent appeal for solace herself.

"They both felt worthless themselves," he added with sudden understanding. "But that didn't make it right to ensure you felt the same about yourself."

She rested her head on his chest. "I know, and most days I'm able to remember that."

"And yet, there are times, like tonight, when it is much harder to remember?" He stated it as a question, and she nodded.

"It's helped me to remind Vienna that she's of worth. The more I said it to her, the more I felt it in here." She released him long enough to tap her finger to her heart.

"Your friendship with her has blessed you both," he said, seeing the situation in a new and clearer light. He could well understand the blessing of having Maggy as a friend. "How did you become a detective after all of that?"

Her quiet chuckle sounded more precious than ever. It told him that she'd been wounded in the past but not permanently.

"After Jeb's death, I wasn't sure what to do. I had no other family around and was living off the kindness of a neighbor. One day I happened to overhear two men talking. To my shock, I learned one was a Pinkerton agent." The soft smile in her voice was unmistakable. "I was intrigued and decided to help him, if I could. I'd always been observant and Jeb's drunken revelations had given me some information I figured the detective might find useful.

"I made sure we crossed paths later that week and told him what I knew, both about his real identity and the information about the mines. I'll never forget the shock on his face." She gave a light laugh. "I assisted him for another few weeks. By then, I was nearly out of what little money I'd taken with me on my walk the night of the fire. That's when the agent Mr. Beckett told me there were female detectives working for the Pinkertons, and he thought I would make a good one myself. The more I thought about it, the more I wanted to give it a try."

The thought of Maggy, determined and brave, deciding to become a detective brought a brief smile to his face. "And that's what you did."

"That's what I did." The confidence had returned to her tone. "Mr. Beckett graciously helped me secure a train ticket to Denver. He also gave me a recommendation to take to the office's superintendent, James McParland. James was skeptical of me at first, but after I successfully completed my first mission, he became my greatest champion."

She turned in Edward's arms to face him. "If I hadn't gone through what I did, I never would have become a detective. I try to remember that, too."

"Yes, though that's still a great deal of pain you've experienced, Maggy."

He was grateful that she seemed to accept his efforts at empathy. But her next question caught him off guard, making him wish she'd thrown out a retort instead.

"What was she like? The woman you were nearly engaged to?"

Edward cleared his throat and glanced away. It would be rude to refuse to talk about Beatrice when Maggy had shared such personal things about herself.

"She was young, from a well-to-do family, and quite pretty."

"Did you love her?"

He sniffed with mild amusement. "I believed I did, but now looking back, I don't know that I understood real love."

"I've felt the same," she admitted softly. "What happened…between the two of you?"

The old pain resurfaced, but this time, it stung only briefly before ebbing away. "I discovered that she was actually enamored with my oldest brother. I was told it was because her family was facing financial difficulties and she knew the unlikelihood of me inheriting."

"Oh, Edward." Her heartfelt compassion was evident in those two words.

He shot her a grim smile. "I would be lying if I said it wasn't difficult. But I wonder now if perhaps she found something with my brother that she and I didn't have."

"So you've let go of the bitterness?"

Edward considered the question. "You know, I believe I have." That realization had him feeling lighter than he had in a long time.

"I think I have, too," Maggy said, though her chin dipped downward. "Especially my bitterness toward God. I thought He'd abandoned me during those years with my father and Jeb. But He didn't. I walked away from Him."

He lifted her chin with his finger. "And now?"

"Now I've walked back. Thanks in large part to you." Fresh tears glittered in her eyes, but he could tell they were tears of cleansing instead of pain. "I know

I'm somebody and I'm realizing that's not just because I'm a good detective. I'm of worth even without that."

Edward rubbed his finger below her lower lip. "Yes, you are."

"Thank you for letting me talk, Edward." She offered him a bright smile. "I feel much better."

"My pleasure."

If he kissed her right now, as he wanted to, he feared she would think he was taking advantage of a vulnerable moment. And he wouldn't do that—not after all she'd shared with him. So he settled for a kiss to her forehead.

"You are of worth, Maggy," he murmured, easing back to see her face. "I'm glad you're not letting the Howes and Jebs of this world convince you otherwise."

Her luminous gaze studied him. "I won't, and you shouldn't, either."

"I don't—"

The look she bestowed on him was as kind as it was sorrowful. "You're of worth, too, Edward, even if your girl chose someone else."

How had she… But then, given her powers of observation, was it really surprising that she'd gleaned his insecurities? "You're right."

"How I love that phrase," she mused with an impish look.

If he didn't let her go, he wasn't sure he could convince himself not to kiss that mischievous mouth of hers. "I imagine you want to head inside," he said, lowering his hands to his sides, "after such an eventful evening."

Maggy swayed a bit as if she'd grown accustomed

to his gentle hold. But he forced himself to step back instead of reaching out to steady her.

Each touch, each smile, each conversation just left him yearning for the next, and yet, the reality was that Maggy wouldn't be staying. The sooner he accepted that fact, the less he hoped it would hurt when he said goodbye to her for the final time.

Two nights later, Maggy dreamt again of Jeb and the fire. Only this time in her dream, when she reached the cabin, she saw a figure inside. She screamed Jeb's name, but when the person turned, it was Edward staring back at her.

She woke with a start, her face and neck beaded with sweat and her heart beating fast. "It's a dream, just a dream," she whispered to herself, though she could still smell the smoke from the burning cabin.

Flipping onto her side to face the window, she tried to settle her mind. But the smoky scent grew stronger. Why would anything be burning in the middle of the night?

Maggy climbed out of bed and padded to the partially opened window. Nothing seemed amiss in the front yard or by the stable. She pressed her nose to the cool glass, trying to get a better view of the side yard. A flicker of light caught her eye. Could the guest house be on—

"Fire!" she heard someone holler. "Fire!"

She spun from the window and grabbed her shoes, her pulse erratic once more. She knew, firsthand, how quickly a building could be consumed by flames. After fumbling with the laces, she finally had her shoes secured. Maggy pulled her arms through her dressing gown as she rushed into the hallway and banged on Vienna's door.

"There's a fire." She didn't wait for the girl to respond, but instead she rushed downstairs and out into the night.

A group of the men, including Edward, had gathered a safe distance from the guest house. The fire had already eaten up one wall and part of the roof. "We'll fight it as best we can," Edward instructed. "But with the way the wind is blowing, we've got to focus on keeping the main house protected." Grim nods ran the length of the group. "We'll start a pair of bucket brigades—one to wet the roof of the house and another to try to fight the blaze."

As the group broke up, Maggy cast another glance at the fire. She felt grateful she'd moved her things into the main house when Vienna had come to the ranch two days earlier. Otherwise Maggy would have been inside the now-burning building… A sudden remembrance had her sucking in a sharp breath of smoke-tinted air. She ran to catch up with Edward who was carrying a ladder out of the stable.

"It was Howe," she said quietly but with conviction. "He thought I was staying in the guest house."

Edward stopped at once to look at her. "How do you know?" he demanded.

"I don't, not for sure. But he asked the other night if Vienna was in the guest house and I told him that I'd been staying there."

She watched the color drain from his face before his expression hardened. "We can't prove anything at this point, so we'd better focus on saving what we can."

"I agree—" But he'd already walked off to prop the

ladder against the porch. A flicker of frustration shot through her.

Reminding herself there'd be time enough for discussing tactics and strategies later, she joined the bucket brigade to save the main house. By then, Mrs. Harvey and Vienna had joined everyone else outside.

Maggy worked as quickly as she could, feeling as invested in saving the ranch house as if it were hers. After a time, the muscles in her arms began to ache and cramp from lifting the full buckets to the first man on the ladder. The exhaustion she felt was mirrored on the faces of those around her, but no one complained. Near the guest house, the members of the other bucket brigade, which included Edward, were working just as tirelessly, though their efforts were making little difference. Flames rose across the guest house roof, and Maggy knew it was only a matter of time before it collapsed.

A sudden cry had her tipping her head back to look at McCall who was positioned on the roof of the main house. "The stable!"

She glanced in that direction and gasped when she saw small flames gnawing at the stable roof. The wind had clearly changed directions. Edward shouted for help to get the horses out of the stable. Several of the wranglers dropped their buckets and sprinted toward the building. Maggy and the other two women did their best to fill in the gaps in the bucket line, since the house still needed protecting. The men across the yard moved their attention from the burning guest house to the stable.

A few minutes later, Napoleon, Persimmon, and the other horses ran out of the building. Maggy offered a silent prayer of gratitude as she took another full bucket from Vienna and passed it to the man on the ladder.

Her dressing gown and nightdress were soaked from all the sloshing water, making her shiver in spite of the heat from the fire. Still, she kept hauling, kept passing. Ash floated through the hazy air. The scene felt eerily similar to her dream—so much so that her heart began to pound. The bucket slipped between her sweaty palms and she rushed to catch it before it spilled, then handed it up the line.

This isn't the same as the other fire, she told herself firmly.

But when the guest house roof caved in, sending sparks and flames skyward, she couldn't draw a full breath into her lungs. The stable was now ablaze, too, despite the group's efforts to save it. Through the smoky night, she watched the men back away from both buildings.

"Maggy." Vienna extended another full bucket toward her. "Are you all right?"

She bit her lip to keep from crying out as she shook her head.

"Do you need to sit down?"

Did she? No, she could do this. This wasn't the night Jeb was killed. He hadn't even been in her dream tonight—it had been… Edward.

Cold alarm rushed through as she searched the blackened faces of the men coming to join the final fight to save the main house. Edward wasn't among them. Where was he?

Maggy grabbed the bucket Vienna still clutched and passed it up the ladder. "I'll be right back," she told the girl. She had to make sure Edward was all right.

Renewed purpose chased away any lingering anxiety. She ran toward the stable doors, which spewed out heat and smoke. A lone figure stood near the open doorway, a bucket still in his hand.

"Edward," she yelled, but he didn't turn. To her horror, she watched Edward square his shoulders and take a step toward the burning stable.

"Edward, stop." She reached out to grab his arm and felt the knotted muscles beneath her fingers. "You can't save it."

The light from the fire illuminated every detail of his determined expression. "Yes, I can. They won't take away everything I've worked for."

"They won't and they haven't."

The grim resolution rolling off his rigid stance didn't change.

"You still have the house, see?" She gestured toward the unburned building, hoping he would look. But his gaze remained fixed on the stable.

"The Cavalry won't want the horses from someone who's a failure, Maggy." The hard tenor of his voice made her wince. He wrenched his arm free and stepped toward the building once more.

Should she run and get McCall to help her? She was strong, but she wasn't sure she was strong enough to stop Edward on her own by sheer force. If she left his side, though, he would likely be halfway inside the burning building by the time she returned with the foreman. She would have to try a different tactic.

Stepping in front of him, she gripped his face between her palms. The heat of the fire baked her back, but she wouldn't give up on Edward, not without a fight. And a fight could well be the result of what she was about to do.

She tipped his head toward her. Then, ignoring the steely quality in his gray eyes, she pressed her lips firmly to his. His jaw stiffened briefly beneath her hands, but Maggy didn't let it deter her. She poured all the fears and joys she'd experienced over the last month into her kiss.

Long moments later, to her intense relief, she felt Edward relax. The bucket in his grasp hit the ground as his hand settled at her waist and he drew her slightly closer. Her pulse treaded faster, no longer from fear but pure contentment as Edward kissed her back.

When the heat from the fire grew too uncomfortable, she lowered her hand from his face to his arm and turned him to the side. His gaze had lost its hardness completely.

"You are not a failure, Edward." She rubbed her thumb against the stubble that covered his jaw. "As the third son of an earl. Or the suitor who was jilted. Or the rancher with a burned-down stable. You are not what you do or what happens to you." Her voice caught as she studied his beloved face.

"Am I the only one who's been paying attention during church services?" she half teased, in an effort to disguise the depth of emotion spilling through her.

His laugh sounded strangled, but it was there nonetheless. "Apparently so." He tugged her wrist downward and kissed her hand. "Thank you, Maggy." His voice came out low and husky.

"For what?" she asked, hating how breathless she sounded. But the way he was looking at her and the lingering touch of his lips against her knuckles had her feeling lightheaded.

He smiled. "For what you said just now…and for that kiss."

A longing rose inside her—to kiss him again and to share her heart. Could Edward possibly feel the same about her as she did for him? Did he share her longing to make their temporary engagement permanent, however impossible that might be?

"You quite possibly saved my life tonight."

Sharp disappointment cut through her. Though the words were spoken tenderly, they seemed to convey only gratitude. "You would've done the same for me," she countered with a slightly forced smile.

He didn't feel as she did, and she'd been foolish to think otherwise. Edward was devoted to his ranch and she was devoted to her career—and securing that promotion.

Thoughts of her promotion brought welcome practicality back to her addled brain. "We need to see if whoever started the fire left any evidence." She released her grip on his arm, pulled her other hand from his, and took a decisive step backward.

Was it her imagination or did Edward look suddenly sad? "Evidence, yes." He cleared his throat. "Once the flames fully die down, we can safely look around. In the meantime, we'll need to ensure the roof on the house doesn't catch fire."

Maggy nodded in agreement as he hefted the bucket at her feet and moved slowly toward the house. As she followed, she glanced back at the spot where they'd been standing. Very soon, she would have to say goodbye to him, to this man she'd come to care for as far more than a friend, but at least she would have the memory of that kiss to carry with her.

Chapter Fifteen

Hours later—after the main house had been saved, after everyone had drunk their fill of Mrs. Harvey's tea, after the wranglers who weren't on guard duty had returned to their beds—Edward was finally able to scout for evidence around the burnt buildings with Maggy. He still wore his ash-streaked shirt and trousers, and though he longed to change and lie down for a few minutes, a fresh set of clothes and sleep would have to wait. Finding possible clues had to come first.

The dawning of a new day threw enough light on the ground to see by. It also illuminated Maggy's long auburn hair and a smudge of ash on her cheek that he longed to smooth away. It would only be an excuse to touch her face, to kiss her again, though he wasn't sure she'd welcome either one.

Each time Edward thought of her tender, potentially lifesaving kiss, his heart gave a jolt. Kissing Maggy had been sweeter and profoundly more affecting than he'd imagined. She'd risked her own life to try to help him, something he didn't take lightly, but what he'd felt for her in return went much deeper than gratitude or friendship.

He cared deeply for her—he knew that now. And yet last night, when he'd begun to think she might feel the same, she'd stepped away from him, shuttered her emotions and turned the conversation back to solving his case.

Fresh regret wound through him as he surveyed the remains of the guest cottage. The charred boards no longer stood as a testament of his hard work and care.

But I am not what I do, he reminded himself, echoing Maggy's truthful words during the fire.

Thankfully, in spite of his own stubbornness, God kept showing him that he wasn't just the son of an earl or a successful rancher. He was somebody simply because he was God's child. And with Maggy's help, he'd finally been able to see and understand that. He had much to feel grateful for—his life, his staff, his ranch—and most of all, for Maggy. She'd infused his rather solitary life with her charisma, and he would never wish it differently.

He turned to eye the stable. It would need to be rebuilt, but it would get a new life, a second chance. Could he and Maggy have another chance? Would she be open to considering a life here, with him?

"Edward!"

He turned toward her, his question on the tip of his tongue, until he saw that she held something in her hand. "What's that?"

"It's a bandanna." She lifted it, her blue eyes alight with familiar excitement. "I think the person who started the fire used it to wipe his face, then accidentally dropped it behind the stable."

Edward took the bandanna from her and examined it. The item looked like any ordinary bandanna, except for what appeared to be initials sewn in one corner. "C.H.," he said, showing Maggy the monogram.

"Chance Howe," they said at the same time. Mild shock gave way to a resurgence of anger. Maggy had been right in suspecting Howe, which meant the other rancher had likely hoped to trap her inside the burning guest cottage.

A glance at Maggy's face showed she was contemplating similar thoughts. She tugged the bandanna from his grip and started past him.

"Where are you going?" he asked as he moved swiftly to catch up with her.

She didn't slow. "We need to talk to Vienna." She threw him a determined look. "It's time we find out if she knows anything and to tell her who I really am."

They found Mrs. Harvey and Vienna in the kitchen, talking in muted voices, empty teacups on the table. "Any ideas how the fire started, sir?" Mrs. Harvey asked.

"Not how," Maggy said, "but who."

Vienna looked confused. "Someone started it on purpose? Why would they do that?"

"We're hoping you might have some insight into that, Vienna." Edward tempered the words with a kind smile, but the girl still paled.

"I don't understand."

Maggy set the bandanna in front of Vienna. She picked it up, her expression becoming even more bewildered. "How did Chance's bandanna get here?"

"I believe he dropped it." Maggy kept her voice gentle. "After he set the guest house on fire."

Vienna slumped against her chair. "W-why would he do that? Is he that angry with me?"

"Not with you, Vienna." Maggy crouched beside her. "I believe he was trying to hurt me." She glanced up at Edward as she added, "And Edward, too."

"You and Edward?" Vienna shook her head. "I still don't understand. I know Chance can be a bear, but I've never known him to hurt anyone." Her cheeks flushed. "Apart from me," she murmured in a pained tone.

Edward dragged an empty chair over for Maggy, but when she indicated he should take it instead, he sat by Vienna. "There's something about the ranch you need to know…"

"I'll make some more tea," Mrs. Harvey announced as she rose to her feet, inspiring a brief smile from Edward. The older woman might enjoy sensationalized stories, but she also knew what a body needed in times of turmoil and stress.

He began by telling Vienna about the first threatening note he'd received, then he outlined the various attacks against the Running W that led to his decision to hire a Pinkerton agent. Vienna's green eyes widened, but she didn't say a word.

Maggy picked up the narrative next. "The first agent Edward hired wasn't successful at finding anything, so the superintendent in the Denver office assigned me to the case."

"You?" Vienna's expression could only be described as astonished. "Y-you're a detective?"

Maggy chuckled. "Guilty." Sitting on the floor of his kitchen, in a soiled robe and nightgown, she looked nothing like the detectives Edward had imagined. But there couldn't be a more skilled, courageous and beautiful one than her. "After my husband died, I ended up helping a Pinkerton agent in our little mining town. He's the one who encouraged me to apply for a job."

"Are you really engaged then?" Vienna asked, looking between them.

Maggy's expression clouded, though Edward wasn't sure why. "We became temporarily engaged," she explained, "so I could join the ranchers' wives' club and dig up clues there."

"Then you aren't staying? Once you solve this case?" The sorrowful note in the girl's voice matched the one squeezing at Edward's heart.

His earlier thought about asking Maggy if she would consider a life here, with him, rang through his head once more. But her next words had his hopes turning to ash, just like his guest cottage and stable.

"I can't stay," she said, more to her lap than to them. "I'm hoping to be promoted to head female detective. In that role, I'd oversee all of the female agents at Pinkerton's. I just need to solve this case first."

It was as if a fist had connected with Edward's stomach. His case had been a means to an end, nothing more, nothing less. Somehow he forced a smile. "Congratulations, Maggy. You'll be fantastic."

"Thank you." The smile she gave him didn't seem as luminous as some of her others, but perhaps she was simply nervous about the promotion or at what still needed to happen to solve his case. "That brings us back to Chance. Has there been anything unusual about his behavior the last couple months, Vienna? Anything he's said against Edward?"

Vienna appeared to be thinking hard. "I'm sorry,

but I can't recall anything." She twisted the bandanna around her fingers.

"What about your aunt and uncle?" Maggy asked. Edward guessed where she was going with that question.

The girl's eyes went large again. "What about them?"

"Has Chance been meeting with them or talking more about them recently?"

Her brow furrowed. "You know, now that I think about it, Chance *has* talked a great deal more about them recently—and in far more positive terms than he once did."

"Was there animosity between them at one time?" Maggy asked.

Vienna shook her head. "Not exactly. They thought he was wealthier than he actually turned out to be. Lately, though, he's been talking about them helping him—helping us. Something about getting more land and horses. I didn't pay much attention."

"If they promised to help him…" Maggy looked at Edward. "My guess is the Druitts promised to help Bertram and Winchester, too, in exchange for their cooperation."

He gave a quick nod. "That must be what Bertram meant when he said the other week that Druitt had promised him a nice deal. And that would also explain why he and Winchester were willing to help with the letters and sabotage. What about the buggy, though?"

"What buggy?" Vienna threw Maggy a puzzled look.

She quickly detailed what had happened the other day. By the time she finished her tale, Vienna had gone white again.

"You think it was Chance that tampered with the buggy as well as starting the fire?"

"Yes." Maggy stood. "I don't think your aunt or uncle were behind either of those." She went on to share Kitt's warning about their friendship. "Chance is angry with me, especially now for my part in you leaving him. He might have even thought that harming me would convince Edward to leave."

Vienna's shoulders drooped. "I'm so sorry, Maggy. I don't know what else to say."

"You're not to blame for any of this," she said with unmistakable conviction. "And you've given us more insight into Chance's reasons for helping your aunt and uncle."

The girl turned to look at Edward. "Why would Uncle Nevil and Aunt Dolphina want you gone?"

"We believe they want a successful and operational ranch to use as leverage." He accepted one of the teacups that Mrs. Harvey handed around. "It would be an attractive incentive for Lavina to move back to Sheridan."

Vienna nodded slowly. "I believe you might be right."

Edward shot Maggy a knowing smile—those words would always represent a private joke between them.

"Each time Lavina visits, they launch a new campaign to convince her to stay." The young woman suddenly clapped her hands. "And yet, I think I know why they've been much more aggressive this time."

Maggy took a sip of her tea, her expression expectant. "Why?"

"Uncle Nevil has been quite ill for the last year or so."

Edward exchanged a glance with Maggy. "I didn't know."

"No one does, not even Lavina. I only know because I happened to stop by their house one day when the doctor was there. My aunt swore me to secrecy." Vienna blushed. "I feel it's important for both of you to know, though. He's desperate to have his daughter close by and hopes to see a grandchild or two born before he passes away."

"The motive," Edward exclaimed at the same moment as Maggy.

Mrs. Harvey set down her cup. "So what do we do now?"

"I think we still wait to force a confession from them at the ball, since it's only two days away." Maggy began pacing the kitchen, her tea now growing cold on the table. "Do you think Howe will be there?" she asked Vienna.

The girl shook her head. "Not likely. He's not too fond of social events, except for the dinners at the inn. I don't plan to be there either, considering the circumstances." Another flush stained her face.

"It's all right. You don't need to be there, Vienna," Maggy reassured.

Edward couldn't stomach any more tea. Placing his cup next to Maggy's on the table, he rested his arms on his knees and voiced the question that had been on his mind the last few days. "How will we get them to confess at the ball?"

"What about a note?" Mrs. Harvey suggested, breaking the thoughtful silence.

He looked at his housekeeper in surprise. "A note? What sort of note?"

"Like one they write in those books."

When she blushed, he knew she was talking about

her dime novels. But he wouldn't dismiss the idea. It had been one of her penny dreadfuls that had inspired him to hire a detective in the first place, which had led to Maggy entering his life.

"The person writes a note to the scoundrel," Mrs. Harvey continued, "anonymous like, and says 'we know what you did and you need to meet us here at this time.' And then the sheriff comes along, too, and hides as the person gives their confession."

Maggy stopped pacing and gave Mrs. Harvey a hug. For a moment, Edward wished he'd come up with such a smashing idea so her embrace might have been his instead.

"Mrs. Harvey, that is brilliant." Maggy's delightful laugh filled the kitchen. "You ought to be a detective yourself."

The older woman's cheeks turned a deeper red, but she was grinning. "Go on, now. It's nothing I haven't read in stories over and over again."

"What about Chance?" The question came from Vienna.

Edward looked to Maggy for the answer. "I say we start with a confession from the Druitts," she said, her eyes meeting his. "They might be willing to give him up to prove that they weren't involved in the arson or attempted murder. Then with the sheriff in tow, we'll confront Howe."

Vienna gave a decisive nod, her expression determined but also sad. "If there's any way I can help, I'd like to."

"Thank you, Vienna." Maggy bestowed what appeared to be a genuine smile on all three of them. "And now…we have a confrontation to prepare and stage."

* * *

"Do I look too…fancy?" Maggy asked, studying what she could see of her coiffed hairstyle and blue velvet dress in the bureau mirror. Ms. Glasen had created a ball gown more fitting for a duchess than a detective. However, Maggy did have to admit, the lighter flecks of sapphire scattered across the darker blue color made her eyes and auburn hair stand out. Even the cream-colored lace at her shoulders complemented her skin.

Vienna smiled into the mirror from where she stood behind Maggy. "You look gorgeous. Mr. Kent isn't going to be able to take his eyes off you. Temporary fiancée or not. Isn't that right, Mrs. Harvey?"

"Just what I was about to say myself, love." The housekeeper beamed as proudly as if Maggy were her own daughter.

A lump of gratitude rose in her throat for these two women. "You both look exceptional, as well." Last minute, Vienna had decided to attend the ball. She'd borrowed an evening dress from Maggy and Mrs. Harvey had donned her Sunday best.

"Maggy?" she heard Edward call up the stairs. "Are you ladies ready? The horses are hitched to the wagon." Most of the staff would pile into the wagon, while the rest would ride their horses.

She threw one last look at her reflection. "We're nearly ready," she called back.

"We'll go first," Vienna said, a twinkle in her green eyes. "Then you can make a grand descent down the stairs."

The last four days Maggy had seen a slight change in the young woman. Vienna was still shy, but she no longer appeared timid. There was a quiet confidence that had begun to radiate from her, and Maggy couldn't be happier.

Except she wouldn't be around to see her friend fully develop her inner strength.

If all went well this evening, Maggy would be leaving in the next day or two. She'd already sneaked a note into Mrs. Druitt's valise earlier that day, when she and Vienna had gone to the city hall building to help put up the decorations for the ball.

Edward had been busy with preparations, too. After he'd accompanied them into town, he'd paid a visit to the sheriff. He had reported that he'd been working with a Pinkerton agent—though he didn't say it was Maggy—and asked if the sheriff would be attending the ball. Some well-placed hints about horse thievery and arson had piqued the sheriff's interest and secured his cooperation.

Vienna and Mrs. Harvey left the room, grinning and chattering like schoolgirls. Grabbing her sapphire-colored gloves off the bed, Maggy hurried after them, pulling her gloves on as she walked. Her pulse jumped when she reached the stairs and saw Edward at the bottom, talking to the other two women. He hadn't looked up yet, which gave her a few seconds to watch him unobserved.

It wasn't as if she hadn't seen him dressed well before. Tonight, though, his ensemble, which included a tailcoat and cravat, had him looking every bit an earl's son—and as fine looking as ever. Not for the first time, she felt proud to be known as his fiancée and friend.

But not for much longer.

Her heart lurched with pain at that thought, and she hurried to draw a calming breath. There would be time enough, on the train ride back to Denver, to mourn over what might have been between them. For now, she would proceed with their carefully laid plans.

She lifted her chin and descended the stairs. When Edward glanced up at last, his jaw visibly slackened. The awed look in his gray eyes made her grateful she'd chosen to wear her fanciest gown after all.

"I'm ready," she announced into the quiet. Vienna and Mrs. Harvey seemed eager to exit the house, leaving her and Edward alone.

He stared at her a moment longer, then offered her his arm. "You are beautiful, Maggy." The low timbre of his voice and the intense way he studied her made it difficult for her to breathe. Then there was the belated but delightful realization he hadn't simply complimented her dress or her look tonight—he'd told her that *she* was beautiful.

"Thank you." She slipped her arm through his. "You look very handsome yourself, Edward. But then you always do." She hadn't planned to share that last part, but it had slipped out nevertheless, and she couldn't take it back now.

His slow grin had her feeling grateful for the support of his arm. "You find me handsome?"

"Yes," she retorted, tugging him toward the door. "And humble, too."

He laughed, and the sound wound its way through her embarrassment and into her heart. Making her long for things she couldn't have. Surely God still wanted her to be a detective. Besides, it wasn't as if Edward felt more than friendship for her. Once his case was wrapped up and he was supplying the British Cavalry with horses, he would forget all about her.

Maggy would never fully forget him, though—or her time as his fiancée.

Please let me make it through tonight, she prayed as Edward led her into the yard, where the others waited in the wagon or on horseback. *Then grant me the courage to say goodbye.*

Edward couldn't keep his gaze from wandering to where Maggy stood with several other women, talking and drinking glasses of punch. While all of the women in attendance looked nice in their best dresses, Maggy—his fiancée—stood out like a ray of sunshine after a long gray winter. She was beautiful, strong and graceful, inside and out.

Did he see her that way because he'd come to know and love the real Maggy?

Love? He started coughing, drawing curious looks from Kitt and Jensen standing nearby. "Excuse me," he mumbled. "I believe I'll get some punch."

He made his way toward the refreshment table, through the crowd of people not currently dancing. A few called out to him. He did his best to smile and nod, but inside he was reeling.

Had he actually associated love and Maggy in the same thought? He certainly admired her, cherished her, cared deeply for her. But *love*?

The last time he'd believed himself in love, things had not gone well. He'd been left alone and heartbroken, which would surely happen again if he confessed his feelings to Maggy. She was leaving, quite possibly tomorrow, and had a promotion waiting for her in Colorado. He had things to focus on, too, like rebuilding his stable and securing a contract with the Cavalry.

And yet… He studied her as he neared the table and felt the familiar leap of anticipation inside his heart at the thought of being near her once more. He wanted to protect her from every evil, comfort her after every loss, laugh at her every joke and hold her close tonight and every night hereafter. Surely that was love.

In that moment, he knew—he was in love with Maggy.

Edward downed a cup of punch and set the empty glass on the table. The notes of a waltz filled the crowded room. He and Maggy had danced twice already, but they'd been more exuberant dances. The waltz was different, more romantic. And he didn't want to dance it with anyone else except his fiancée.

Making his way over to her side, he extended his hand. "May I have this dance, Miss Worthwright?"

Her cheeks glowed a pretty shade of pink as the women around her tittered in approval at his request. "I'd be delighted." She set her gloved hand in his palm and he led her to a spot on the dance floor.

"Are you enjoying yourself?" he asked, feeling suddenly nervous.

Maggy nodded, then gave him a rueful smile. "At least as much as I can before ten o'clock." That was the hour they were to meet the Druitts in an anteroom of the city hall building, with the sheriff in tow.

"I know what you mean." Though his nervousness had less to do with the confrontation and more with what he'd finally realized about his feelings for her.

He pulled her closer. "Maggy?

"Yes?" She lifted her wide blue eyes to his.

Did he dare confess his heart? Would it be fair? If he told her what he felt, she might feel obligated to stay, instead of pursuing the promotion she clearly wanted. "I…"

Her brow furrowed. "Is something wrong, Edward?"

"No," he said, making a decision. He loved her, yes, and wanted nothing more than to make her his wife. But he loved her enough to put her happiness first, to see her continue in a job she excelled at doing. "It does occur to me, though, that I don't know your real last name."

She looked a bit surprised at the change in topic. "Do you really want to know what it is?"

"Very much." It would be something else real, beyond his feelings for her, that he would hold on to after she left.

Maggy smiled, and the radiance of it nearly made him forget they were supposed to be dancing. "My maiden name," she whispered, "and the one I go by now is Worthing."

"Maggy Worthing."

A mixture of sorrow and gratitude swelled within him just as the music did around them. Her full name was no longer a mystery to him and neither was the identity of the woman who'd fully and completely captured his heart.

Chapter Sixteen

Maggy had to resist the pull to become caught up in the music, in Edward's embrace and in the deep and tender way he regarded her. Maybe she should've turned him down for the waltz, insisted they sit this dance out. Except she'd wanted to be the one whirling about the room in his arms as though they actually belonged together. She wanted to draw out every moment of their time tonight.

"Tell me something about you—something I don't know," she said, glancing away.

If she kept staring into those beloved gray eyes, she might not have the courage to walk away tomorrow. She had an incredible opportunity before her with this promotion. She had little here, beyond friends, if she stayed. And she couldn't settle for friendship with Edward—not anymore.

His brow furrowed as if her question had caught him off guard. "Something you don't know?"

"Yes." She searched for something to ask, something to distract her from the pull between them. "W-what was the name of the girl you loved?"

"Her name was Beatrice." His intent focus remained on her face when she looked at him. "And I didn't love her."

Maggy found it suddenly hard to form words. "But the other night. You said you thought you loved her."

"I was wrong back then, Maggy." When had they stopped dancing? He still held her hand, which he gave a gentle squeeze. "I didn't know what real love was, but now I do. And I know I don't have the right..."

Her heart beat so loudly she could hardly hear him over the music. Did his feelings run deeper than she'd thought? Movement across the room caught her attention. Vienna was standing in the doorway, waving at Maggy to join her. Her face had lost its earlier color and her expression appeared anxious.

"I'm sorry, Edward. Can we finish this conversation in a little bit? I think Vienna needs something." She motioned to the other side of the room as she stepped away from him.

Though he looked disappointed, he nodded. "Would you like me to come with you?"

"No." If Vienna needed to talk about her husband, then she wasn't likely to welcome Edward's presence as she and Maggy conversed. "I'll be back soon."

She smiled at him, hoping to convey how much she wished to keep talking. When he returned her smile, she felt better. She'd hurry and see what Vienna wanted and then come right back.

Slipping into the crowd, she moved around the guests toward the other side of the room. But, by the time Maggy reached the doorway, Vienna was no longer there. Baffled, she glanced up and down the hall.

"Vienna?" she called.

The click of the outer door straight ahead indicated her friend must have gone outside. Maggy followed, eager for some fresh air herself. Hopefully that would help cool her cheeks before she spoke with Edward again. Pushing through the door, she found Vienna standing beside a parked wagon.

"There you are." Maggy smiled and took a step forward. "Is everything all right?"

Vienna hung her head. "Oh, Maggy," she murmured in a tortured whisper. "I'm so sorry."

"So sor—"

Strong arms grabbed her from behind and a hand clapped over her mouth before she could cry out. "Well, if ain't the high-and-mighty Miss Worthwright," Howe jeered in her ear. "Getting you to leave the ball was as easy as I expected."

Alarm pooled in Maggy's stomach as the gravity of her situation became apparent to her. Howe had used Vienna to get them both to leave the protection of the ball.

"Now, listen real good. You're going to get up into this wagon. And you aren't going to make any noise." He lifted the hand not covering her mouth to reveal a gun. "If you so much as take a step toward the building, I'll shoot Vienna."

His wife let out a whimper that tore at Maggy's heart and made her want to fight Howe. But she'd witnessed his unhinged anger the other night. There was no doubt in her mind he would make good on his threat, and she wouldn't knowingly put her friend in danger.

She dipped her head in a submissive nod. Only then did Howe loosen his iron grip on her. He marched her toward the back of the wagon, where some torn cloths and coiled lengths of rope sat waiting to be used.

Howe gagged her mouth with a cloth, then tied her wrists together in front. Lastly, he ensured she couldn't untie the gag by lassoing rope around her upper arms and torso. Everything inside Maggy cried out to fight, but she squelched the feeling as he half lifted, half tossed her into the back of the wagon. The thought of Ms. Glasen's beautifully crafted ball gown being torn or dirtied made her cringe with frustration and empathy. And that made her nearly laugh out loud. When had she come to care about the proper maintenance of feminine clothes? Probably about the time she'd started to fall in love with Edward.

Edward! If only she'd accepted his invitation to come with her. Moisture burned in her eyes. She might have unknowingly jeopardized their meeting with the Druitts by walking right into Howe's trap. Which also meant they might not get the confession they needed to finally put Edward's case to rest. An overwhelming sense of despair settled inside her.

Howe gagged and tied Vienna in the same fashion before putting her in the back of the wagon, too. After ordering them to lie down and keep quiet, he climbed onto the seat and urged the horses forward. The wagon rattled beneath them as he increased the team's speed.

In the dying light, Maggy could see Vienna was crying. She wished she could tell her not to worry or to blame herself. But she was struggling with similar thoughts and self-accusations.

Maggy shut her eyes and did the only thing she could think of to do. She began to pray—for her and Vienna and Edward. When she opened her eyes, she saw Vienna's were now closed. The hope that her friend was also petitioning the Lord brought a surge of comfort and pushed back at her despondency.

The light disappeared as the wagon rumbled onward. Maggy could only see a square of darkening sky above them, which gave little indication of which direction they were headed. After a long time of praying and dozing, she felt the wagon's movement growing rougher. Then tree branches loomed overhead.

At last the wagon came to a stop. Maggy wished she could rub her aching jaw. Her back felt stiff and sore after the jarring ride, and her arms were chaffed from rubbing against the rope.

"We'll wait here," Howe announced as he leaned in to grip Vienna's arm.

Wait for what? Maggy wondered with a shiver. *Where are we?*

She soon learned the answer. Howe wrested her out of the wagon and onto her feet, dragging her toward a nearby fence. Vienna sat against one fence post, and Howe pushed Maggy to the dirt beside another. The man had a lantern, which threw light and shadow on the ground as he moved from the fence to the wagon and back. After a bit, he started a campfire a short distance from where he'd left them, then he extinguished the lantern. He looked up every few minutes, his gun in hand, as if watching for someone.

With the aid of the glowing campfire, Maggy turned her focus from Howe to studying the fence line. She soon realized it encircled a corral—one that she recognized. This was the hidden corral she and Edward had discovered weeks ago. Wild hope rose into her throat as she pulled her knees to her chest. Edward knew this place existed, and now she just had to pray he'd remember it before Howe lost patience or anyone else showed up.

Edward danced three more times—once with Matilda Kitt, once with a girl he didn't know and lastly with Lavina Jensen. Based on her answers to his questions about the ball and the evening in general, she seemed entirely unaware of the pending meeting her parents were to attend. He looked for Maggy between each dance, but he didn't see her. Her conversation with Vienna was running longer than he'd expected.

When he finished dancing with Lavina, he searched the room and the nearby hall for Maggy. A glance at the clock inside the main room showed it was a quarter to ten. Perhaps she'd gone into the anteroom early. Edward glanced inside, but the small room stood empty. Where had she and Vienna gone?

He returned to the ball and walked among the guests a second time to see if he'd missed them coming back inside. But neither young woman was there. Had they gone outside to talk? He exited the city hall and circled the building. No one was about, save for a middle-aged couple taking a stroll. His wagon and all of the ranch horses were in the same spots where they'd left them.

Uneasiness gnawed at him as he went back inside. Something was amiss; he could feel it, even if he didn't know what was wrong. He found Mrs. Harvey and asked her if she'd seen Maggy and Vienna, but she hadn't.

"Is something wrong, sir?"

Edward frowned. "I'm not certain. I can't think of any reason the girls would leave the ball."

"Unless they didn't leave by their own choice." Mrs. Harvey tapped her lined chin with her finger. "What if they were taken?"

Torn between worry and surprise, he half growled out, "By whom?"

"I would think that obvious, sir."

Edward glanced at her raised eyebrows and felt his heart drop when he realized what she was implying. "Howe would do that."

"My guess, as well."

Dread mingled with determination in his gut. "In that case, we're going to have this little meeting earlier than we planned. The Druitts might know something that will help us find Maggy and Vienna." He started toward the opposite side of the room, where Mrs. Druitt was conversing with a group of ladies. The woman's husband had conveniently disappeared from the room, but Edward didn't want to waste time looking for the man. They only needed one member of the Druitt family to start this meeting. Mrs. Harvey stayed right behind him as he moved through the crowd.

"You're coming, too?" he asked her.

"Yes, sir." She shot him an arched look. "Those girls are as close to being my own flesh and blood as they come."

Her presence—one that had been a part of his life for years now—brought a modicum of calm. As did the prayer he silently uttered for help before reaching Mrs. Druitt.

"Evening, madam," he announced with a false smile. "I need to whisk you away."

The woman looked confused. "For what purpose, Mr. Kent?"

"I'll explain on the way."

Seeing Mrs. Harvey behind him must have helped her decide to go with him. "I'll be back shortly, ladies," she said before sauntering toward the door. Edward caught the eye of the sheriff and nodded. Ten or not, it was time for their meeting.

"This way to the anteroom," Edward said when he reached the hallway. He gripped Mrs. Druitt by the elbow and steered her in that direction. "We're a bit early, but being punctual is important, don't you think?"

Her cheeks instantly drained of color. "The...the anteroom? You mean you..." She attempted to recover as she tugged backward on his hold. "I don't know what you're talking about, Mr. Kent. And I'll ask that you unhand me. Oh, look, Sheriff Tweed. Will you kindly ask this gentleman to leave me alone?"

"Of course, Mrs. Druitt." The sheriff smiled as he tucked her arm in his and began walking forward—toward the anteroom.

If Edward hadn't felt so wound with concern, he might have laughed, especially when Mrs. Druitt threw him a smug look. "Thank you kindly, sheriff. I appreciate your..." Her voice faded when they stopped in front of the anteroom. "Wh-what are we doing here?"

"We," Edward said, moving past them to open the door, "are here for your meeting."

Mrs. Druitt released a squeak, but since she was still on the arm of the sheriff, she couldn't escape. "I don't know anything."

The sheriff's gaze narrowed at her guilty reaction, but his tone was polite when he said, "We'd simply like to talk to you, Mrs. Druitt."

The woman huffed as she dropped into a chair. Mrs. Harvey took a seat, as well, while the sheriff perched on the corner of a nearby table. Edward took up a post beside the closed door.

"Is there anything you can you tell us, Mrs. Druitt, about the threats against Mr. Kent here?" The sheriff nodded at Edward.

She turned to face the wall. "I have no argument with Mr. Kent, other than this rudeness tonight."

"So you don't know what happened to several of his horses," Sheriff Tweed continued, "or the feed he ordered or the fire someone set to his stable?"

The woman whipped around, her expression indignant. "I had nothing to do with any fire. Or with that buggy accident."

"He didn't mention any buggy accident," Edward said with satisfaction, which only increased when Mrs. Druitt turned ashen again. "Where is your husband?"

"He's around here somewhere." She sniffed as if disinterested. "Perhaps he went over to the inn."

Edward folded his arms and leveled her with his firmest look. "I doubt that. My guess is wherever he is, that's where we'll find Mr. Howe. As well as Maggy and Vienna."

"They're missing?" the sheriff asked, his expression confused and concerned. "How long have they been gone?"

Mrs. Harvey spoke up. "Quite a while, sir. We're awfully worried."

"I don't know where Maggy and Vienna are, and that's the truth," Mrs. Druitt said as the three of them looked at her. Edward didn't think she was lying—but she wasn't telling the whole truth, either. She hadn't responded to the mention that the women were missing, as if she knew it already.

The sheriff leaned forward, bringing his face closer to hers. "Do you know the penalty for horse rustling, Mrs. Druitt?"

"Yes." She swallowed hard, then appeared to make a decision. "I don't know where Nevil went, but I do know it was to meet Chance Howe."

Edward smacked his hand against the wall as fresh apprehension and anger coursed through him. "Why was he meeting with Howe?"

"He said Chance has become a loose cannon." She seemed to realize what she'd admitted because she began to wring her gloved hands. "He hoped to talk some sense into the boy…and pay him the ransom."

The sheriff reared back and exchanged an alarmed look with Edward. "A ransom for whom?"

"Chance has just been so upset since Vienna left him," Mrs. Druitt said, ignoring the direct question. Tears rolled down her round cheeks. "He's not thinking clearly. I didn't know he would take Miss Worthwright, too. Truly, I didn't. I just want this whole thing over."

Sheriff Tweed scrubbed his hand over his jaw. "Why would Howe demand Mr. Druitt pay a ransom for the return of his wife?"

"I don't believe he intends to return Vienna." Mrs. Druitt pressed her lips together as if she didn't plan to say more.

"What was the ransom for then?" The sheriff's hard tone didn't allow for argument or silence.

"For us—Nevil and myself. He threatened to… to…turn us in otherwise." She hid her face behind her hands as she noisily wept.

It was the closest thing to a confession they'd gotten, but it would have to suffice for now. Edward was desperate to find Maggy and Vienna before more time passed.

He doubted the sincerity of the older woman's apparent grief, and yet, they needed her help if they were to locate the girls. "Mrs. Druitt?" He crouched beside her. "Can you recall the place where your husband was to meet Howe?"

"No," she half wailed. "He wouldn't say. Only that it was a hiding spot very few people knew about."

Edward rose to his feet and began pacing the narrow space beside the door. "You can't recall any other details?"

When she didn't answer, Mrs. Harvey voiced a question. "Have you or your husband been to this spot before?"

Edward stopped walking and glanced from her to Mrs. Druitt. "I haven't been there," the woman answered. "But Nevil has. More than once, I think. All I know is that it's south of our ranch, near your place, Mr. Kent."

"That's it." He faced the sheriff, feeling the first seeds of hope. "I know where they are."

Sheriff Tweed looked doubtful. "You sure?"

"I believe so."

His answer seemed to satisfy the sheriff. The man propelled Mrs. Druitt to her feet. "You'll need to wait at the jail until we find your husband and Mr. Howe." He didn't let her bluster deter him one bit; he simply talked over her. "Once I get her to the jail, we can ride to this spot of yours, Kent."

"I can't wait." Edward opened the door and stepped into the hallway, Mrs. Harvey behind him.

The sheriff led Mrs. Druitt out of the room right on their heels. "How come?" he asked Edward. "You don't know what you're riding into."

"No, I don't," Edward said with a glance at his housekeeper. He hadn't confessed his feelings for Maggy out loud to anyone yet. *In for a penny, in for a pound.* "But I know *who* I'm riding toward and that's my fiancée. The woman I love."

Mrs. Harvey shot him a smile, though it looked far more knowing than surprised. Had she suspected for some time what he'd only realized?

In contrast, Sheriff Tweed frowned. "I don't like it. But I can't force you to wait, unless I arrest you." Edward felt a moment of panic as the man seemed to consider doing just that.

"I don't want to wait, sir."

"Which I can understand, son, having been married twenty-five years to the woman I adore." He matched Edward's level gaze with one of his own, though his held understanding as well as firmness. "Still, there's an advantage to having more men riding together. If you wait, I'll round up one of my deputies to ride with us and you can bring along someone else of your choosing. And that, Mr. Kent, is the surest way to help your lady love."

Edward itched to go now. But he recognized the wisdom in the sheriff's plan.

"McCall can go with you," Mrs. Harvey said. "That'll give you four to their two."

Blowing out a breath, he nodded. "All right. I'll get

my ranch foreman and we'll meet you at the jail." He hurried back to the ball with Mrs. Harvey.

The ordeal of the last hour or so had made one thing abundantly clear to him—he didn't want to live without Maggy in his life. Even if he didn't stand a chance of convincing her to stay, he had to at least try—after he helped rescue her and Vienna.

Chapter Seventeen

Maggy startled awake at the sound of a horse approaching. Had Edward found her? She straightened against the post, her backside numb from sitting on the hard ground for what felt like hours. Bitter disappointment coated her gagged mouth when the rider entered the circle of light created by the fire. It wasn't Edward; it was Mr. Druitt.

She turned to look questioningly at Vienna a few yards away, but the girl shook her head in response. Vienna hadn't expected her uncle's arrival any more than Maggy had. They knew the two men were colluding—but why meet here and now? Had Mr. Druitt known about this planned kidnapping?

"Did you bring the money?" Howe asked as Druitt dismounted.

The older man nodded. His expression looked grim and a bit peaked. He wheezed as he approached the fire, a valise in hand. Maggy remembered what Vienna had said about her uncle being sick. A tiny flicker of empathy sparked inside her. She certainly didn't agree with his choices, but she could understand how his illness had made him desperate to have the one thing people wanted most before dying—to be surrounded by those they loved.

"Is it all there?" Druitt blocked her view of Howe's face, but she could hear the skepticism in his tone.

Druitt dropped the bag. "It's there. Did you really mean to rat us out, after all we promised you?"

"You were taking too long, old man. Besides, none of those threats of yours were working. It was time to try something else."

Stalking to the fence, Druitt wheezed again, making Maggy wonder if exertion or agitation made his condition worse. "So you resort to tampering with that buggy, setting things on fire and kidnapping your own wife as a way to scare Kent?"

"They weren't meant to just scare him—they were supposed to get his fiancée out of the way, too." His vehement tone sent a shudder through Maggy. She might have been right about him, but she hardly felt victorious as she sat here bound and gagged by his hand. "I did it to send her and Kent fleeing for the hills so she'd leave Vienna alone."

Druitt whirled on him. "But she didn't flee, did she?"

"How was I to know she wouldn't keep driving that buggy?" Howe argued as the older man marched back to the fire and sank to the ground. "Or stop sleeping in the man's guest house?"

A chill swept through her at his words. Once again she'd been correct about his motive—he'd meant to harm her—but she felt no pride in her skills this time. Druitt wasn't likely to hurt her; Howe still might. And what about Vienna?

Please help me, Lord.

She wrestled against the ropes around her arms and hands, but they held fast. Glancing around, Maggy realized that she was covered entirely in shadow. The light from the fire illuminated the two men, Druitt's horse, and part of the fence, but it didn't reach where she and Vienna sat. Which meant if she could come in at Howe's back… She didn't have a clear plan; she only had a growing determination to move, to act. Edward would trust her instincts, and she needed to do the same.

Thoughts of Edward increased her desire for action, but they also tugged painfully at her heart. If she ever saw him again, she would tell him how she felt. She'd tell him what was most important to her—and it wasn't the promotion, as fulfilling as that would be. The people in her life were most important to her. Like Mr. Druitt, she longed to remain in the company of those she loved. Starting with the man she loved.

She lowered herself onto her stomach, grateful Howe hadn't tied her feet together, and crawled beneath the lowest rung of the fence. The train of her dress dragged behind her, but it couldn't be helped. She scuttled forward, keeping her gaze locked on the two men talking by the fire. Druitt was attempting to placate Howe with more promises of what the young man could have if Kent gave up his ranch. Whether the man meant what he was saying or was merely trying to confuse Howe, Maggy couldn't say. She was grateful, though, that the conversation kept them focused on each other rather than on her and Vienna—and that she was getting the full confession she'd feared she had thwarted.

As she drew closer to the fire's circle of light, she slowed. She'd have to inch around it to avoid being seen, which meant more time would pass in which she could be spotted. And if she were caught, she wasn't sure Druitt would be able to convince Howe not to dispose of her.

Weeds scratched at the exposed skin of her arms between the loops of rope, and her heart beat hard and fast. She continued forward, though, circumventing the beam of light. Howe's face was visible now— he looked annoyed and impatient. Maggy picked up the pace of her laborious crawling as best she could. When she reached the fence on the far side of the men, she allowed herself a few moments to catch her breath. Then she kept going, making sure to stay in the shadows behind Howe.

She would need to find something to knock out the man or at least render him unmovable. Hopefully long enough that Druitt could get Howe's gun, giving all of them the advantage.

Angling herself toward Howe's back, she searched the ground for something to heft. She couldn't see much in the dark. There were no rocks and she couldn't tear something from the rickety fence with her bound hands. Besides, that would make too much noise. There was the darkened lantern, though...

She inched forward, painfully aware of the way her dress rustled with each movement. Timing would be everything if she hoped to be successful with using the lantern.

When she reached it, she stopped and carefully moved from her stomach to her knees. One look at the men revealed they were still engrossed in conversation, but that might end at any second. It was now or never if she hoped for the element of surprise.

Maggy bunched the yards of fabric from her dress around her knees, then locked her fingers around the lantern's handle. It creaked when she lifted it toward her lap. She froze, along with the men. Her pulse pounded loudly in her ears.

"Did you hear something?" Howe asked, glancing to his left where he'd parked the wagon.

"Probably just the horses," Druitt said.

Forcing steady breaths to slow her heartbeat, Maggy scooted forward. She winced at the pebbles that embedded themselves into her knees. She was close enough to Howe that she could easily reach out and touch his coat. Thankfully his broad back and shoulders still provided cover for her. She repositioned her hold on the lantern handle.

As she braced herself in preparation to stand, she heard the unmistakable sound of oncoming horses. The men did, too. Both of them swiveled toward the noise. If she didn't act now, she'd lose her opportunity, especially if the riders were friends of Howe's instead of a rescue party.

"Those aren't our—"

Maggy sprang to her feet and swung the lantern at the back of Howe's head. The man's sentence ended in a grunt as he pitched sideways into the dirt, along with the broken pieces of the lantern. Druitt cried out and lumbered to his feet at the same moment a firm voice hollered, "Hands in the air. You're under arrest."

The old man threw his arms up, though he continued to gape at Maggy as if he'd seen a ghost. She dropped the broken lantern as four riders breached the tree line.

She recognized the sheriff and guessed the man on his left was a deputy. Her gaze shifted to the rider on the sheriff's right. It was Edward. Her bravery gave out at the sight of him and she sank to the ground.

Within seconds he was kneeling before her. "Maggy! Are you all right?"

She couldn't do more than nod with the gag still in her mouth.

Fumbling with the knot at the back of her head, Edward untied the cloth and tossed it aside. Maggy pulled in a deliciously full breath through her mouth as he crushed her to his chest. "Did he hurt you?"

"No," she managed past her dry throat. "But he knew I would go after Vienna. He forced her to lure me outside and was waiting for me there." The tears she'd been too afraid and then too determined to allow came cascading down her likely dirty cheeks. "I should've had you come with me, Edward. I'm so sorry."

He eased back to hold her face between his hands, his thumbs brushing at her tears. Maggy shut her eyes at the wonderful feel of his strong fingers. "You didn't know, my dear. None of us knew what Howe was planning."

"He demanded a ransom," she said, opening her eyes and glancing at Druitt. The sheriff was leading the older man, his head dipped low, toward his horse.

"I know. Mrs. Druitt confessed that much."

She felt a rush of relief. "You still had the meeting?"

"We had a meeting of sorts." He gave a rueful chuckle. "Mrs. Druitt did let enough details slip out that she's currently waiting at the jail."

Maggy lifted her bound hands as high as she could.

"Can you untie me? My arms ache from being tied up and smashing Howe with that lantern."

"You rendered him unconscious?" Edward asked, his tone full of awe as he turned to look at the prone Howe. "Even tied up as you are?"

She nodded. "I also ruined my lovely ball gown by dragging myself through the corral so I could come in at his—"

Edward's kiss stole the rest of her explanation, along with her breath. But Maggy didn't mind. Kissing him felt marvelous and right. This time wasn't about saving him from walking into a fire either, or for the benefit of an audience. This time she felt promise and hope in their kiss.

Eventually he released her to locate a knife and cut the rope from her hands and arms. Edward helped her stand, though he pulled her close again as soon as she was on her feet, as if reluctant to have any distance between them. Maggy happily obliged by wrapping her arms around him.

She could see McCall talking with Vienna. The expression on their faces hinted at the familiarity she'd witnessed between them over the past few days. The girl was no longer bound and gagged either, but stood gripping the fence post as if for support. Maggy felt a wave of sorrow for her friend. Vienna had witnessed the full measure of her husband's malice tonight.

"Let's get Howe in the wagon before he wakes," the sheriff directed as he approached the unconscious man. "I'm surprised Druitt had the gumption to knock him out."

Edward tucked Maggy against his side, so they were both facing the lawman. "On the contrary, Sher-

iff Tweed, it was Maggy here who knocked out Howe."
The proud look he gave her filled her full of warmth
and love. She longed for everyone else to disappear so
she could tell him what was in her heart.

"You knocked him out?" The sheriff tipped up his
hat and regarded Maggy. "Bound and gagged?"

She lifted one side of her dress. "And in a ball gown."

"You see," Edward interjected with a smile at her,
"Maggy is not only my fiancée. She's the Pinkerton
detective I told you about who's been solving my case."

Sheriff Tweed shook his head. "Well I'll be… Once
we get everything settled at the jail and you let me
know what charges you intend to press, Mr. Kent, I'd
like to hear the full story of your investigation, miss."

"It would be my pleasure to share it," Maggy answered.

The sheriff and the deputy each grabbed Howe by
the arm and hauled him, groaning, toward the wagon.
Edward glanced at them, then cleared his throat.

"Maggy, there's something I need to tell you."

The seriousness of his tone resurrected her erratic
pulse. Was it possible he'd come to the same conclu-
sions she had tonight? "I have something to tell you,
too."

"If it's about leaving…" His expression turned wary.

She shook her head. "Not exactly." Gathering her
courage, she opened her mouth, but she didn't get a
word out before the sheriff interrupted.

"We need to get moving, folks." He climbed onto
his horse. "We've still got to ride back to Sheridan and
then everyone has a lot of explaining to do."

Disappointment flooded Maggy, though it lessened
when she caught a similar look of remorse on Edward's

handsome face. "Should we see if we can get a full confession from all three of them this time?"

"I do relish the thought of that," Edward said with a nod. "But only if you and I can speak privately later."

Her heart pattered with anticipation, especially when he pressed a tender kiss to her forehead. "I'd like that, too."

Edward felt exhaustion all the way down to his bones, in spite of catching a few hours' sleep at the Sheridan Inn in the wee hours of the morning. Judging by Maggy's soft breathing, her head resting against his shoulder, she was just as tired. Mrs. Harvey, Vienna and McCall were likely dozing in the back of the wagon, as well.

The confessions at the jail had lasted far longer than Edward had anticipated. He'd sent his wranglers home after returning to town with Maggy and Vienna. Bertram and Winchester had fled the party by then.

Edward's housekeeper and foreman had both insisted on staying in town. And he had been grateful for their trusted company as he, Maggy and Vienna shared with the sheriff all that they'd discovered and experienced over the past month, ending with the kidnapping.

When the three of them had finished, the sheriff thoroughly questioned the Druitts and Howe. They'd each made a full confession, though the Druitts appeared to be the only ones who felt any real remorse over their actions. The sheriff insisted everyone, except for the Druitts and Howe, get some sleep before reconvening at the jail to hear what charges Edward would press. Instead of driving all the way back to the ranch, he'd gotten rooms at the inn for him and McCall and the three women.

Sleep had come easily at first, but then he'd woken, anxious about what to do when it came to pressing charges. He'd spent that last hour or so in prayer, asking God what to do, before the tired group had trooped back to the jail. And though Edward had felt his decision was the right one, it wasn't until Maggy had told him that she'd also been praying that a sense of real peace had come over him.

Edward scooted her closer to him on the wagon seat and urged the horses to pick up their pace. They'd had to delay their intended conversation—the one in which he planned to tell her that he loved her—but once they reached the ranch, he didn't plan to wait another minute. He only hoped what Maggy had to tell him was something similar.

"Are we there yet?" she murmured sleepily as if she'd sensed he was thinking about her. She probably had—she featured in his thoughts more than any other person or thing these days.

Edward rubbed her arm beneath the lace sleeve of her ruined ball gown. "Almost."

"We missed services." She lifted her head to look at him, her expression deadpan. "And at the Running W, everyone attends church services."

He chuckled, enjoying the smile it brought to her mouth. "I think God will understand this once."

"So do I," she said, linking her arm through his. "Especially with how merciful you were to the Druitts and Howe."

Eying the bridge up ahead, he frowned. "Do you think I did the right thing?" Now that his case was solved and everything had been decided, he felt a moment's doubt.

"Edward." She waited until he looked her way. "I would have done the same in your position. The Druitts were genuinely sorry, and with Mr. Druitt so ill, I think it was absolutely the right choice to drop any charges of horse theft."

The couple had agreed to return his stolen horses posthaste and compensate him financially with the ransom money for their other misdeeds. Also, Mrs. Druitt had agreed, albeit reluctantly, to step down as president of the wives' club. In return, Edward had agreed not to divulge their wrongdoings to their daughter or the news of Mr. Druitt's illness. Nevil Druitt promised to share his condition with Lavina and Felix before the month was out.

Edward had chosen not to seek out and force a confession from Bertram and Winchester. He felt confident the Druitts would be instrumental in discouraging the two men from trying anything of a nefarious nature in the future.

"What about Howe?" he asked Maggy.

A frustrated expression settled onto her beautiful face, then disappeared as she released a sigh. Edward could well understand her reaction. He still felt anger each time he thought about the fire at the ranch and Howe's treatment of her and Vienna.

"I think you were merciful with him, too." Maggy leaned her head on his shoulder again. "Charges of horse stealing would have put a noose around his neck, so I think having him return your horse and charging him with arson was appropriate."

Howe would have to stand trial and would go to

prison if convicted, but despite the man's crimes and his despicable behavior toward Vienna, Edward didn't want to see him swing—not on Edward's word. And neither did Maggy and Vienna. After learning from Maggy that Vienna was with child, Edward had offered the girl a permanent home and employment at the Running W for as long as she wished, which she'd tearfully accepted.

"Who's that?" Maggy sat up and pointed at a buggy parked in front of the ranch house.

Edward shook his head. "I don't know." He didn't recognize the carriage. Hopefully the unexpected visitor wouldn't stay long. He needed to change out of his wrinkled evening clothes and have his private talk with Maggy.

As he stopped the wagon beside the buggy, a woman with gray hair in a long dress stood up from the rocker and stepped off the porch. "Edward. Where have you been?"

"Mother?" He blinked in shock. "What are you doing here?"

"What am I…" She lifted her eyes to the sky for a moment. "Do you even read my letters? I informed you more than a month ago that I'd decided to come to visit."

Now that he thought about it, there *had* been several of her letters he'd put off reading with all that had been going on. "Forgive me." He threw Maggy a tight smile, then climbed down from the wagon. "I'm glad to see you."

"And I you." She smiled fully as he approached. Back in England he wouldn't have embraced her, but it had been so long since he'd last seen her.

Throwing propriety to the wind, he gathered her tightly to him. "I'm very glad you came."

"Me, too," she whispered in a voice choked with emotion. "I've missed you, my boy."

When he eased back, she placed her hand on his face. There were tears shining in her own gray eyes. In that moment, he realized he'd been a fool to think his family didn't care.

"Did you hire a buggy?" he asked, releasing her.

Her expression conveyed irritation once more. "I had to since you weren't at the station to meet me. Except the livery man said the strangest thing." She glanced from him to where Maggy and the others were exiting the wagon. "He told me you were quite popular with your relatives these days and that I wasn't the first to come visit. What in the world did he mean, Edward?"

He looked at Maggy who was doing her best to suppress a grin, but he couldn't contain a burst of laughter. "That is a rather long story, Mother."

"I like long stories," she said, arching her eyebrows. "Perhaps you can also explain why you are dressed as you are. Or why it looks as if you had a fire here recently." She motioned to the burnt rubble of the guest cottage and stable before nodding politely at his housekeeper. "Hello, Mrs. Harvey. A pleasure to see you again."

The housekeeper dropped a curtsy. "Lady Healey. Nice to see you again, too."

"Are these other people friends of yours, Edward?"

Edward motioned to McCall. "This is my ranch foreman, West McCall, and the young lady there is Vienna Howe. She's come to help Mrs. Harvey." He stepped away from his mother to take Maggy's hand in his. "And this…this is my fiancée, Maggy Worthing." Maggy had told McCall last night that she was a detective, so Edward felt no qualms about sharing her real name.

"Your fiancée?" his mother repeated in an awe-struck tone. "Let me guess. That is another long story."

It was, but Edward refused to wait another moment to learn if the ending to his and Maggy's engagement story would be the one he'd been hoping since yesterday. "I would be happy to explain everything to you soon, Mother. But first I need to speak with Maggy. Why don't you go with Mrs. Harvey and get yourself a nice cup of tea?"

"That's right, my lady. Let's get you settled, shall we?" Mrs. Harvey threw him a perceptive wink as she guided his mother toward the house.

Vienna hurried after them, a faint smile on her face. "I'll help."

With Maggy's hand still gripped in his, Edward led her down the drive, calling over his shoulder, "McCall, find something to do."

"Yes, boss," he said with a laugh.

Edward didn't stop until he reached the bridge. Only then did he turn to face Maggy, who watched him with equal parts amusement and confusion. "I imagined this scene going differently," he admitted.

"Differently than having your mother show up or differently than having spent most of the night in the jail?"

He laughed as he stroked his thumb along the back of her hand. "Both." He felt a sliver of fear at the thought of laying bare his heart to another woman, but he fought it back with the reminder that this wasn't just another woman. This was his Maggy.

Or at least he hoped she'd agree to be his.

"Maggy, there's something I've been waiting all night and all day to share with you." He gazed into her blue eyes and felt himself relax. "I don't want you to be my temporary fiancée anymore."

Her brow pinched with bewilderment and what looked like a twinge of hurt. "That's what you wanted to say?"

"Yes. I mean…no." He shook his head. "This isn't coming out right. What I'm trying to say is that I love you." He let go of her hand so he could cup her face as he'd done after finding her near the corral. "I love you, Maggy Worthing. And I want you to be my fiancée for real this time. To marry me and stay right here. But…"

She cocked her head. "But what?"

"But I know you have a wonderful opportunity with this promotion of yours." He tangled his fingers in her hair as an ache filled him. If she still wished to go, he would let her. "You are an amazing detective, Maggy. And I hate to see you throw that away—"

She pressed her fingers against his mouth, silencing the rest of his speech. "Will you give me a chance to share what I wanted to earlier?" When he nodded, she smiled—the sort of smile that had made him fall in love with her in the first place. "I've worked very hard for that promotion, and it would be everything I dreamed of for my career. But…" She lowered her hand.

"But?" he repeated with a smile, his hopes rising.

Her chin dropped and her voice shook with unshed

tears. "I realized last night that I don't want that promotion as much as I want…other things."

"What do you want, Maggy?"

He nudged her with his finger until she was looking at him again. "I want to stay here, Edward. With you. As your wife." She smiled through her tears. "Because I love you, too."

With a whoop of joy, he gathered her to him and swung her around. Then he set her on her feet and kissed her for a long time.

"Are you sure you don't mind giving up your career to marry a rancher?" he asked when he finally released her.

Maggy threw him a smug look. "Who said anything about giving up my career?"

"But you…"

He couldn't resist kissing the impish grin that appeared on her mouth. "I believe I might have come up with a way to do both."

"Have you now?" He wrapped his arm around her shoulders as they headed back toward the house. "And what is that?"

She snuggled into his side. "You'll have to wait and see."

Two months later

"Does it look straight?" Maggy couldn't quite tell from her position on the top rung of the ladder. She glanced down at Edward.

He studied the sign she'd hung beneath the ranch's archway. "A little more to the left, I think."

She reached out to correct the sign's angle. Her husband—a title she felt certain she would never tire of using—had volunteered to hang the sign for her, but Maggy had wanted to do the honors. After all, it was her detective business, though she suspected Edward would be a great help now and then. Just as she was with the ranch.

"Better?" She inched back slowly.

When he nodded his approval, she grinned. Now the arch not only stated the name of their ranch but also the name of her business—Kent & Harvey's Detective Agency. She didn't expect a great deal of cases, and most of them would likely be minor thefts or crimes or assisting the sheriff now and then, but she was still grateful for the chance to keep honing her skills.

"Let me climb down and then we can go find Mrs. Har—"

Edward grabbed her from behind, making her squeal as much from surprise as delight, as he settled one arm around her back and the other beneath her knees. "You still haven't shown much remorse for stealing away my housekeeper."

"She promised to do both," Maggy replied, fiddling with the lapel of his coat. "And Vienna agreed to pick up any slack in the kitchen."

He pretended to glare at her. "See? No remorse."

"I'm truly sorry, Edward…" She had to swallow a giggle before continuing. "I know it must pain you to have your exceptional housekeeper promoted to assistant detective."

He started to carry her toward the house. "I knew letting her read those dime novels would prove fatal."

Maggy laughed. "I think that is what's made her all the more skilled."

"True. And I suppose I ought to thank her."

She rested her head in the crook of his neck. "For what?"

"For reading those stories in the first place." He shifted her in his arms as he stopped walking. "That's what gave me the idea for hiring a detective in the first place."

Lifting her head, she placed her hand alongside his jaw. She thanked the Lord every day for bringing them together. "Do you regret that decision?" she half teased. "Because you certainly got more than your fair share of trouble with that request. You got a detective, a fiancée and a wife."

"I don't regret it for a moment," he said before kissing her soundly. "I do suggest, though, that as you go forward, you keep one very important thing in mind."

She feigned an innocent expression. "And what is that?"

"Only this, *Mrs. Kent...*" He grinned in a way that made her heart race with joy, gratitude and anticipation. "That you remember you are my detective first, last and always."

Leaning close, Maggy whispered against his lips, "I will."

* * * * *

Dear Reader,

On a research trip to Wyoming for one of my other Love Inspired Historical Westerns, I visited Sheridan and the nearby small town of Big Horn. The beautiful landscape and a lovely preserved 1890s ranch house looked like the ideal spot to set a story.

Those weren't the only reasons I set Edward and Maggy's story near the foothills of the Big Horn Mountains, though. Like Edward, a number of gentlemen from the United Kingdom settled in the area and established horse and polo pony ranches. The British Cavalry did, in fact, contract with ranchers in the area to supply horses for use in the Second Boer War. And though that war didn't start until 1899, for the purposes of my story, I have the Cavalry interested in Edward's horses the year before. Also of interesting note, Queen Elizabeth and Prince Phillip visited the Sheridan area in 1984 and purchased polo ponies from there.

The ranchers' wives' club is my own creation, though the Sheridan Inn is an actual building and was the hubbub of social events back in the day. Buffalo Bill Cody was part owner of the inn and was reported to have auditioned acts for his Wild West show on the inn's front porch.

The Pinkerton National Detective Agency opened a branch location in Denver, Colorado, in 1886. James McParland became the superintendent of the Denver office in 1888. As one of the most famous of Pinkerton's detectives, McParland is best known for infiltrating a gang of assassins in Pennsylvania in the 1870s. And while the position of head female detective is fictional as far as I know at this time in the agency's history, Allan Pinkerton, the agency's founder, did employ the first female detective in the U.S., Kate Warne, in 1856.

My hope for this story is that readers will enjoy Edward and Maggy's adventure, their chance at love and their realization that we are all of unchangeable worth, regardless of what we do or what has happened to us.

I love hearing from readers. You can contact me through my website at www.stacyhenrie.com.

All the best,
Stacy

Get 2 Free Books,
Plus 2 Free Gifts—
just for trying the Reader Service!

*When the most influential women in Seattle ask
successful matchmaker Beth Wallin to find a wife for
deputy sheriff Hart McCormick, she can't turn them
down...even if the handsome lawman once refused her
love. But when she realizes she's his best match,
will she be able to convince him?*

Read on for a sneak preview of
FRONTIER MATCHMAKER BRIDE
by *Regina Scott*, *the next heartwarming book
in the **FRONTIER BACHELORS** series,
available March 2018 from Love Inspired Historical!*

"Beth, stay away from the docks. There are some rough
sorts down there."

The two workers hadn't seemed all that rough to her.
"You forget. I have five brothers."

"Your brothers are gentlemen. Some of those workers
aren't."

She really shouldn't take Hart's statements as anything
more than his duty as a lawman. "Very well. I'll be careful."

His gaze moved to the wharves, as if he saw a gang of
marauding pirates rather than busy longshoremen. "Good. I
wouldn't want anything to happen to you."

Beth stared at him.

"I'd hate to have to explain to your brothers," he added.

Well! She was about to tell him exactly what she thought
of the idea when she noticed a light in his eyes. Was that a
twinkle in the gray?

Beth tossed her head. "Oh, they'll take your side. You

know they will. They always say I have more enthusiasm than sense."

He shrugged. "I know a few women who match that description."

Beth grinned. "But none as pretty as me."

"That's the truth." His gaze warmed, and she caught her breath. Hart McCormick, flirting with her? It couldn't be!

Fingers fumbling, she untied the horses and hurried for the bench. "I should go. Lots to do before two. See you at the Emporium."

He followed her around. Before she knew what he was about, he'd placed his hands on her waist. For one moment, she stood in his embrace. Her stomach fluttered.

He lifted her easily onto the bench and stepped back, face impassive as if he hadn't been affected in the slightest. "Until two, Miss Wallin."

Her heart didn't slow until she'd rounded the corner.

Silly! Why did she keep reacting that way? He wasn't interested in her. He'd told her so himself.

She was not about to offer him her heart. There was no reason to behave like a giddy schoolgirl on her first infatuation.

Even if he had been her schoolgirl infatuation.

She was a woman now, with opportunities, plans, dreams for a future. And she wasn't about to allow herself to take a chance on love again, especially not with Hart McCormick.

For now, the important thing was to find the perfect woman for him, and she knew just where to look.

Don't miss
FRONTIER MATCHMAKER BRIDE by Regina Scott,
available March 2018 wherever
Love Inspired® Historical books and ebooks are sold.

www.LoveInspired.com